SCRIBES & SCOUNDRELS

Scribes & Scoundrels

A NOVEL BY

George Galt

ECW PRESS

CANADIAN CATALOGUING IN PUBLICATION DATA

Galt, George, 1948–
    Scribes & scoundrels

ISBN 1-55022-333-X

I. Title. II. Title: Scribes and scoundrels.

PS8563.A48S36 1997   C813 .54 C97-931520-4
PR9199.3.G27S36 1997

Cover image: *The Usurers* by Marinus van Reymerswaele,
courtesy of Museo Stibbert, Florence, Italy.

Permission is gratefully acknowledged for use of the lines on
page 5 from "I Cried for Us" by Kate McGarrigle, Garden Court
Music, copyright Library of Congress 1981 from the recording
"Love Over and Over" by Kate and Anna McGarrigle.

Author photo by Susan Ross.
Design and imaging by ECW Type & Art, Oakville, Ontario.
Printed by Webcom Ltd., Scarborough, Ontario.

Distributed in Canada by General Distribution Services,
30 Lesmill Road, Don Mills, Ontario M3B 2T6.

Distributed in the United States by General Distribution Services,
85 River Rock Drive, Suite 202, Buffalo, New York 14207.

Published by ECW PRESS,
2120 Queen Street East, Suite 200,
Toronto, Ontario M4E 1E2.

http://www.ecw.ca/press

PRINTED AND BOUND IN CANADA

CHAPTER I

April 13

On Max Vellen's car radio, a song about love. "I'll put this note/Inside your coat/And leave the gate unlocked." That could be the beginning of an affair, but in these lyrics, which always stuck to him like an insect trapped in his ear, it was the end, good-bye, it's over. The words brought back his last face-to-face with Sarah, her anguished early morning voice, the shouting: it's not working, you're unfaithful, you don't have enough time for me, you're too wrapped up in yourself, your own needs, your own ego, you never really listen. Good-bye, I loved you, good luck.

Max flicked off the radio as the McGarrigle sisters' song wound down. He could still be sucked through the thin ice of everyday chores into the dark swirl of his break-up with Sarah. Half a year later, she was under his skin, maybe would be a long time, but please not always like this, holding him hostage, yet never returning his calls.

"Mea culpa!" he shouted in the rusty old Pontiac as it sped down the Danforth, past Shopper's Drug Mart, the Ford dealership, the old Roxy cinema where he had watched Bogart movies twenty years before. "Mea culpa, Sarah McDermott!" He passed the cement-block mosque on the south side, its men in white and coloured skull caps, ankle-length robes, and cheap running shoes, standing in groups out on the sidewalk.

Constantinople, he thought as he waited for the red light to change at Donlands, and Islamabad. Who'd have thought Mohammed's children would one day be living alongside refugee Incas, dispossessed Ojibway, Somalis on the run, and villagers from the Peleponnese? The city was now a polyglot patchwork sewn hurriedly onto the snow-white sheet that Methodists and Presbyterians had been shaking out and scrubbing and ironing for eight generations. Max had no nostalgia for that starched antiseptic whiteness. He was relieved whenever he saw pieces of the bright new quilt. Yet it seemed to him that Toronto, burdened by a stiff emotional reserve, hadn't found much comfort in its changed self. Sarah had seen it differently. "Immigration is like an arranged marriage," she had said. "It takes time for both parties to find each other." Clear-eyed, tolerant, articulate, that was Sarah, appealing to the world's better nature.

As he was thinking about her — her largeness of heart, all that she had offered, and all that he had carelessly thrown away — he noticed a thin whisp of vapour escape from under the Pontiac's dented hood. It was a sunny morning, the beginning of Toronto spring, cool with patches of warmth on the sidewalk, about ten degrees. Certainly not radiator-blowing weather. He had slept badly — maybe the vapour was behind his eyes. But a moment later it was unmistakeable. He was driving a piece of mobile theatre — dry ice was all he could think of as he rolled down the Danforth with steam puffing and rolling off his hood. And then the smell. The smell? Holy Jesus, he realized, *I'm on fire!*

Pulling up at the curb, he scrambled out, ran into the nearest variety store, and interrupted a gabby old sidewalk rat who was buying a lottery ticket.

"Your fire extinguisher — please!" Max said sharply. The Korean woman behind the counter responded with a cocked head and a neutral smile. "Quick," he insisted. He stepped in closer and pointed outside. "Your fire extinguisher. Please! Fire! Quick!"

Looking frightened now, she handed him a cannister with a little hose attached. He ran out and yanked open the Pontiac's hood, fanning a huge flame that licked the engine's metal lid. A hostile headline flashed through his mind as he sprayed foam over the engine: MAGAZINE EDITOR EXPLODES NEIGH-BOURHOOD. The Korean shopkeeper was now standing in her doorway yelling at him in her native tongue. It occurred to Max that she probably wasn't inviting him to dinner. The fire sank, died. No-one would be charging him with criminal negligence.

Down the street he spied a phone booth where he could call the fire department and a towing service, but as he went along the sidewalk feeling his pockets for change, he realized the Korean woman was tailing him, still shouting angrily. He turned, apologized gently, handed back the cannister, and offered her money.

"Police. Police. Call police. Police," she was now yelling.

"Yes. Yes," he replied. "Police and fire department. I call. Don't worry." He pointed towards the phone. In his face she shook the twenty-dollar bill he'd just given her, let go what sounded like a vicious curse and, dangling the spent cannister from one hand, waddled back to rejoin her small daughter who had been standing guard at the entrance to the store. "Police," she shouted again angrily as Max reached the phone booth.

He'd be late for the editorial meeting. Better do some damage control — phone Chaser first. Tell him there's a terrorist group bombing the editors, one by one, he's next. For a nanosecond, thinking of all the freelance writers Chaser had deceived and provoked, Max felt such a campaign might not be that much of a wild fantasy.

Chaser Makepeace, the editor of *Berger's*, came on the line.

"Chaser, it's Max. I've been delayed. I had to put out a fire." He explained that his engine had ignited.

7

Max was interrupted with a tale about Chaser Makepeace's car, the time it had gone kaput in an African game park when he'd been posted in Johannesburg. As Makepeace stories went, this one was colourful, with a disloyal driver and a pride of lions, but Max was in no mood. He cut Chaser short, said he'd be in after lunch, and then he called the first east-end towing number that caught his eye under the A's in the yellow pages.

As he waited for AAA Afghan Towing to show up, Max thought of Chaser's lions prowling the game park. If you had a story about a wolf, Chaser replied with one about a lynx. He'd killer-shark your dolphins and Himalaya your Andes and Alzheimer your arthritis every time — a one-upmanship junkie whose favourite voice was always his own. Max, thinking about his heart-pounding fright over the smoking engine, imagined a cartoon, someone gasping for air, exhausted after a boating mishap, floundering in the wet, when along comes Chaser in a canoe. "I almost drowned once," Chaser would say, looking down at the poor sap in the water, and before lending a hand, Chaser would light a cigarette and self-dramatize for a satisfying moment while the swimmer swallowed more of the lake.

A strange duck, Chaser, with the unstoppable voice gushing from the small body, the straight shoulder-length white hair and wire-rimmed glasses that made him look like a middle-aged Victorian boy, the old-fashioned, rote churchiness that made him sound like a corrupt Anglican deacon out of Trollope, and the lust for the spotlight that always sent him puffing into the centre of any conversation. More than once at *Berger's* Max had been given the impression that Chaser was paying close attention to someone else's story. But the truth was that anyone else's anecdote was only another platform-in-waiting for Chaser. He would listen carefully for as long as it took him to study the ground and find a foothold for himself. Then he would climb nimbly up on your story, barge in, and hold forth with his own little tale in which he was almost always the principal actor.

A popular reporter and columnist at the *Tribune*, where he had worked for twenty years, Chaser had won the *Berger's* job on the strength of a stellar newspaper career. He was new to the magazine business, but his inexperience hadn't dampened his many large and, in Max's view, ignorant opinions about how *Berger's* should be run.

Chaser is nimble, Chaser is quick, Chaser is often a nasty little prick. Max saw the tow truck pull up. *Ever so hollow but oh so slick*, he added as he approached the man from Afghan Towing, who was now looking down at the engine of the Pontiac. To Max car mechanics and rocket scientists were equally gifted. He tried to wear a knowing look as the man explained why no-one would ever be able to drive this twelve-year-old junk heap again. Peering down at the scorched pipes and hoses, he decided against a second opinion and agreed to ride down to the car graveyard and sign a paper. The burned-out Pontiac would be sold for scrap to AAA Afghan Towing for a hundred dollars — less fifty for the service call.

"Why does a car catch fire?" Max wondered aloud in the cab of the tow truck as they rode down the hill towards the lake.

"You keep a car too old, you got problems," shrugged the driver, a hint of contempt in his voice. "You keep a car too old, anything happens."

"I don't know much about cars," Max said.

The driver smiled and nodded. "What job you have?"

Max thought how great it was he had one. "I'm a journalist. I work for a magazine."

"Ah, newspaperman! My cousin know big Toronto news-paperman. Was in my country. Afghanistan. Mockpiss."

"What?"

"Mockpiss. Is his name. Big man in newspaper business. Mr. Mockpiss."

"You don't mean Chaser Makepeace?"

"Yeah, maybe. I think it's the name."

"How would your cousin know Chaser Makepeace?" asked Max incredulously.

"Mr. Mockpiss do good things for Afghanis here. He help my family come in Canada." Max concluded they were probably talking about someone else, and he was curious who the good Samaritan might be. Selflessness was not a common characteristic among the journalists he knew. Nor did many get involved personally in stories they covered. This was sometimes described as a "principle" of the trade. Don't get emotionally involved. As a principle Max found it self-serving. More often, though, journalists didn't feel any need to invoke it. They simply acknowledged their own cynicism and moved briskly on to the next assignment.

The truck turned up a ramp and through a shabby corrugated-iron fence on Eastern Avenue. Max watched the tow truck dump his dead Pontiac beside a seven-carcass-high pile of stripped-and-rusted wrecks, then followed the driver through the sloppy, greasy yard into a makeshift hut that served as an office. In the dim light that seeped through one dirt-caked pane of glass, Max could see sets of car keys hanging from nails in the wall. Filthy, yellowing invoices were pinned in no apparent order behind the desk. On it sat a rotary-dial black telephone and two half-finished coffees in grimy paper cups.

The man picked up a note lying on the second desk and then looked dolefully at Max. "Sorry. My cousin is out from office. You come back tomorrow for sign papers. I am only driver."

"Back here?" exclaimed Max.

"For sign papers. It is necessary."

★ ★ ★

A cab dropped Max at the old sandstone building off Yonge Street where *Berger's* and several smaller trade publications were housed. His shoes were still smeared from the scrapyard and he saw he was leaving a trail of brown streaks as he walked through the lobby.

"Hey, Max!" Nick Mannella, the managing editor of *Phrase Mocker*, followed him into the elevator. Before taking his job at *Berger's*, Max had contributed to *Phrase Mocker*, a hip monthly critique of books and media. Nick, with his long black hair combed neatly back from his broad forehead, was wearing an expensive black leather jacket and high-shine motor-cycle boots. Max guessed he had just come from a fashion shoot. Nick supplemented his small magazine salary by working as a model.

"You look like you're about to appear in *Vanity Fair*."

"*House and Garden*, if you can believe it, man. One of those images where they co-opt the brute underclass to sell slick consumer trash. In this case crystal stem ware. Very whorish. Very well-paid." He eyed Max's pant cuffs and shoes. "You look like you just waded through a cow barn."

"My car exploded. So I had it towed to Kabul. AAA Afghan Towing."

"Most potent dope I ever smoked was in Kabul," said Nick as he stepped onto his floor. Holding the elevator door with one arm, he leaned back in and said, "Take some of that Afghan mud with you into *Berger's*. It could use a shot of unsanitized reality."

As the doors closed, Max could hear Nick reproaching him, many months earlier, when Max had said he was about to accept the job at *Berger's*. "Don't do it, man. You'll become another stuffed editor glued to a chair. You'll be doing twelve-hour days."

Chaser Makepeace had arranged for the last part of the prediction to come true. Even so, Max felt a lift most days when he arrived at work. *Berger's* regularly offered up a heady punch bowl of social gossip, headline news, and political rumour, and Max drained his cup as greedily as anyone when the bowl passed his way. He thrived on the buzz as he looked for ways to make his mark. And twelve-hour days weren't altogether unwelcome. The daily rush of claims on his time, the letters, the calls, the meetings, and endless production deadlines, all had helped to fill the hole left in his heart by Sarah.

CHAPTER 2

Feeling for her straw basket of spices deep in the cupboard over the back stairs, Sarah McDermott discovered the wad of old letters wedged between two jars. She dimly remembered having stuffed them there one day a couple of years earlier. Someone had been coming over. She'd wanted the letters out of sight.

The spices weren't in the cupboard at all. She found them in her mother's old bread box. Where Max had left them — Max, chaotic and self-obsessed. She felt a tingle of anger. A man moved into your life, then out. Always moving, and moving on. She reached up to the open shelf for her white mixing bowl. Most relationships with men had a built-in obsolescence. But somehow this one had promised more.

She took the stewing beef out of the refrigerator. After the break-up, cooking in these empty rooms had repelled her. Aromas that had been as good as a body massage had turned acrid and unappetizing. First she'd lost weight. Then, with all the restaurant meals, with the bread, the retsina, and the Greek olive oil on her salads, she'd gained seven pounds. Irritable, she'd dieted, taken up yoga again, and seen her old therapist, all of which had helped chase from her mind the worst of her memories of Max.

She ran her paring knife through the sharpener, trimmed the fat from the chunks of beef, cut them to size, and dropped the pieces into the marinade bowl. It felt good to be back working with food at this table, the noonday April sun painting a sharp stripe across her pine shelves, illuminating the titles of her cook books. She lifted up a handful of the red beef and took a full sniff. It looked male, smelled male, and, come to think of it, males liked to eat it. She'd made this stew in honour of males all her cooking life. Max had loved it.

She chopped the carrots and onions and ground some pepper over the meat, then looked for some red wine. Down under the back stairs, she found three dust-covered bottles. The last of Max. Everything else she had banished and expunged, wanting to repossess these rooms, wipe him from her daily life and make the place all hers again.

She drowned the meat in wine, poured herself a glass, and sat down. The smell of the pepper and onions and wine conjured up, unbidden, the French word *gîte*. A picture darted into her mind: sheep grazing by a stone cottage in Provence and herself cutting a sprig of thyme in the garden. Mauve and jonquil wildflowers grew against the stone walls. Across the hill behind the property stood gnarled dwarf trees from a Van Gogh painting. Someone, probably Martin, the man who would share her stew, was somewhere nearby, chopping wood. Yes, it was probably Martin. But when she pictured Martin, he was wearing tasselled loafers, a pair of pressed charcoal suit pants, and a blue-striped business shirt, and he was consulting a dictionary for the French translation of a phrase he'd come across in *The European Wall Street Journal*. Not that Martin was a dull bean counter or a wimp. Far from it. He was athletic, and strong-minded, and no slouch at pleasing a woman. A tax lawyer with a large firm, he wasn't without taste and style. But he wasn't exactly funky either.

Salt. She'd forgotten it. She stood and reached for the box.

To her friends Sarah defended Martin. Pouring a teaspoon of white crystals into her palm, she remembered Jill at that dinner they'd had a week ago with one of Martin's partners. It had gone badly and Jill had made it clear the next day that she didn't want to meet any more of Martin's colleagues. There had been too much shop talk at the restaurant, and too much of it about limiting the tax bite on wealthy corporate clients. This hadn't sat well with Jill, a reporter with the *Herald*.

"Sarah, dear, you know I think Martin is very nice, and it's true that I'd like to meet someone who's both bright and solvent, but please, no more blind dates from McGimme, Pinge, Trough, and O'Slooze," she had said, laughing. Sarah had felt guilty and hurt.

Rinsing the salt from her hands at the sink, she saw herself in the kettle, an image that gave her an extra ten pounds. But she knew the natural glow of her skin was back. Even her big dark curls, now down to her shoulders, looked healthier.

"Beautiful guileless eyes," he had once said.

Nuts to you, Max. She peered at herself, bloated by the kettle. *Not so guileless as you might think.*

She picked up her glass of wine. Martin reappeared in front of the *gîte*, looking more relaxed this time in his desert boots and khaki shorts and one of his Hawaiian shirts. But he was reading that awful, reactionary book they'd argued about at his apartment last week, *The End of History*. A dreadful, pseudo-intellectual tract that Sarah had wanted to throw against the wall.

Suddenly Martin was gone from the picture.

She could feel a dark presence looming, threatening to breach the borders of her French terrain. It would be a car, probably an old *deux chevaux*, all banged up, and he'd step out with two bottles of good white wine, hoping to appease her. He'd be grinning and apologizing and spinning a wild yarn about mishaps en route, all to stall her anger, because he'd be late, maybe a couple of hours, maybe a couple of days — you could never tell with Max.

No. She wouldn't allow it to happen. *She wouldn't even tell him she'd found a place.* If, that is, she did find one. *She wouldn't even tell him what country, the son-of-a-bitch!* Of course, he'd find out eventually. They had too many people in common for him not to. Which was fine. Maybe he'd even feel a twinge of travel envy.

That end-of-the-road shouting match, that last time he had stood her up, the long wait alone, then going over to his place, waking him in the small hours, screaming at him in his own bedroom. So humiliating. But unavoidable. At first he hadn't believed it. The phone messages and notes dripping with polite contrition. She'd had her fill of it all. They never ate together again.

She reached for the bundle of old letters.

Dear Attractive:

I have never replied to this kind of ad before, but nothing ventured, nothing gained, right! I admit I do look at the personals — for entertainment. Your ad caught my fantasy. I'm like you, I read a lot, and maybe we could enjoy going out.

You say you like visiting France. I have nothing against the French. I like French fries! (Joke) And some other French things too.

You say in the ad you work with words. I wonder what you do. Maybe a librarian — very nice people. I spend many hours in the library every month. Mostly what I read is philosophy, but I can read anything. I mean and talk about it.

I also have a hobby. But I'd better wait and tell you about that one on one, in person.

Then there's what I do for a living. It's related to philosophy, because I believe human happiness is the goal we all have to aim for. Don't you! I work in a restaurant. Who can be happy on an empty stomach! Well, like I tell people, it may not be solving all the world's problems, but it's a start.

I am 49 and I have never been married but some day I
hope. I have strong arms from my work. Right now I don't
have any girlfriend, so I'm free.
   If you'd like to meet somewhere sometime, give me a call.

There had been a number of letters like this, dispiriting
expressions of loneliness and social ineptitude. Between the
lines you could sense repressed howls of grief and longing.
They could have been writing anyone. And maybe they did
write the same letter over and over. Then there were the
mysogynist cranks who had written. And the single-minded
pornographic bores. Some guy had put his large flaccid penis
on a piece of paper and traced it, adding only the words
"This is a picture of me lying down. But wait till I get *up*."
And he'd given his name and phone number. Another deluded
male had proposed a straight exchange: she'd cook him a good
dinner and he'd give her great oral sex for dessert. Apart from
those with below-the-belt obsessions and those with marginal
IQs who could barely string sentences together, most of her
respondents had written faceless, matter-of-fact replies that
suggested dull lives mired in ennui.

But a few letters had struck her as possibilities. Her ad had
been cryptic; she hadn't said that she worked in publishing.
"Love touts," she called the personals, and sometimes "love
tarts." She'd been embarrassed about shopping for romance,
and hadn't been very disclosing. Her ad had supplied a short
list of nouns: "France, Alice Munro, irony, risotto, reliability,
salt water, intelligence, a wooden chopping block, a garden
spade; attractive female wordsmith, 34, wishes to be wordsmitten. Tell me who you are."

Some guys had caught on and written amusing notes. She'd
met them for coffee or a drink at the end of the day, five or six
encounters in all, about two and a half years ago now. But most
hadn't been the person she'd imagined from reading their

words on paper. Two, used up and apparently desperate, had lied extravangantly about their ages. Another had confessed, near the end of a promising conversation, that he was married, but looking for a quick exit. And another was an honest, intelligent man, but — she could still visualize him, his name was Frank — he had very thin carrot-coloured hair, a long bony nose, and leached blue eyes, and she couldn't imagine ever going to bed with him.

Riffling through the remaining letters, she stopped at the only one with familiar handwriting on the envelope. She pulled it out and reread it.

```
Dear Fellow Wordsmith:
    I'll bite if you will. It hardly seems fair
for me to have to spill out my life on this page
when I don't even know your name.
    I too work with words. So here's a proposition:
we exchange a few letters to see whether we might
be interested in each other. I've answered ads
before, never successfully. It's an artificial
process, a hot-house mating technique that's
better suited to thoroughbred poodles and show
horses than to most humans. I swore off it,
frankly, not being one to jump through erotic
hoops on command, but am still addicted to reading
the personal columns, and can't resist sending
you this note because we seem to have so much in
common. Of course, as you've found out by now if
you've been meeting men through your pitch, most
people out there lie about themselves, both in
the ads and in the answering letters, so you may
not be "attractive and ironic" at all, and I may
be a fraud too, for all I know.
    On the other hand, maybe we're both for real.
```

Let's go ahead on that assumption for now. Here are a few personal details on my side. I'm a thirty-eight-year old raggedy-ass writer, surviving and content with my work, so if you want a dude with a closet full of suits and a swimming pool, try the next guy in line. I loathe opera and John Cage but love horn concertos. I'm not into drugs and rock'n roll. I am into green sex, by which I don't mean we both cover ourselves in extra-virgin olive oil (well, that might be negotiable). I mean green as in ecologically sound. Ask me about this some time.

I travel when I can — I too like France — never wear a tie with grease spots on it, and read voluminously. My favourite novels are The Third Policeman, Animal Farm, and One Hundred Years of Solitude. You seem to like eating. My preferred summer drink is vodka. I hate mustard. My winter drink: red wine. Which I like to have with a beef daube.

That's enough. Write me if you care to.

Max Vellen

She looked at her bowl full of beef and red wine and felt a sudden urge to pitch it all out and start another meal. For a moment the kitchen seemed infested with Max, his peculiar culinary likes and dislikes, his sardonic magazine articles, his insane laughter, his self-dramatizing. Then he was gone. She was, after all, over it.

She examined the letter again coolly. As he'd suggested, they had written many times back and forth before meeting — she still had all of his letters in a file in her office. At first she hadn't replied to him. There had been something defiant about the letter which she hadn't liked; that and "green sex" had put her off. He sounded as though he could be pretty dreadful, maybe a little weird. But then she'd had those disappointing encounters with the other men who'd written. When they'd all fizzled out, she'd looked at Max's letter again and had second thoughts.

He was an ardent flatterer by mail, and an entertaining screwball commentator on whatever subjects she raised. She'd been infatuated with the idea of him before they'd ever met. And when they did finally get together, it had been as good as she'd hoped. She could see now, that like all her relationships, this one had been a bell curve: accelerating erotic obsession and romantic optimism that hit a high point and then rolled downhill into disillusionment and decay. For a while she'd believed she would beat the odds. But the closer she got, the more evasive he became. She could hear his voice now, irritated, promising: "Do I have to give it to you in writing, or what?" The usual bravado. He was an emotional escape artist. Not exactly a missed opportunity, though. Marrying Max would have been like riding a canoe into a hurricane.

Do I Have To Give It To You In Writing? The phrase sat stubbornly in her mind, sounding a lot like a title. And an idea began to take hold.

CHAPTER 3

That sunny April morning, as he walked briskly past the King Edward Hotel, the editor of *Berger's* magazine was waylaid by a familiar face.

"Chaser!" the face boomed. It belonged to Michael Rector, a tall man who wore a leather jacket and a beret. He hid his chinless condition under a grey Vandyke. "Belated congratulations. From Red Square to Clubbland. That's one hell of a career move." Rector grinned down at the editor, who was shorter by a head. They shook hands.

"You're back from London," Chaser said. "Big changes for us both."

"Not for me really. I'm starting a national column in two weeks. 'Rector At Large.' Meanwhile I'm Rector at rest. Finding my feet after the loopy, upside-down politics the Brits practise. It's quiet here by comparison. But your days must be full of piss and vinegar with Edward Clubb on the scene. I hear he's a phonaholic. How do you stand all that polysyllabic bombast?" Rector's grin now had a twist of malice in it.

Edward Clubb, as had been reported in a local gossip magazine, favoured late-night phone calls to his most senior employees, of which Chaser was one.

Chaser ignored the goad. "I'm off to see his nibs right now," he said. "It's my first annual report. *Berger's* is doing well.

Ad lineage is holding and we're getting new writers in. Lots of great stories in the pipeline." He could see Rector wasn't impressed. Chaser changed course. "Clubb's not bad to work for, you know — God bless him — despite the multisyllabic midnight calls. He actually reads the magazine from cover to cover. And occasionally makes a useful suggestion. Some dreadful ones too."

"Remembering my own magazine days, I'd say a publisher with any useful opinions for the editor is a rare bird." Rector had edited *Best*, a national magazine that had gone bankrupt in the early eighties. Then he'd gone to work for the *Herald*.

"Opinions Mr. Clubb has plenty of," Chaser replied. "He hated the piece I did on *glasnost* and the fall of the Wall. He believes Reagan conquered the Soviet empire. Whereas I implied the people rose up and howled their own governments down. And he loathed our piece on trickle-down economics. . . ." Chaser suddenly stopped himself. The economics commentary hadn't been published yet. Which meant Clubb shouldn't have seen it. He glanced quickly at his watch. "Let's have lunch," he said. "I've got to run."

In the flatiron building on Wellington Street, Chaser slid open the brass accordian grill that served as an elevator door. He stepped into the antique wooden cage, and looked at himself in its polished glass panels. He appraised his reflection as the cage rose. He stared at his small hard eyes. He clenched his jaw. He adjusted his horn-rimmed glasses and straightened his red bow tie.

On the top floor he stepped into the lobby. The words JANUS CORPORATION were emblazoned across one wall. Under them appeared the corporate logo, two halves of a globe. Beneath this stylized split sphere sat Edith Crutchlow, Edward Clubb's assistant. As Chaser well remembered, she had been with the family firm ever since Mr. Clubb senior had managed it. Chaser had once toiled as a summer apprentice at the Dominion

Publishing Company, the firm's original name. His charms had never worked on Mrs. Crutchlow.

"Morning, Mrs. Crutchlow. Beautiful day."

"Not so far," she replied, looking up from her video monitor. Tight grey curls crowded her head, framing a face that wanted you to apologize. "But it might improve. Tread lightly is my advice." She looked at her watch. "If you'd been here five minutes ago, I'd have sent you in. Now he's busy. You'd better take a seat."

Chaser perched on one of the dainty upholstered armchairs that filled the waiting area by the window. He sat for ten minutes, looking down onto the Front Street shoppers and around the room at all the Victorian furniture that had been moved from the old Dominion Publishing Company offices. Then he walked back over to Mrs. Crutchlow's desk.

"Are you sure he knows I'm here?"

"You always were an impatient boy."

"Bless you, Mrs. Crutchlow — that was thirty years ago. Weren't you impatient when you were seventeen?"

"That was a lot more years ago than I care to remember." She pointed to her telephone console. "See that little white light? It's his line. He's still talking."

"Can you buzz him and let him know I've arrived?"

Mrs. Crutchlow narrowed her eyes. "You seem a little daffy today, Chaser. You know how he dislikes being interrupted. If you want to barge right in, I'm too small to stop you. Or, tell you what, I'll turn on the speaker here and you can shout into it and interrupt him that way, okay?" She pressed a button on another console and suddenly they could hear an aggressive, nasal voice speaking rapidly.

". . . and that's the way to orchestrate it. Your minions are just plain in error, Jack. I know precisely the avenue I want to pursue with this debenture and, as I'm certain you are aware, it's our credibility on the goddamn line, not yours." Chaser looked at Mrs. Crutchlow, then leaned closer to the speaker. As he did, his arm brushed her empty tea mug, dislodging it from the shallow ledge around her work area. The mug landed on the ancient intercom and broke into pieces.

Then they heard, "Hold on a second, will you, Jack. . . . What the hell is going on out there, Edith?"

"Chaser Makepeace just dropped a tea cup on the intercom, Mr. Clubb. I'm terribly sorry."

"Send him in here where I can hold on to his dog collar."

Chaser picked up his briefcase and slipped quickly into his employer's office.

Edward Clubb, Korean war veteran, proud inheritor of old money, scourge of Toronto's left-wing press, and chairman of the Janus Corporation, sat in the far east corner of the large triangular room. He was leaning back in a leather swivel chair and barking into the phone.

Chaser sat down and opened his briefcase. "See where DBRS pegs the credit rating," the chairman was saying. "Not that I trust those egregious snoops. But the market gives their view some weight."

Chaser pulled out a file labelled BUDGET. He opened it to a page headed EDITORIAL PROJECTIONS. He looked around the room. The tables and cabinets were dark cherry and oak. The walls were painted a stifling shade of maroon. He touched his bow tie, wiggled his finger between his Adam's apple and his collar. His throat was dry.

He watched Edward Clubb put down the phone and pick up a fresh cigar from a wooden box that had "Monte Cristo" stamped on it. The chairman came around his desk and shook Chaser's hand. Then he wandered over to the south window, clipped the uncut end of his cigar, and dropped the nick of tobacco out the window onto the street.

"Edith's given you tea or coffee, I presume." Before Chaser could answer, he added, "I've got lawyers and brokers crawling all over me today. You're a refreshing change." He lit the cigar and rested a heavy forearm on one of the glass cases that were filled with platoons of tiny toy soldiers.

"Comic relief," Chaser said. "As opposed to one of your profit centres."

"But you will be, one of these days, Chaser. Profitable. *Berger's* will not limp along as a permanent ward of the house of Janus. We are not a charity hospital for ailing publications. But I am willing to supply you with a measure of latitude. Temporarily. As I've said."

Edward Clubb, bulky and rumpled, had been a handsome young man — tall, dark, with the sleek insouciance that money endows. Now, pushing sixty, he was freighted with a lot of surplus body weight.

Chaser sat with a pencil in one hand and his file folder open to a blank page in the other. He found himself scribbling a note of the kind that he'd written every working day of his life as a *Tribune* reporter. "Ed Clbb," he scrawled in his own shorthand. "Post-phrmaceutcl, bloated Elvis lk-alike."

". . . precisely what it is that's on your agenda," Clubb was saying.

"Yes. Well, the magazine. There are some ideas I wanted to try on you."

"More aggressive and less slavishly puerile political commentary is what you need," declaimed the publisher, punching the air with his cigar. "Some sharp, economically literate analysis in tune with the revivified conservative Zeitgeist. I've developed some ideas about this myself."

"Really? Ah, well . . . I welcome them, of course." Under "Elvis," Chaser scratched, almost illegibly, "King of neo-con lard-belly publshrs."

"But after you. It's your meeting."

"Alright. It's been twelve months now, and we're holding our own with circulation and advertising. It might be the right moment to try a modest editorial expansion. I think *Berger's* would benefit from a regular international feature. But we couldn't do it on our existing budget."

The Janus chairman exhaled a puff of smoke. "Where is it exactly that you wish to go?" His nasal voice was unfriendly.

"Oh, no, it's not for me. We'd do it with freelancers."

"I would never look to *Berger's* for my international news."

"No. Of course not. We're not *The New York Times*."

"*The Economist*," snapped the chairman.

"No, not that either. It's not news-gathering we're good at. We couldn't afford it, God bless us. I'm thinking of more reflective commentary."

"Ah." The voice sounded grudgingly appeased.

"Another idea. I'd like to start a column called 'The View from There.' Prominent journalists and experts from abroad commenting on things Canadian. But we'd have to pay for it." Chaser watched the chairman's face tighten into thin-lipped hostility. "The bottom line: if we want to hold on to our momentum at *Berger's*, we have to be nimble and keep readers interested. We're still losing money, but . . ."

"Damn right you are. Almost a million in the initial ten months. I verified that with Nutley this morning. It's imperative that you be aware I did not purchase this title to incur losses of that magnitude. Why do you always scribble during meetings?"

Under "lard-belly," Chaser had been writing "Col. Flabass, field commder., 7th Tin Sldr. Brigade. Scorch-earth tctics." He looked up quickly and said, "Sorry. Force of journalistic habit."

The chairman rested his half-smoked cigar on the lip of a marble ashtray. At its centre was mounted a brass replica of a World War II tank. "I want you to be cognizant of my views on the *Berger's* balance sheet. This is not a severed artery for Janus. Thus far, you have inflicted only a flesh wound, irritating but not irremediable. *Berger's* is a handsome property, well worth some small measure of additional investment, as I have maintained all along. But you are going to have to discipline yourself and address those rebarbative losses. *Nunc aut nunquam*, Chaser. I won't wait another year." He moved away from the window towards his visitor.

"That's definitely the plan," the editor replied as he scribbled, "Empror Agustus threatns exile." He watched the chairman lumber past him into the other half of the office. Chaser shifted and asked over his shoulder, "What do you think of my content proposals?" He saw Clubb's long, fat fingers pick up an envelope from the top of a two-tiered cabinet.

"I might be interested in the commentary on foreign affairs," the chairman replied. "Let's give that some more reflection. I imagine you could do it without any painfully sacrificial infusion of new cash. Meanwhile, I have my own modest proposal for you."

He turned and rolled back over the plush blue carpet to the coffee table. Bobbing towards Chaser, Edward Clubb's heavy, venal face melted into the chubby, expectant mien of a ten-year-old — a little boy offering his teacher an apple.

The publisher gently proffered a brown envelope. "Chaser Makepeace" was typed on the white address label. The proprietor of *Berger's* smiled shyly and turned away to his desk.

Chaser had seen it dozens of times over the past twelve months: the yearning face of the hopeful writer. Everyone in the country with any intellectual ambition or pretension wanted the imprimatur of *Berger's* on his work. Defeated cabinet ministers, eminent professors, crusading freelance journalists, underappreciated poets, has-been film critics, scrappy left-wing academics, neo-conservative crusaders, novelists with a cause, unemployed book reviewers, would-be satirists, think-tank directors, television commentators who thought they were essayists, bookish clergy, authors flogging their next title — the best authors in the country but also every literary crank and con artist — they'd been knocking on his door in a steady stream since the day he had arrived last spring.

Edward Clubb had just joined the queue.

"Fuck," Chaser scribbled, and closed his file folder. He tried to look pleased. "What's this, Edward?" he asked, pulling a typescript halfway out of the envelope. He glanced at the title page. The words "SOME CHICKEN" were typed in boldface capitals. He quickly shoved the typescript back inside.

"It's an essay I've prepared. On, I believe, a significant matter of global dimensions. Take it with you. I don't want to prejudice your reaction in any way, but I believe I've been able to convey *multum in parvo*. I'd be most grateful if you could read it. And I'd like you to consider publishing it in *Berger's*. . . ." He relit his cigar. "Unless, of course, you feel it's not sufficiently well written."

"No, no, no." Chaser held up one hand like a traffic policeman. "Naturally, I'm delighted to have some of your, um, thoughts. I'll get right to it."

"You know," said the chairman, all deference gone, "I think it might very aptly inaugurate this new column you're proposing. You can consider that idea tentatively approved. Cost it out for me. We'll arrange something modest, at least for a probationary period." He looked at his watch.

"Great," croaked Chaser. He picked up his briefcase and turned to leave.

"That file belong to you?"

"Yarrrrh!" Chaser gurgled, spinning around to grab the blue folder in which he'd tucked the notes he'd been making.

"How long does it usually take?"

"Usually? I'm not sure I . . ."

"For the editor to let a writer know."

"Oh. Not long. I'll get back to you soon. Give me a few days. I'll fast-track it."

★ ★ ★

"God bless us! Unbloodybelievable!" said Chaser. He was standing in Max Vellen's office with the "SOME CHICKEN" typescript. The editor had undone his bow tie and was loosening his collar. "I read most of it on the way back here. At first I was afraid it might be a treatise on the controversy over whether force-fed broilers are hygienic. In that case I'd have been well and truly screwed. Can you imagine the headlines? 'FOWL PLAY AT BERGER'S.' Or 'EDITOR LOSES INDEPENDENCE IN GAME OF CHICKEN WITH PUBLISHER.'" He paused and looked down at the typescript in his hand. "Then again, maybe that would have been better than what this really is."

"What exactly *are* we dealing with?" Max asked, craning to look at the title page.

"You really do have to read the thing to get the full experience. It's about the fall of communism. Sort of. It's also about Edward O. Clubb and his colossal ego. As usual he doesn't merely opine, he thunders. High-volume polemics. Written in his trademark convoluted-Edwardian prose — no pun intended. I seriously doubt it's publishable in *Berger's*. I'm not running a vanity press here." Chaser fidgeted with his open collar. "Sorry about your own bad luck today," he added as an afterthought. "You weren't hurt, were you?"

"The car's a write-off, that's all. It was towed to a scrap yard."

"I was in Moscow for the fall of the Wall, you know. I survived early *glasnost* and *perestroika*. Nothing I had to do to keep my job at the *Tribune* ever compared with what's required to stay alive in this place." He handed the "SOME CHICKEN" typescript to Max. "Can you read it and tell me what you think, a.s.a.p.? I'll be in my office."

When Chaser had left, Max settled in to read the twenty-five pages. The essay was a bizarre self-indulgence locating its writer at the centre of world events. The self-aggrandizement began with paragraph one: "My eighth birthday coincided with Winston Spencer Churchill's address to the Canadian Parliament early in World War II. On that day, December 30, 1941, speaking to parliamentarians in Ottawa, Churchill recalled the ominous forecast of the French Commander-in-Chief General Weygand, who had predicted the year before that Britain would soon have its neck wrung like a chicken. 'Some chicken!' Churchill drily observed. 'Some neck!' As I grew older, my father with great fondness would repeat that Churchillian incantation at the dinner table on Sundays whenever he was carving roast fowl. A non-observant Anglican, my father informed me that those phrases were a substitute for grace, because we who had survived the war owed as large a debt to Churchill as to God. I incline to agreement with that view, and have been so inclined for forty-five years, since I first began reading about Churchill's political principles and career."

There was more, much more: Churchill's dogged fight against Hitler, applause for his fierce anti-communism, approval for his support of the counter-revolutionaries in Russia after 1917, and then a long section on the raising of the Iron Curtain in 1989 which, in Clubb's words, "finally finished the war that Churchill won." Through it all were woven strands of Clubb's personal history, including his enlisting in the Princess Patricia's Canadian Light Infantry right out of high school, his service in Korea, the opposition some years later to his master's thesis on Churchill at the University of Toronto, and his family's presence in London in 1965 at the time of the great man's funeral. The last paragraph of the essay read: "Today, it ill behoves us, all beneficiaries of the blood spilled and treasure expended by the generation led by Winston Spencer Churchill, to bite and snap ungratefully at the heels of history. Those who carp, as the snivelling, envy-mongering mob of ill-informed socialist scribes have been doing of late, about the rapacious shadow of capitalism falling over Eastern Europe as Churchill's Iron Curtain is lifted, are in reality inviting that suffocating black sash to drop again. Churchill saved the neck of *his* chicken and left us with peace and prosperity in the 1950s. It remains to be seen whether we are intelligent and robust enough in the 1990s to save our own necks from the doom sellers and vultures of the left who are today ready to make a meal of us."

Max leaned back in his chair and grinned happily. He wrote on a yellow sticky note, "Definitely not *Berger's* material. Over to you, chief." He scribbled his initials, attached the note beside the words "SOME CHICKEN," and took the typescript down the hall to Chaser's in-basket.

CHAPTER 4

Arnold Sturgess lifted his craggy face from his hands and smoothed his bushy silver eyebrows. He was confronting his "affliction," the affliction he had alternately resisted and appeased all his journalistic life. He had won newspaper awards. He had won magazine awards. The affliction had never been cured.

First sentences did not visit him as gifts from God, the way they dropped into the heads of other writers. Arnold had to struggle for them. Or wish desperately for them. Or even lift them.

Having to survive the new editor of *Berger's* only made this anxiety worse. Chaser Makepeace was a difficult man to work for and an impossible one to respect. *Slippery little Mr. Snakepace, always coiling around the office, head poised to strike. Rigoletto, doing his master's bidding, with malice aforethought.*

Arnold had imagined other endings for himself. To finish as an employee of the malignant dwarf Chaser Makepeace — town crier, court jester, scandal-monger, and self-promoter *sans pareil* — was an indignity the older man found hard to bear. Chaser had a habit of using his power to make people look foolish, and Arnold was damned if he was going to end his working life looking like an old fool.

The telephone honked. It was Sheila Moses. Could she have a minute?

"For you, my dear, the whole afternoon. How about the opera tonight? I have tickets to Lucia di Lammermoor. I am" — he paused for effect — "one of the few old rakes left in the garden, as you may remember." Once, just after he'd left his second marriage, Sheila had amicably reproached him for being a rake, which he had taken as a compliment.

She laughed. "When are you going to get Alzheimer's like the rest of us?"

"I have it. I forgot to tell you."

"Can you help me, Arnold dear," she said sweetly. "I'm doing a piece on Edward Clubb for *Uptrends*. And hoping you can fill in some gaps for me."

He replied that he had heard *Canadian Investment* magazine was about to come out with the same story.

"Arnold, it's called herd journalism. We can all smell the same tasty meal."

There was no escape. Every friend he'd ever had in the business had called him in the year following Clubb's purchase of *Berger's*. Arnold disliked these calls — they were an inevitable reminder that his own professional ambitions as perpetual editor-in-waiting had again been quashed, this time forever.

And prying questions could expose his wobbly position in the new regime, an unhappy fact that Arnold never admitted outside the office.

Sheila Moses was saying that she'd picked up some street buzz about *Berger's*. "I'm hearing Edward Clubb isn't pleased with the huge loss the magazine is running. And that he's thinking of dumping the title." Was Chaser Makepeace feeling any heat? And was it true about the massive losses?

"Well, let's just say you wouldn't know it judging by my salary, Sheila. If there are hefty losses, they've been lost some place other than in my pay cheque. No, I doubt Clubb is shopping us around. Very unlikely." There were schemes afoot, he told her cryptically. Schemes that he couldn't discuss, but — off the record — she'd be safe in assuming that the plans bore no relation to the rumours she'd been hearing.

"And how about Mr. Clubb's bow-tied boy wonder? Has Chaser Makepeace made the transition between newspapers and magazines without causing any bodily harm?"

"I don't think Rigoletto — as I've privately christened him — has hurt himself at all. Other people here are suffering from assorted mishaps in his wake, though. I personally have developed a massive brain injury from reading manuscripts that Rigoletto has brought in, most of them penned by old cronies of his. And *that* is definitely off the record." Arnold paused, then ended more cautiously. "But I've been through it enough times to know that every new editor can be depended on to create havoc."

As he put down the phone and pressed the do-not-disturb button, Arnold felt a mixture of relief and disgust. Scrambling to stay ahead of Chaser Makepeace was an undignified game.

He yawned and stretched. The clock on the bookcase read just after eleven. His monthly column on media was beginning to take shape on his desk. The proverbial headless horseman. Begun in the middle, with no top.

My curse.

He read through what he'd written and felt uneasy scanning the last paragraph. Moving over to a pile of back issues by the window, he checked an article on the same theme that he had done for the March issue.

"Other than the flash of an exploding bomb, television is the only light we know that adds to the sum of human darkness," he had written in the concluding paragraph of his March column. And just now, for the June issue, he had read his own sentence about the tube being "the light that failed." Too close, he decided, tossing the old issue back on the pile.

But it was the absent lead that bothered him most. He took

Understanding Media by Marshall McLuhan from his bookshelf and began thumbing through it.

★ ★ ★

Late that day, Chaser carried the "SOME CHICKEN" typescript as well as Arnold's freshly written media column down the hall to Dorothy Scrivener's office.

"How's my senior editor today?"

"I'm reconstructing a piece the writer has already rewritten twice. It mostly got worse each time he did it." Her face gave away nothing but a hint of irony in the smile. The straight red hair framed a pale, lined face that was masked by heavily tinted glasses.

"I still don't entirely understand it," he said. "All these magazine freelancers who regularly need two or three rewrites, they wouldn't last a week in newspapers."

"A lot of them *are* in newspapers," she replied crisply. "That's their problem. They mistakenly believe that readers slide through magazines the way they skim newspapers over coffee in the morning. Our pages have to stand up to month-long scrutiny. They are not tomorrow's fish wrap."

Chaser had heard this little lesson almost weekly since he had arrived from the *Tribune* in the fall. "Speaking of which," he said, "could you do me a favour and read these two pieces? I've got difficulties with both of them."

She glanced at the cover pages. "*Edward Clubb*? He wants to appear in this magazine?" She pursed her lips, signalling mischief, and added, "Who's going to edit him?"

"That's the least of my problems with that essay, believe me. I'd just like your opinion on whether it's publishable."

She looked at the other title page. "What's your cavil with Arnold's column? He's one of the most reliably interesting magazine writers in the country."

"Yes, yes, of course. Bless you. He's a crackerjack craftsman. I just think this media column is getting tired. And it's got a from-on-high tone I'm not keen on. I think the media column might be a good perch for someone younger."

Dot glared at him. "Most of the young freelancers who come through this office can't string three sentences together without help. Experience does count for something in this business, you know."

Chaser smiled. "That's why I rely on you so much."

"Have you talked this through with Arnold?"

"No."

"Has he seen Clubb's piece?"

"Max has seen it. I don't want too many chefs stirring this pot. Tell me how it strikes you, and I'll take it from there."

"Don't you think your deputy editor should see it?" Her deep, smoker's voice now had a resentful edge.

Chaser stood up to leave. "Actually, I'd prefer he didn't, if you'll do me that favour. I don't want Clubb's piece to be fodder for anyone outside the magazine. But I'd very much like your discreet take on it. And on Arnold's piece too. Just between you and me, okay?"

CHAPTER 5

April 14

After he had pulled Max into his office, Arnold offered to get them both morning coffee, and Max sat waiting for him. He looked again at all of Arnold's things, the awards framed on the walls, the bookcases stuffed with knick-knacks and worn volumes — reference works, essay collections, a dozen books on opera, and shelves of Canadian novels. This was a traditional journalist's lair, unlike the other spaces at the magazine. Chaser's much larger room was decorated in Man-of-Letters-Bombast and the other editorial offices were all Utility Modern. Arnold's, by contrast, felt lived in.

Among the awards hung on the walls were a bright Miro print and Arnold's touchstone epigrams. Over his typing table, Voltaire advised, "One should always aim at being interesting rather than exact." And framed on the side wall was a passage from Samuel Butler, which Arnold had copied in his own hand. It was taken from *The Way of All Flesh*. Arnold had added the words "A Cautionary Tale" as a headline:

Sometimes his articles were actually published, and he found the editor had edited them according to his own fancy, putting in jokes which he thought were funny, or cutting out the very passage which Ernest had considered the point of the whole thing, and then, though the articles appeared, when it came to paying for them it was another matter, and he never saw his money. "Editors," he said to me one day about this time, "are like the people who bought and sold in the book of Revelation; there is not one but has the mark of the beast upon him."

Arnold walked in and set the coffee mugs down on his desk. "Here's the problem I have." He looked sheepishly from under his feathery silver eyebrows. "What seems to be happening is that Rigoletto wants to marginalize me. I'm hearing he dislikes my media column. I also know I'm not privy to things I probably should be. My antennae may not be what they once were, but I'm still pretty good at smelling blood, especially when it's my own. I have a hunch he views me as a culture snob, a sort of useless antique."

Hell, thought Max, office politics. He had never heard Arnold speak of Chaser in this way. The Rigoletto joke had been running for months, but it was offhand and light-hearted, and seemed to spring naturally from Arnold's ironic nature and his passion for opera. But with this talk of bloodlust a line had been crossed. "I'm one of your fans," Max said. "You already know that. I'll certainly stick my paddle in, for what it's worth."

"It would be useful if you could let me know what you pick up in the corridors. If I can, I'd like to stay a step ahead of our tiny helmsman." Arnold gulped the rest of his coffee, rolled his chair away from his desk, and leaned back. "Chaser Makepeace is a talented man in his own peculiar way, you know. But he doesn't really understand his position. He can have my head if he wants. I can't stop him. But it won't help his cause. I'm reminded of that wonderful line of Chamfort's: 'Rank without merit earns deference without respect.' He'll get the deference alright. That comes with the job. But you can tell he wants more than that."

"Mmmhmm," Max nodded. "Pure unadorned deference doesn't have enough calories for Chaser. It's just an hors d'oeuvre. He needs the full juice-dripping meal of respect, adulation, and envy. I've noticed more than a few people in our line of work with that kind of appetite."

Arnold's sagging face lifted. "And most of them manage to do very well. Have I ever told you my simple, two-word diagnosis for what ails this business?"

Max shook his head.

"Shit floats," Arnold croaked with a broad smile. "The worst writing, the worst people, the loudmouths and the power-mongers, they all rise to the top. I've come to regard it as a natural law. Clear thinking and deft writing always have to fight like hell to get even a breath of oxygen in the swamp."

He swung his chair away to face the window; then he stood and, staring distantly out over the department store opposite, ran his fingers through the silver hair that grew wildly from ear to ear.

"Of course, it's been said better. Yeats, for one. 'The worst are full of passionate intensity.' Except I've always believed that line has a note of tabloid journalism in it." Arnold laughed grimly as he wheeled around.

Max, to his surprise, saw that Arnold looked embarrassed.

"Do you know the marvelous Caruso line about shit?" the older man went on, his eyes suddenly merry again.

Max didn't.

"It's a lovely one." Arnold inhaled deeply and extended his arms. " 'You know whatta you do when you shit? Singing, it's the same thing, only up!' " He dropped his arms. "No-one in our business would dare say anything like that publicly about journalism. People would think they were referring to our product rather than our effort." Then he looked apologetic again. "This is a tough business, as I'm sure you know, but I've always loved it. Lots of my friends got out, went into advertising or into public relations. They've got pensions now; some of them made a lot of money. I'm chronically broke. But I've had a helluva good time." He stopped for a moment and then murmured tentatively, "I suppose I also like to think I've occasionally written some good stuff."

When he left the deputy editor's office, Max carried a period picture in his mind's eye. Sometimes he imagined sepia prints of Arnold, a vulnerable creature who belonged to a more cultured age. In this faded photograph, the older man was wearing a new fedora and a lamb's-wool overcoat. He sat in a dusty 1940s Buick sedan. It was winter, and the snowbanks were piled high. On a dark country road, the car's engine was cold.

CHAPTER 6

April 15

At eleven o'clock in the morning Chaser Makepeace was staring at Dot's opinion written in her cramped spidery hand on a series of yellow sticky notes.

"I see a problem with E. Clubb's essay. He is not an expert. He has done no research. He employs a very mannered *son et lumière* prose style — with too much *son* and not nearly enough *lumière*. There is far too much about Himself and not nearly enough hard analysis about why the Soviet empire is collapsing.

"But — why not turn all this to our advantage? If he wants to be a journalist, let's make him one. He has access, through his business connections in London and New York, to people most writers wouldn't even think to call. Ask him to do some interviews. He can give us a window onto how High Capitalism views the end of Communism. It won't be hot news, but it might be a fascinating slice of social reality. As it is, all we have are his private ruminations and pontifications, which are an embarrassment."

"Fuuuuuck," groaned Chaser out loud.

He read on. "Re: A.S.'s media column. I think this is his usual perceptive, elegant essay. It's written for those who read rather than those who watch TV. A bad thing? Isn't that why we exist?" Dot had appended her initials.

"Dot," Chaser began a note. "We cannot keep this magazine afloat if we continue to cater to geriatric subscribers, some of whom have been reading us since before they even *owned* a TV. Yes we should have well-crafted essays in the book. No we shouldn't ignore the cathode-ray-tube generation. They are exactly who we should be trying to seduce into our pages. We . . ."

He stopped, reread his note, crumpled it up, and was about to toss it away when his secretary appeared with the day's mail.

Chaser pushed aside his work and eagerly took a handful of letters.

Dear Editor:

    I have been reading <u>Berger's</u> magazine since the hungry thirties when my mother used to scrimp on housekeeping expenditures so we could afford a subscription. You are the inheritor of a proud Canadian tradition. But are you living up to it?

    I would like to know why you published the sensational exposé of transvestite people in Vancouver. Canada faces many problems. Your magazine should be discussing them, not pandering to pornographers and hedonists. I hope this is a momentary lapse and not a sign of the new direction you intend for the magazine. You will lose people like me unless you publish articles that reflect community values.

Arthur McClintock

East End, Sask.

Dear Mr. Makepeace:

    Whatever happened to your monthly food page? The world is changing so fast all around us. The food page has been part of our lives since the

1950s, as reliable as my kitchen table. Perhaps
you don't realize how much your readers have come
to depend on certain features. I don't mind the
new design which you started last month. You seem
to be putting in more pictures now. Fine. But I
hate it when the headlines jump all around the
page. And please bring back Margery Steadman on
cooking. We rely on her sure culinary hand.

Beatrice Frellick
President, Seabright Cooking Circle,
Seabright, Nova Scotia

Dear Mr. Makepeace:
Your recent article, written from a Moscow
perspective, on the fall of the Berlin Wall was
excellent. We have too few first-hand accounts of
world events written by Canadians in the Canadian
press, which depends too much on American sources.
Your article was a refreshing exception. I admire
the changes you are making at Berger's, where I
believe a shake-up was long overdue. Keep up the
good work.
Prof. Nathan Binstock
Dept. of History
Dalhousie University, Halifax

Chaser plucked this one from the pile and placed it in a folder
marked "For Publication." He read on through the pile. Most
of the letters were complaints about how the magazine had
changed since his tenure began. A few were cancelling sub-
scriptions because of articles readers had found offensive.
There were a couple of commendations. About two-thirds of
the way down in the pile he found a neatly typed letter with a
Montreal address.

43

Dear Editors:

  I noted with particular interest the article by Arnold Sturgess in your April issue. I am doing research on communications theory here at McGill, and so I try to keep an eye on what the media has to say about itself.

  Here are the first three sentences from Chapter 11 of Amusing Ourselves to Death by the American communications gadfly Neil Postman: "There are two ways by which the spirit of a culture may be shriveled. In the first — the Orwellian — culture becomes a prison. In the second — the Huxleyan — culture becomes a burlesque."

  Now take at look at the opening three sentences of the Sturgess article: "The spirit of a culture can be shriveled in one of two ways. It can be squeezed in an Orwellian vice to become a prison. Or it can descend into Huxleyan parody to become a burlesque."

  Frankly, I found the Sturgess article fascinating and nicely written. Why would you stoop to near-plagiarism in the opening paragraph? Surely that is unnecessary. In academe, careers are ruined by this kind of stunt. I had always assumed a distinguished popular journal such as yours would espouse high standards of intellectual integrity. Now I'm not so sure.

                              Jonathan Pluman
                              McGill University

Chaser reread the letter. He walked across the room, picked up a copy of the April *Berger's*, and checked the quoted passage against the article.

Then he walked down to Arnold's office.

Arnold looked up from a page he was editing. "Hello, Chaser. Had a chance to look at my media piece?"

"Yes. Well, not entirely. I'm not quite ready to talk about it. Actually I need a favour for something else I'm working on. Do you by any chance have a copy of Neil Postman's book *Amusing Ourselves to Death*?"

The older man seemed startled. "I think I did have one at some point."

"Bless you, old trout. Could I possibly borrow it, if it's still around?"

Arnold glanced unenthusiastically at his book shelves. "Sure." He stood up and ran his eyes along the rows of titles. Then he turned to Chaser. "Thinking of taking over my beat?" Even with his slight stoop, he was six inches taller than the *Berger's* editor. He looked down on Chaser with a sardonic smile.

"No, no, of course not. It's not for an article."

Arnold went back to his shelves. "Here we are." He pulled out a paperback and removed the bookmark. "Happy reading."

Chaser took the book back to his office. Standing by his desk, he checked the Postman passage against Jonathan Pluman's letter, then snapped the paperback shut. The editor laid the letter on his desk. Looking out the window, he saw a faint outline of himself against the light. He watched the reflection move as he raised one hand and gave the glass a satisfied thumb's up.

CHAPTER 7

April 21

Max arrived late at Saint Simon the Apostle Church on Bloor Street. The sun was blazing, the trees were brushed with the first tufts of green, and the day was so unusually warm that the mourners queueing outside the church were carrying their coats. A few faces had been browned by the Florida sun. Max thought most people in the crowd looked happier than they should. But Arnold might have liked it that way.

For his part Max felt queasy, even more so when he realized that from here on Bloor Street you could almost see where it had happened.

The line at the church's side door stretched out to the sidewalk and down the street. Toronto's media establishment appeared to be out in large numbers for the event. Max saw several familiar faces as he made his way to the end of the queue. Jeremy Glass the novelist, Michael Rector the political columnist, Andrew Rice the publisher, and Lilian Tillerman the television personality were all engaged in conversation as they stood in line. Max caught an interesting snippet as he passed, and hesitated for a moment.

". . . reputation as a randy old goat."

"So the sexual harassment story is true?"

"'Swhat I hear."

"Yeah, but that's hardly a capital offence."

"I'm told it wasn't the first time," Lilian Tillerman said, and then she became aware of Max lingering on the sidewalk. She beamed at him warmly. "Max Vellen!" Then she dropped her smile. "We're so distressed by what happened. You all know Max Vellen, don't you?"

"Hello all," said Max. The other three seemed unusually friendly too. They opened up their circle to include him. Normally, Max mused, Lilian Tillerman could barely summon his name. Once, in a supermarket, she had looked right through him, as if he'd been nothing more than a few notes of Musak. And Andrew Rice: "No-one knows who you are" were the words Max remembered from the time he had approached the publisher with a book idea two years earlier.

"Were you and Arnold close?" Lilian purred. The other three looked on intently.

"A great guy. But almost impossible to know," Max replied as he began to move away. He gestured down the line. "I'm meeting someone."

Vultures.

At the end of the queue he found himself standing beside John Bowen, a wunderkind newspaper reporter-turned-radio host, and Annabel Schon, the new entertainment editor at the *Herald*.

"Do you know what led up to it?" Annabel asked cheerily. Max felt vaguely alarmed by his attraction to her big, delicious, gossip-hungry eyes. "Was there any sign of deep distress? I've heard some weird stories."

Looking over her shoulder at the line growing behind them, Max said, "All I know is that Chaser Makepeace practically went into cardiac arrest when he got the news. What have you been hearing?"

"There's a story going around that Arnold was about to be taken to court for sexual harassment. But no-one seems to know who the alleged harassee was."

"I'm sure I'd have heard," said Max. "*Berger's* is a very small place."

"Money worries," John Bowen announced. He spoke with a mannered cadence, as he did for a living on his CBC radio program. He cocked his head back slightly, so that his thick, rock-star curls bounced on his shoulders, and added, "Money was the grim reaper here." He looked hard at Max, apparently letting the insight sink in. "Arnold told me more than once that he had almost nothing put by. And no pension. I foolishly disbelieved him when he said that he dreaded ending his life as a security guard."

"I didn't know him that well," Max shrugged. "I could tell he wasn't happy being passed over for the *Berger's* editorship, but that was many months ago. I just assumed he'd made his peace with it."

"Maybe he'd just had enough. Of everything," said Annabel.

John Bowen looked offended. "I'd say exactly the opposite. Arnold was a man of appetites. Never enough of anything! He was a boon companion over a shot of whiskey, I can tell you. A wonderful five-o'clock man." He turned to address Max. "I think you're right about the *Berger's* editorship. The last time I saw him he made a sharp remark about your Mr. Makepeace. Arnold had adopted a pet name for him. From a favourite opera." He rubbed his carefully unshaven chin.

"Rigoletto," said Max.

"Yes! Rigoletto."

"I forget who that was," Annabel said.

"Rigoletto is a malign dwarf in the same-name opera," said Max. "As far as I could tell, Arnold used it as a friendly pejorative."

"But I'll bet he never used it to your boss's face."

"It was definitely a third-party thing." Max smiled.

"He was emphatic as all hell," the radio host declaimed in his smooth baritone, "that he would never be able to bond with Chaser Makepeace."

Max remembered his last serious talk with Arnold. "There were tensions alright. How could there not be? Arnold had twenty years behind him in magazines and saw Makepeace as a brazen interloper with well-oiled connections." He stopped, eyed them both. "This is off-the-record, all this stuff, okay? I'd like to keep my job."

He pointed across the street. "Eerie, no? That's where it happened, down the street on that foot-bridge over the ravine, in full public view. An early morning jogger found him just after sunrise. Apparently he used to walk over to come to church here, every Sunday. I always assumed he was an atheist."

They filed into Saint Simon's. Hundreds of people were crowded into the small church; additional chairs had been carried in to accommodate them all. Max saw two former *Berger's* editors seated in pews nearby. He took his place just off from the side door in one of the last available portable chairs. He could see into part of the chancel, and across the nave to the far side of the church where Arnold's sister and niece occupied a front pew. Beside them sat several men and women who looked to be in their sixties and seventies. Max recognized one of their faces from a picture in Arnold's office — the second Mrs. Sturgess.

The service began. He looked into the back end of the church and tried to guess how many mourners there were.

I am the resurrection, and the life: he that believeth in me . . .

Six or seven hundred? Arnold, if you had only known. But would they have attended, say, the book launch for your memoirs?

Naked came I out of my mother's womb, and naked shall I return thither: the Lord gave, and the Lord hath . . .

From where he sat, Max could see the draped coffin. Migawd Arnold, what angst-ridden mental space did you find yourself in, your richly painted world reduced to nothing but a frigging all-purpose nylon cord? Why, with all your words, a precise paragraph-maker over lunch and neat gin, an easy yarnspinner with red wine after work, a maestro who made ideas sing on the page — why did you finish in silence?

For am I persuaded that neither death, nor life, nor angels, nor principalities, nor powers, nor things present, nor things to come, nor height, nor depth, nor any other creature . . .

A formal, operatic exit. But no curtain call. And, so the police said, no libretto.

Awfully frigging strange, that part.

The rector's voice was a signal intermittently received. Funerals are like warm baths, thought Max, who preferred a hot shower. You lie there and slosh around and occasionally you're conscious of being in the tub, but more often you drift off somewhere else.

For a thousand years in thy sight are but as yesterday when it is past, and as a watch in the night.

Thou carriest them away as with a flood; they are as a sleep; in the morning they are like grass . . .

Max searched his brain for some word, some hint. There had been that last afternoon heart-to-heart, pessimistic but not what anyone would have called life-threatening. And the next morning Arnold had been effusive about the opera, as high-spirited as he ever was.

The days of our lives are threescore years and ten . . .

In the afternoon the old boy had been closeted for a while in Chaser's office. After which he had gone straight to his own room and closed his door, not his usual practice.

. . . for it is soon cut off, and we fly away . . .

The next morning he had not appeared at the magazine.

So teach us to number our days . . .

And the morning after that, they found him.

As everyone sat, Max watched Chaser Makepeace walk up the centre aisle from his pew. He turned to the right, mounted two steps, his straight white hair bouncing on the collar of

his navy blue blazer. Then he laid on the brass lectern a sheet
of paper that he had pulled from his breast pocket. He was
wearing a purple bow tie.

An oily speech, thought Max.

But as Chaser began, Max could hear it was a poem, not a
speech.

"Sunset and evening star
And one clear call for me! . . ."

The sister must have asked him, Max decided, with the best
of intentions: honour thy brother. He watched his employer,
only slightly taller than the lectern, bat out the century-old
lines like tennis balls. To Max he sounded like a little barrel
organ being turned through an old dance-hall melody.

Tabloid verse, Arnold would have called it.

"For though . . .
The flood may bear me far,
I hope to see my Pilot face to face
When I have crossed the bar."

Phew! Chaser stepped down and strutted back to his seat. A
hymn was sung. As prayers were led by the rector, Max's eye
settled on the downy blonde that feathered the neck of Annabel Schon, who was seated in front of him. She was wearing a
wide-brimmed black straw hat.

The prayers ended. He looked at the order-of-service. Psalm
23. He waited for someone to step forward to do the reading.
Instead a woman, with her silky auburn hair braided and
pinned, emerged from the choir stalls. The organ sounded a
bar and she began to float the words in a rich soprano.

"The Lord is my shepherd . . ."

Her voice looped through the air like a swallow.

They got this right, thought Max. A silly headline popped
unbidden into his head, as often happened now that he was
writing them for a living: DIVA'S SONOROUS LAMENTATION
BIDS ARIA LOVER ADIEU.

As the music soared and fell, Max focused again on the neck in front of him.

"*. . . leadeth me beside the still waters.*"

He examined the zipper that divided the back of Annabel's black dress. The zipper and the downy neck. He imagined himself leaning forward . . .

"*Thou preparest a table before me in the presence of mine enemies . . .*"

And laying a long, gentle lick on her downy skin with his tongue.

"*. . . in the house of the Lord forever.*"

Hold that tongue!

"The time you first licked me in public," he could hear her say, "you could have gone to jail for sexual assault."

The soprano turned and disappeared into the chancel.

Say a prayer for the old boy, thought Max with a pang of guilt. Maybe I just did.

He looked down at the order of service. "Eulogy: Mr. Alexander Campbell."

From the front row where the sister and ex-wife were sitting, a stooped, grey-haired man even older-looking than Arnold made his way up to the lectern.

He took a pair of reading glasses from his pocket and placed them carefully on his nose.

"Those of you who knew us both knew that Arnold and I were on the Normandy beaches together. After that we attended the same university. We went back a long way.

"Arnold, you may also know, left McGill after receiving his arts degree and immediately went back into newspapers, which is what he'd been doing before the war. He was a bright student. I tried to persuade him to join me in graduate school.

" 'I don't want to sit around parsing dead writers,' he told me then. He said he wanted to become a writer himself. And so he did. He wrote for his living for almost half a century, first in newspapers, then in magazines. Many of his best essays were collected in his two books, which are both, if I may offer my opinion as a professor of English literature, superb volumes.

"Look back at those books and you will find an erudite commentary on the flowering of modern Canadian literature. You will also find a Canadian voice and a Canadian sensibility. The dear friend and writer we remember today began life in Montreal and worked as a newspaper editor in Manitoba and Saskatchewan before finally settling in Toronto. He knew his country."

Max's attention drifted away from the professor's worthy words and back onto the little blonde hairs on the back of Annabel's neck. Chicken parts, he thought, annoyed with himself. Neck, breasts, thighs. Not supposed to see female flesh in this neanderthal way anymore.

He imagined Annabel's breasts, lifting with her breathing. He looked desperately back to the lectern.

". . . can there be any doubt about that. I think it fair to say that he fought for his country in more ways than one. He cared deeply about being Canadian, and made good on that commitment all his writing life. He saw us struggling to build a culture and a literature that was our own, not a colonial copy and not a borrowed import . . ."

You don't even know whether you *like* Annabel, Max reflected. This is how you get into serious trouble.

". . . believed in making a contribution. About ten years ago I told him I thought it was appalling he was not better known in this country. I remember his sardonic reply. 'Fame,' he said, quoting the philosopher Emerson, 'is proof that the people are gullible. . . .' "

Max glanced at the draped coffin. The grave's a fine and private place. Suddenly in his mind's eye Sarah's face appeared, eyeing him reproachfully. Then she moistened her lips with her tongue. Max blinked and tried to focus again on the professor.

"... but why shouldn't we? In a less temperate moment, he once said to me, 'Canadians eat their young, of course. But they know how to carve up their middle-aged colleagues too.'"

Necrophagia? You could hear a rustling in the pews. Max looked over at the faces in the front rows and thought he could see some eyes widening and lips pursing with alarm.

No knives in church, please.

Professor Campbell looked up from his text and smiled reassuringly. "That's just a brief nod to ironic realism. I'm sure Arnold would have urged us, above all, to turn our attention to realism today. We are here to console ourselves, yes, but also to remember him as he was, with all his splendid barbs and edges . . ."

Too bad, thought Max. Would have made a great send-off. Heated discussion of corporate cannibalism just before they wheeled him out.

The professor finished with a tribute to Arnold's love of art and music. As he stepped down, Max could see the heads of two men making their way out of the choir stalls to the middle of the chancel.

The next item in the order of service, he read, was the "Church sonata by Petronio Franceschini." He gazed at the carved timbers, warm against the white stucco ceiling, and waited for the organ and voices.

Instead he was startled by a single long note blown from a horn.

Like a liquid drum roll poured into the air.

He looked down and saw that both men in the chancel had trumpets pressed to their lips. The second player joined in on the fourth lachrymose note.

The pure, clear sounds of the horns vaulted across time and space, taking Saint Simon's with them. Max envisaged

Arnold's stone with nothing but Franceschini's first four notes carved on it.

Pallbearers emerged from their pews to wheel the casket out.

The trumpets played on. Max could see him now, as everyone who had heard the full story must have seen him in their minds' eyes. Dressed as for the opera in starched white shirt and dinner jacket. The aluminum stepladder kicked over on the bridge. An old man swinging lightly in the early morning air currents, the nylon cord tightly squeezed above his perfectly knotted black bow-tie.

CHAPTER 8

April 29

Sarah sat at the computer in her bedroom typing frenetically, still hoping to meet a May target date for the September title she was editing. The author, Frank Gitlin, had been late. He regularly missed the manuscript deadline for his Zeke Mud-cutter books. Privately she thought of Gitlin's series as the "Cudmutter Books," because the author adopted a hick-farmer persona to write hee-haw sallies on contemporary issues. Sarah had once suggested in a planning meeting that the publishing house produce scratch-and-smell bookmarks to promote these titles, but her editorial director, who had escaped a small farm in the Ottawa Valley when he was eighteen, had told her that too many middle-aged Canadian readers had grown up near the odour of real cow shit — farming was too close a condition to romanticize. "Frank ridicules it. That's a different thing," he'd explained.

Well, okay, but how could a bookmark that smelled of clover and pig swill *not* be ridiculous?

Sarah typed: "Now yew take thet there Mr. Gorbychuff. I'm all fer thet glass-nose pulissy of his wich lets all them Rushuns reed a buk. But the danghest thing is, he's also got this here poor-he-strikes-ya thingamabob that isn't leavin 'em any of their rubbles to buy a buk *with*. Now if that don't sound like Canada! First, Prime Muffer McGravy sez he wantsta fight illyatiteracy — that's a diseese ya get when ya don't lern yer Ableyseas. Then he takes out the old sharpenin stone and puts the tacks on buks. Juss lookin in a bukstore now practikly makes yer fingers bleed. Ya juss can't win."

In two hours Sarah had written twelve pages, flying through it on her computer. This was her sixth Cudmutter title; with each one she had to write more chapters herself. The titles had become solid moneyspinners, both for Gitlin and for Fulton House Press. A dreadful commentary on Canadian book publishing, she felt, but in a moment of sophomoric folly she'd recommended the firm buy the first one, and now she was stuck with one a year, an unshakeable little profit centre in hard times. Even Frank Gitlin counted on the sales, though he had long ago lost interest in producing the manuscripts. As she typed, Sarah could see a small picture of him in her mind's eye: a squeaky-voiced, five-foot-five actor with a white goatee and a cigarillo, who liked putting on overalls and performimg his Mudcutter routine at men's service clubs.

After he'd delivered the third title, he'd told Sarah that writing the material had become a grim chore. This time he'd managed to come up with only two-thirds of a book. She was keeping in a separate folder all the pages she'd done herself. If she was going to co-write these dumb bestsellers, she wanted some of the credit.

Jill rang, calling from her desk at the *Herald*. Sarah stretched her cramped fingers and confessed she was feeling torn between pride and disgust. "I've been making cow pies since six this morning. Cutting mud, to be precise. Twelve pages. I'd be elated with my progress if this drivel weren't so shameful."

"Poor Sarah. Behind every stumblebum author stands a brilliant editor. Or co-author, in this case."

"Yeah. The invisible angel. Maybe it's this anonymity that's got me thinking of writing a magazine article of my own."

"Really? About how female editors are exploited?"

"No, no. About . . . other stuff."

"Yes?"

"I'll tell you when I've figured it out."

"You should talk to the editor of *Wellington*. Best magazine in town."

"I'm not sure. It may be more of a women's magazine piece."

"Have you seen the new *Wellington*? The May issue? It has a profile of Edward Clubb in it. And migawd, does the writer ever stick the knife in. The word around here is that Clubb is suing. Apparently his lawyers have already filed. He's particularly pissed about the way some of his business deals have been maligned."

"Who wrote the piece?"

"Jeremy Glass," said Jill. "Do you know him? I think he writes books."

"Yes. Thrillers. Quite good, the two I read."

"Well, he's in for a few thrills himself. He used words like 'bully' and 'browbeat' and 'railroad' to describe Clubb's negotiating tactics. Which is asking for trouble. Those people at *Wellington* must have a death wish. They're going to get Clubbed with a vengeance."

"Maybe Clubb will just buy the title," Sarah suggested, as she pictured him pop-eyed and jowly in his unfashionable and rumpled suit, standing like a beached whale amid the *Berger's* Christmas party year before last, with Max — still a freelancer then — teetering drunkenly in the background, making a gargoyle face behind his future employer's back. "He could merge it with *Berger's*. They could call the new magazine *Burgherton*. Sounds very old Toronto."

"Ha. Or *Wellburger*. The guy could use a few of those. Anyway, they may have to just call it quits. Mr. Clubb takes no prisoners. But it was a fun piece. One of my favourite lines was the description of his bloated face and oversized eye teeth. I've got it here. Lemme read you a bit:

"'Clubb certainly does not resemble Toronto's typical squash-playing WASP business executive. He lumbers around town in baggy grey suits, perhaps to mask his wide girth, and his face looks like a cross between a wolverine on steroids and Orson Welles with a hangover. His eye teeth dangle like sharp little daggers, and when he opens his mouth wide to laugh — by all accounts an infrequent event — you can see some of his illiquid assets, two gold crowns on molars that had chewed one chestnut too many.'"

Jill hooted with laughter. "Jeremy Glass is a brave man. I'd like to meet him. While he's still got bus fare."

"I'll pick it up when I'm out. Which should be just about now. I have to be at the dentist in half an hour."

"You haven't told me anything about Martin," Jill protested.

"I'll call you later in the week. Promise." Sarah felt relieved as she put down the phone.

Later, walking west along Bloor to her dentist's office, she thought about what she hadn't wanted to say on the phone. For days now she'd been waking in the early grey light, brewing coffee, staring at the soggy April backyard, and trying to imagine how she would feel if Martin were there with her every morning. The prospect didn't excite her, didn't even reassure her, and she had been feeling angry with herself that she had let the entanglement go this far without admitting that he was wrong for her. She knew now she should have waited longer after Max before getting involved with someone. But she'd been lonely, and loneliness could so easily trip you up. After a long spell of it the heat and excitement of discovering someone new rushed in to fill the empty space. And the rush had thrown her off. She thought of herself as self-sufficient — God knows, she'd had to be — but not as a loner, not at all. She'd always imagined being with someone, a permanent link, and so she did feel she had in her life an unoccupied space, a reserved seat, carefully kept, for a male.

She had told Martin she needed some time to think. That had been ten days ago. He'd been phoning, probably sensing that something had gone awry. She'd have to face him soon.

The day had turned glum. Clouds blotted the sky now and a cold wind left over from March was raking the street. She felt the weariness of the long winter, the annual climate fatigue that had lifted for only a few merciful days this month when the April sun had slipped through. But, as she'd tried to explain recently to Martin, spring, never dependable in Toronto, was really a colonial concept, mostly hope and illusion. He'd given her a puzzled look. *Geez, Martin, clue in, it's obvious.* One week you're still living in late winter, the next you could be plunged into a hot, soupy, summer day — not like gentle Europe. But when she used terms like "colonial" with Martin, he retreated into what she thought of as his "biznology bafflegab." He'd say something defensive and deeply infuriating like: "Colonialism was the beginning of the global economy. Where'd we be without it? Cleaning horse dung out of some stable in Yorkshire, I have no doubt."

Bits of paper and dust lifted into the air. Sarah squinted as her hand touched the front-door handle of the three-storey red-brick building where her dentist had his office. The door swung open before she could pull it and an unshaven, middle-aged man stepped out, pushed past her, and went back towards Spadina Avenue. The face — a balding, oversized head with clumsily cut features, like an Easter Island statue of some sourpuss Polynesian god — she thought familiar, but couldn't place it. A friend of Max's? No. But somehow there seemed to be a Max connection. Another writer?

She was sitting in the dentist's chair with her jaw frozen and one of her rear molars being ground down for a gold cap when she remembered: Jerome Segal. She'd met him once at a party Max had taken her to — Segal, the aggrieved left-wing media critic whose carefully constructed public persona of fearless truth-teller, anti-corporate crusader, and avant-garde male feminist was complicated for those who knew him by his private obsessions: doing damage to his competitors and preying on young women.

"Is Jerome Segal a patient of yours?" Sarah asked as she wrote out a cheque at the reception. Her lips were puffy from the anaesthetic.

The secretary looked blank. "Never heard of him," she said. "Should I have?"

Sarah smiled crookedly with her swollen mouth, and shook her head.

After two hours in Dr. Jordan's chair, she was feeling light-headed. On the way out at the bottom of the stairway she brushed past the postman, who was stuffing a fat wad of letters into one of the mailboxes in the little vestibule. More letters than any dentist would get, she thought idly as she walked back towards Spadina, her frozen tongue trying to feel the temporary plastic cap in the back of her mouth.

Then she thought of Edward Clubb's golden molars, as pictured in a recent issue of *Poop* magazine, and then, as often happened when Clubb's name entered her head, she thought of one of his employees, Max Vellen.

CHAPTER 9

"I want that insect Glass crawling on my carpet, begging for a reprieve!" bellowed the chairman of the Janus Corporation into his phone. "I want a twenty-one-gun, royal fucking apology from him *and* his publisher. Or we go to court and give them the reaming they so richly deserve. These snivelling termites think they can chew into my reputation and defecate it in slimy little black lines on the page. Not with impunity, they won't, Justin! And spare them no pain. I want to see some squirming." He banged the receiver down.

"Justin Carrier relishes a good fight — but then why wouldn't he? It's all *lucri causa* on his side. What he really relishes are the fees I pay him."

Graham Nutley, Clubb's financial vice-president, nodded.

"Likes a good fight alright. Likes the money better." Tall, bearded, and balding, Nutley wore the sagacious mien of a rabbi, but was in fact an accountant raised as a Presbyterian.

"Precisely," said Clubb. "But Justin lacks backbone. His letter to Glass's counsel was far too mild in my estimation. Justin, of course, disagrees. Says he demanded an unequivocal apology. But I was appalled when I read what was patently a polite appeal for a settlement."

"It's appalling," Nutley intoned.

"I don't even *aspire* to a settlement. Not yet anyway, not until they've had to quiver and sweat for a few months."

"No," said Nutley.

"No?" Clubb leaned back in his swivel chair and glared.

"What I mean is, yes. Yes, we don't want a settlement."

"I should have drafted the letter myself. I'd have issued exacting conditions: the complete and unqualified disavowal of every slanted assertion in the article, an admission of professional wrongdoing by *Wellington*, and a binding undertaking by them to purchase newspaper notices recanting Glass's excesses. That's what Justin should have insisted on."

"Absolutely," Nutley echoed. "Should have insisted."

"An apology might be honourable, but where is the punishment?"

"Balance the books. As it were."

"Crush them!"

"Yes, of course."

"Crush them to a pulp."

Nutley shifted in his chair. "The *Tribune* has already called," he began. "What's our position?"

"Why do we need a position? I'm not beholden to every gutter pressman who calls my number. We're the plaintiffs. Our grievance is spelled out in the writ. We don't need to elaborate any further."

"No."

"Our *opponents* require a position. Glass should find himself a position. Preferably on his knees. With his palms together in the air." Clubb reached for the wooden box by his telephone.

"Absolutely. On his knees."

"Refer all enquiries to the offices of Carrier & Trench. Say Mr. Clubb is unavailable for comment." He lit a cigar and pressed a button on his desk. The screen on the cabinet beside him crackled alive with parallel trains of letters and numbers moving from top to bottom. "Let's see how the market is doing."

He swung his chair around to have a good look at the screen. "DOW up 7, TSE down 13, consumer products down 4, oil and gas up 12, management companies down 2, gold & silver even, communications & media even. Well, that's in line with the recent trend."

"Right in line."

"Janus is down 3/8; Christ, we've skidded down to $8. That's a firesale price! Inferior to where we stood before my father's death, despite all the value we've created since then. If you calibrate it a certain way — and no doubt many people do — that renders *me* a *negative quantity* in the market."

Clubb glowered at Nutley.

"Uhhhh," said Nutley, glancing nervously out the window. "Nuhmmm." He cleared his throat and looked back at the screen.

"What?"

"Well." Nutley straightened a shirt cuff. "Possibly as a temporary misconception, I suppose."

"So you do think people would see it that way?"

"No. I mean not exactly. On the other hand, you have a point. It's just conceivable that that kind of minority view on asset value might have been factored into the current price in some remote and imponderable way. Today an apple costs twenty-nine cents, next week thirty-nine. It's the same apple. The market is a strange animal, as you know."

"Sometimes you're hard to follow."

"Yes."

"But certainly the slanders that Glass has fabricated do not enhance our image. The pusillanimous little twit! I think it's imperative that he be discredited."

"Right."

"What is the purpose of owning publications if you can't enlist their support when you a need a helping hand? I believe it's incumbent on a magazine like *Berger's* to take a well-defined view on this kind of public issue."

"Uhhhh, yes."

"I'll talk to Chaser Makepeace. Steer him onto that libelous miscreant Glass. Publish an editorial. A rousing polemic. Make Glass look like the mendacious jackass he is."

"Mmmm," said Graham Nutley, staring at the floor.

Clubb's fleshy finger punched the *Berger's* line on his telephone console.

CHAPTER 10

Chaser Makepeace sat in his office flipping through the latest issue of *Poop*, Toronto's six-month-old scandal sheet. He bought it regularly at lunch every other Thursday and in good weather scanned it from cover to cover as he beetled down the sidewalk back to *Berger's*. His first concern was always any mention of himself. He considered it, on balance, helpful that *Poop* fingered him in almost every issue. His professional credo was: keep your name afloat, have it on the tip of every influential tongue in town, and always make sure you're one of the loudest bees in the buzz. But he'd begun to feel some dismay at *Poop*'s Chaser Makepeace items.

The publication had adopted a cluster of national media stars as pet targets, and he could see that he was in danger of sliding into that much-mocked group. One prominent Ottawa television commentator, "Laffy" Moffat — so called because his roly-poly face was stretched into a permanent grin — had been awarded a regular half-page of vicious satire and innuendo. The magazine lampooned his drinking habits, his uncritical coverage of the governing party, and his sexual pecadilloes. The editors of *Poop*, Chaser had heard, even assigned a scavenger to sift through Laffy's garbage for a month. He was currently suing the magazine, but the libel action had only raised *Poop*'s profile and endowed it with added clout.

In the current issue, Chaser reread an item he wished would go away. The editors had run it as part of their regular feature headed "Mediocre Media." It was only a one-paragraph squib, but it stung: "Unimpeachable sources have been whispering some heretofore unknown facts about *Berger's* editor Chaser On-The-Makepeace, well-known Toronto loudmouth and Establishment stenographer. The unctuous Makepeace — who receives a six-figure salary for shining the shoes of his megalomaniacal owner — will soon be saluting the triumphant entry into *Berger's* of one of Canada's most powerful, most despised, most controversial, and most opinionated writers. An unparalleled coup for the sleepy old rag, which has never published this widely feared scribbler before. The writer's name is — we can hardly believe it ourselves — none other than Edward Ossington Clubb himself. Most magazines would kill for that byline. Kill the article, that is. But who said vanity publishing is corrupt and undignified? Nonsense! As the Great Clubber himself might reason, what's a loyal valet good for if not to smooth, polish — and publish — his master's prose?"

How had they got wind of his difficulties with Clubby? He'd told only Max and Dot. And both knew they had to keep it quiet.

He reread the second item, which wasn't bad at all: "Chaser On-The-Makepeace had more than the Great Clubber's megaphone voice in his face this month. The Grim Reaper came around for a visit too. Long-time *Berger's* hack Arnold Sturgess, in the *Tribune's* immortal phrase, 'died suddenly' the morning of April 18.

"Did Sturgess suffer a fatal stroke? Was he run over by a truck? Attacked by an angry writer pissed off at *Berger's* nose-in-the-air editorial policy? You'll never know by reading the *Trib*.

"Police were informed by an early morning jogger that an impeccably dressed stiff was swinging from a lamp post over the pedestrian cross-way linking Rosedale with Bloor Street just east of Sherbourne. The technical cause of death was, as they say in the trade, self-inflicted asphyxiation. Sturgess hung himself over the public walkway with a household nylon cord.

"It has come to our attention that sexual harassment charges were about to be laid against the ancient *Berger's* windbag, who was a noted heterosexualist. Several pretty young things at *Berger's* magazine had apparently complained of his grey, sweaty presence.

"Sturgess was passed over three times in the past fourteen years for the *Berger's* editorship, which must have beaten down the old goat's ego. He continued to pump out his trademark bilge on Canadian culture, which has silted up vast acres of the *Berger's* book over the past two decades.

"Relations were cool between the Jurassic Age culture hack and his new editor, who, Sturgess told friends, was a corporate suck, an indecisive manager, and a brain-deficient scribbler unable to write up to the high standards of *Berger's*.

"On-The-Makepeace appointed Sturgess deputy editor, but in an editorial department of six, who needs a second-in-command? Reliable sources say that the title had no responsibilities attached, and no salary upgrade.

"Sturgess was apparently short of funds for any legal fees that might have have been owing in the near future. (*Berger's*, incidentally, is without a pension plan, and under its current owner, Edward Squeeze'em-Dry Clubb, will not be getting one.)

"The pure maidens of *Berger's* were saddened to learn that no complaint can be laid against the deceased.

"Arnold Sturgess was a great Canadian.

"RIP."

Chaser grinned.

He leafed back through the cheap newsprint pages to the third item that had caught his eye down on the sidewalk. It was another piece that mentioned Clubby, this time on the "Toronto Tattler" page. "Coronary candidate and board-room fog horn Edward "Praise-Me-or-I'll-Bury-You" Clubb will advance into triple-bypass territory when he reads *Wellington*'s May profile of Himself. The scalding bio, written by thriller novelist Jeremy Glass, could have been titled 'Eddie the Clubb, or How a Rich Rosedale Bullyboy Got Richer by Clobbering His Friends and Enemies and Intimidating Complete Strangers.' Eddie, you remember, attended summer school in Palermo between semesters at Upper Canada College. How else to explain his Italian sense of honour? Familiar with the smell of blood, the 800-pound carnivore capitalist is bound to let loose his private pack of trained field legals to bring Mr. Glass to ground. Good luck, Eddie — hell, why use a pop gun when heavy artillery is affordable, eh?

"Was it Eddie who said one gagged critic is worth a hundred PR flacks? Just asking.

"Funeral services will be held for *Wellington*, we believe, in about six months.

"Jeremy Glass was last seen meeting with his travel agent."

Chaser was anxiously walking over to the antique mahogany gaming table where he kept his current magazines spread out in a fan — he wanted to reread the piece in *Wellington* more carefully — when his phone rang and he saw line eleven winking at him. Line eleven was the only one he couldn't ignore.

CHAPTER II

In his office with the door closed, Max sipped his fourth styrofoam cup of coffee, trying to rinse the fug and ache from his brain. His phone was on do-not-disturb, in part because he was still recovering from a beer-sodden night and couldn't tolerate any cranky writers in his ear, but also because he was behind in his work. He examined his photocopied production schedule for the July issue and carefully pencilled notes in the margin, knowing all the while that he was engaged in an utterly futile activity. The writer's final deadline for the cover story — a definitive profile of the prime minister — was today.

Max was the editor responsible for the article, and the only way he could get it into the system was if Leonard Freeman would send him a first draft. Or even half a first draft. Or at least discuss with him why the piece was moving so slowly. But whenever he called Leonard, the writer would say only that he had done some "great interviews" and had got some "dynamite material," but that he was still accumulating his research. "Anyway," Leonard had snorted the last time they'd talked, "what's the hurry? It's not even spring yet. Tell your uptight production people that long before the sun is strong enough to tan them, my piece will be in."

"Leonard," Max had scolded, "it is, in fact, spring, and your first draft is due *now*. You may have to do some rewriting. I have to edit it. We have to fact-check it. The art director has to look at it and commission a photo shoot. This is bigger than you and me, buddy. You're a pro. You know all this stuff. We're counting on you. Hell, me and my job here, we're *really* counting on you."

Talented, prickly, and acid-tongued, more impressive as an enemy than as a friend, Leonard carried an overpumped sense of pride and a lofty estimate of his literary talent. Always ready with a sadistic tale about the nervous editor he was currently dangling over a cliff edge, he was known in the magazine crowd around town for his deadline-defying, irreverent profiles. In the old days, when they had both been freelance writers, Max had admired Leonard's calculated deliquency, his fuck-you attitude and self-made rules.

Not anymore. Now Leonard seemed distinctly unfunny and sophomoric, and Max couldn't think of a move he could make to squeeze his old friend into delivering.

There was just no damn leverage, other than upping Leonard's fee dramatically or threatening to kill the assignment altogether, and neither option would enhance Max's standing at the magazine. If he didn't somehow reel in this story on time he risked a longstanding black mark on his infant editorial career. For months to come, he imagined, there would be snide references to "Max's lost summer cover story." Dot Scrivener — "Dame Dorothy" as Chaser, behind her back, called the magazine's matriarch — would pounce gleefully.

He could think of only one thing to do. Get up to Leonard's place in the Annex. Plead and cajole. Have a look at the story-in-progress. Make a judgment call. Max punched in the number, heard the smoky baritone voice, lingered long enough to be sure it wasn't the answering machine, then hung up.

He was at home — all that Max wanted to know. No use asking for a meeting. Leonard wouldn't let himself be pinned down at short notice, certainly not on home turf. The house was only a fifteen-minute cab ride from downtown.

But first, one small chore that had to be ticked off on Max's list. The art department had been chafing since late yesterday to have two lines added to a piece he'd edited. Earlier they'd had him take seventeen lines out, but apparently they'd miscalculated. It was amazing to him that grown-ups spent this much time shuffling letters around a page. The *Berger's* art people had a horror of unplanned gaps in their scaffolding of type — to them columns of text were like sturdy, interchangeable two-by-fours that propped up the photography and illustrations. If the columns weren't quite the right size, you had to saw them off or glue on extra chunks. No-one in the art department, Max had observed, was much interested in prose style or subtleties of meaning. He wasn't even sure that Giorgio, the art director, could read English all that well. Giorgio regarded the print columns grudgingly as necessities, and his assistant Celia talked about "pouring" type, as if there were a large faucet somewhere in the editorial department where beautiful words splashed out.

Max walked to the bank of filing cabinets where he could find the original version of the article Celia wanted him to "pad out." The cabinets stood in a long line beginning at Chaser's office, and if the editor had his door open, as he often did, and you were positioned nearby, you could hear his side of telephone conversations. Standing at the files, Max twitched when he heard Chaser say with alarm, "No, no, Edward, I didn't mean that. . . ." This sounded promising. Max slid shut the drawer he was looking in and moved to one just outside Chaser's doorway.

"No, I'm not defending him," Chaser continued. "I'm just saying it might be dangerous for the magazine if I were to condemn him publicly. I think . . ."

There was a long pause as Chaser was cut off and forced to listen. From the deferential tone, Max thought it a good bet the editor was talking to Mr. Clubb.

"I'm just trying to explain it as I see it," Chaser went on in a strained voice. "It wouldn't be like commenting at arm's length on any garden-variety libel suit. A piece written by me on an action brought by you would have its own set of consequences. This magazine depends for its survival on the national writing community and . . ."

Another long pause. Was Max imagining it, or could he faintly hear Edward Clubb's voice hollering over the line?

Chaser resumed, speaking quickly. "Yes, yes, yes. It goes without saying we'll take a position. No, depend on it, we're not at all timorous. It can be worked out. Some kind of response." Pause. "Yes, a *vigorous* response, Edward. I'll brood on all this and get back to you." Hearing Chaser hang up, Max pushed the file drawer closed and returned to his office.

To hell with Celia's two lines, he thought. He was still grinning as he stepped out of the old elevator onto the ground floor. It was an uncommon pleasure to see Chaser wince when someone had him by the balls. A trail of fuming, exasperated, and occasionally damaged people stretched behind Chaser, yet he managed to emerge from almost every professional dust-up with his career plans unscathed and his smirk intact. Max, who had rarely seen Chaser in a tight bind with no way to wriggle free, floated giddily out to the cab stand knowing that Toronto's moral balance had been temporarily restored.

CHAPTER 12

The cab headed west, up University Avenue, around Queen's Park, along Harbord Street, and up Spadina into the Annex. Someone had left the front section of the *Herald* on the back seat. The headline PM SAYS NO TO PREMIER ran over a picture that made Prime Minister McGarvie look like a deranged felon. Max saw from the caption that the photo had been taken in Toronto at the Royal York Hotel. And he remembered that McGarvie was in the city to give the keynote address to an international trade conference — apparently he'd added on a meeting with the Ontario premier. The politics of it didn't interest Max so much as the fact that today the PM was a quick ride away from Leonard Freeman's tape recorder. Was Leonard making any effort to be there?

Just short of Bloor Street the cab touched a sore spot. Sarah's street, Sarah's apartment, right there on Washington Avenue, a part of the world Max had been avoiding. A picture of her seized his mind: Sarah sitting at the kitchen table, a pile of manuscripts to one side, her pen on a page, her mouth moving as she talked to herself in that trance-like state of high concentration he'd found beguiling. And then the picture dissolved and he was aware of another one from much later in the piece. One of his last images of her, after she'd reached her limit, her face flushed, her mouth ugly with hurt and anger.

They'd been on a roll. And then it all went wonky. Why?

74

Somehow he'd figured her all wrong at the end. And he'd made some uncouth moves. The missed dinners, the drinking, those other nights. . . . And her mean temper. Was that it? Max still felt puzzlement when he retraced it. Puzzlement and anxiety — the emotional sink-hole sucking at his heels.

As the cab neared Leonard's place, another image, somehow connected with Leonard and the old days of freelancing: Jill at a party, about the time Max began dating Sarah. Were he and Sarah sleeping together? No. They'd just met, he hadn't made a move, and at this first party, she had introduced him to Jill, her best friend. A good-looking babe, more "in your face" than Sarah, more brazen. He could remember the conversation, which must have occurred before he'd gotten clumsy-drunk — an excess ending in the first of a hundred apologies.

"So how did you get into journalism?" Jill had asked.

"Stumbled in. Like most people."

"I mean, did you go to J school? Work your way up in a newspaper?"

He could remember the tight red sweater she'd been wearing. And the earrings, dangling loops. Her bright hazel eyes, darting over their subject the way they always did, as if snapping a hundred little pictures.

"None of the above. I just began to write."

"Ah. A *writer*. How does that happen, anyway?"

"Probably as an act of defiance. It was less risky than crime. Though it's never paid as well."

"You mean you weren't trying to be Hemingway."

"Hemingway is in fact a conspiracy, a mind-altering substance developed by transnational media corporations to fool their journalists into thinking this life could one day lead to a higher purpose. Don't count on it."

"I've never tried that particular drug. Maybe it's for men only."

"They put out a female version — called Martha Gellhorn. But it never sold as well."

"I went into reporting," Jill had said then with a shrug, "because I didn't want to be bored. Defiance wasn't an issue."

"You can't be all that defiant on a salary anyway," he'd said, attempting to provoke her. "You have to be willing to slam the door and walk."

"Didn't you ever want security?"

"No. Money, yes. Money I crave. You?"

"I'm content at the *Herald*. Sort of. As content as you can be in the nineties. It's a job."

"A job is a sentence. I like to be able to tell my employer off if he annoys me. That's my idea of security."

"You freelancers need a union."

"The only unions I like are sexual."

He remembered saying it, not just thinking it. Dumb move. He'd been oblivious to Sarah. Something about the way Jill had looked at him had given him hope. As soon as the words had tumbled out of his mouth, she had snorted derisively and moved away. But there had been signals from her. Definitely.

As the cabbie pulled up, Max saw an expensively dressed woman in her thirties close Leonard's door behind her. He waited for his change and watched her walk down the brick path to the street. She had a striking face, with high cheekbones and large black eyes.

When he had pocketed his change and climbed out of the cab, the woman was there on the sidewalk, giving him a pleasant smile. She bent down and asked the driver if he was free. Max heard a trace of what sounded to him like a Quebec accent. Leonard, he mused, is definitely over his divorce.

Standing outside his friend's flat, which occupied the ground floor of a three-storey, late Victorian house, Max suddenly felt foolish, like a martinet school principal snooping on a truant. Reluctantly ringing the door bell, he thought: I'll quit *Berger's*, Leonard and I will go for lunch like we used to, have a beer or two, shoot the breeze. . . .

"Max. What's up?" Standing at the door with bare feet, Leonard looked surprised.

"I had an errand around the corner. Thought I'd drop in and see how you're doing." Leonard's shirt was unbuttoned. He looked peacefully bleary-eyed.

"C'mon in." For a nervous moment Leonard's eyes darted into the street. Then he relaxed into his easy smile and padded through the flesh-toned living room, its blasted brick walls hung with framed Andy Warhol and Roy Lichtenstein posters. In the kitchen, standing in the flood of April light, he cleared away two coffee cups and took down clean ones from the cupboard.

"There's fresh coffee. Give me a minute while I finish dressing." He disappeared into the bedroom.

Max had been there for dinner with Sarah once when Leonard had been married. The flat had a wide, modernized kitchen that gave onto a deck through sliding glass doors — an elegant reno. But the garden had grown shabby in the year and a half since Carol had left. Uncut, the backyard was a field of matted grass, strewn with stray paper and all the unraked leaves from the fall. The grungy scene reminded Max of his own bachelorhood. He stood up and looked in the fridge. A clump of mould sat on the top grill. On closer inspection the mould turned out to be an ancient lemon. Beside it stood a six-pack of Molson's Export and a bottle of white wine. On the second shelf sat five boxes of Kodak Tmax 400 black-and-white film, two cans of tonic water, a jar of pickles, and half a pint of coffee cream. There was a plastic take-out carton of leftover Chinese food on the bottom shelf, and some old processed meat that was mutating into something else.

Not a vegetable. Not an egg. Not a drop of milk or yoghurt. Definitely no female in residence. Max felt a twinge of sadness as he closed the door. He also felt reassured. His own fridge looked much the same.

Leonard had had a good supply of the folding green not so long ago. In the early eighties there had been a film deal for one of his books. He'd bought this building, and later, Carol had moved in. They had married, remodelled the kitchen, built the deck, and stripped all the walls down to their basic brick. Exactly in that order, as Leonard had lamented one night after a litre of wine. Then Carol had remade the garden, possibly intending, Max had thought at the time, to remake Leonard too. But after three years, it was over. Carol was gone, leaving Leonard quietly bitter about his impending divorce settlement. Max wasn't given all the details of the collapse, but you didn't have to look very hard to figure out that Leonard was more boulevardier than backyard husband. For years he had mocked the condition of the dutiful married man. His own wedding had been not so much a compromise as an act of daredevilry. "Our vows were postmodern," he had told Max in front of Carol. "We tied a slip knot." And Carol had shown only her enigmatic smile.

Leonard stepped back into the kitchen, and poured himself coffee. "You feeling some heat about my piece?" he said. "You don't need to worry. I'm half done."

"That's good to know," Max replied. "Maybe we should mark the moment with a drink. Gin and tonic. With a slice of that bronze-age lemon you're preserving in the fridge."

"I don't eat here anymore," Leonard replied flatly. "Cooking for one is like autoeroticism. I prefer chastity. Actually, I prefer dinner for two at a good restaurant, when I've got the money."

"You don't invite your lady of the hour back here for Fettucine al'Leonardo or Leo's coq au vin?"

"No. Nothing culinary. Getting tactile with skillets and garlic presses sends the wrong signal. I'm not looking for that kind of intimacy." He hesitated, then went on. "Let's just say I like female company of an evening. Anything more than that these days seems ruinous." He stood facing the sliding glass doors, surveying his sloppy April garden. Six feet tall, with dark hair, grey eyes, and a long, lined face, he was normally self-possessed and full of brio, but today Max thought he looked disconsolate.

"Do you really want a shot of gin?"

"Actually what I'd like is to have another coffee while I look at what you've written. I need to have some sense of where it's going. To stay ahead of the piranha fish at the office."

"I don't know," said Leonard, suddenly enjoying himself. "I never show anything before it's finished."

"Jesus, man. Don't hang me out to dry."

Leonard hesitated for another delicious moment, then grinned. "Okay. I'll get what I have."

What Leonard had, it turned out, was not altogether re-assuring. The typescript exhibited his trademark mannerisms: the chic sharpshooter voice, the ironic subtext, and the scathing metaphors. Prime Minister McGarvie, noted in the public imagination for his mellifluous voice, his collection of expensive Italian footwear, and his free-trade/open-for-business policies, was described as a "silver-tongued, Gucci-shod auctioneer who could take the foreign bids on his country's future faster than a bailiff moving used carpets at a bankruptcy sale." Throughout the piece Leonard self-consciously spoke of himself as "the Evolved Voter."

"An autumn storm of political half-truths and false prophecies," the first paragraph began, "barrelled into Ontario with hurricane-force winds last year. It marked the climax of Barton McGarvie's bid for national vindication. A sour electorate was snorting and pawing the ground, and the PM had nothing more to offer than a fistful of sugar lumps.

"The Evolved Voter, witnessing the eighth general election of his adult life, took notes as McGarvie coined one more sickly sweet promise forty-eight hours before polling day. The words were spoken at Toronto's Fairhaven Mall. 'A vote for me is a vote for your own prosperity,' crooned the PM. 'Don't cast your ballot for Bart McGarvie. Vote for yourselves! This election is about your own future! About your children's prosperity! About the dream we call Canada!' McGarvie's conceit being that polling day would offer not so much a referendum on himself as an existential exercise in self-affirmation. A vote for oneself! How could any somnambulent suburban nag say no to this lo-cal candy offered up on the late-night news? McGarvie, our national sugar-daddy with the detergent-commercial voice and the hockey player's smile, belonged that day not so much on the hustings as on some middle-of-the-night, pep-talking TV show entitled 'The McGarvie Message: Ten Steps to Personal Success' in which Barton sells you a set of 'powerful, life-changing tapes for only $89.95.'

"The Evolved Voter couldn't help noticing two years later when the Fairhaven Mall, owned by the Zitrec Corporation, changed hands at half its estimated 1986 value. The deal was designed to mollify Zitrec's angry bondholders who were threatening to send the heavily leveraged development company into bankruptcy. Is Victor Toney, chairman of Zitrec (and recently appointed to the Senate by his old pal the prime minister), more empowered after he 'voted for himself' and his old college buddy? Or is it possible that, in light of McGarvie's disastrous economic policies, the newly impoverished senator now believes that a man who votes for himself has a fool for a candidate?

"McGarvie, on the other hand, would still, would always, vote for himself. 'Inflation,' he declaimed this winter, 'is lower than it's been for fifteen years.' And he's right. No dollars in your pocket buys just as much now as it did in the 1930s."

Max read on with alarm. *Berger's* was not in the habit of handing over five or six of its pages to a writer who wanted to vent some indignation or parade some sharp attitude. Granted, the article was still rough and raw; it was a first draft. But that wasn't the problem. Max was troubled by all the writerly sneers and snickers, which he couldn't defend unless they arose naturally out of fresh research Leonard had done. And Leonard appeared to be operating on a lofty rhetorical plane well above research level. Except for a sprinkling of tart-tongued quotes from some nameless source inside the Prime Minister's Office, Leonard appeared to have interviewed no-one but himself.

There was another reason Max could see the piece would present difficulties for him. Barton McGarvie was an old acquaintance of Edward Clubb's, who shared the PM's conservative leanings. Leonard inclined gently to the Left; his intellectual reflexes had been conditioned by the 1960s, and he viewed McGarvie's neo-conservatism as a repudiation of everything that decade had wrought. Chaser Makepeace was already uneasy about giving Leonard a platform. The simplest dodge for the anxious editor would be to pay Leonard off and bury his piece. Max was sure that's exactly what Chaser would do if he could dismiss the article as inferior journalism. Which, arguably, it was as it read now — a rant rather than well-grounded reportage.

"What happened to your interview with McGarvie?" Max asked.

"The PMO's still dodging my request. You don't like it so far?" Leonard had the wounded-child look that settled on the most overweening writers when their manuscripts weren't praised. Max had learned in his time as an editor that they began with the wounded-child look. Then, if you didn't soothe them, they got surly and vengeful and wanted to hurt someone — preferably the editor.

"No, no. I do love it," Max replied, choosing his words carefully. "You're marshalling your usual verbal cannon power here. I just think you need more of a factual anchor. We didn't commission an editorial, after all."

"I have opinions about this guy," said Leonard testily.

Max shrugged. "Sure. It's no big sweat. And anyway," he added hopefully, "this looks to me like an easy fix. Just a question of spending a day on the telephone, talking to people who've known and worked with McGarvie. And slotting in some quotes from him after you've done an interview. Who's your source, by the way? He's giving you some very juicy comments on his boss."

"I can't say," said Leonard, looking out into the garden. "I can't attribute any of it, but it's reliable, that I promise. There are several people in the PMO who aren't very enamoured of McGreedy." Leonard habitually used the daily-news reporters' pejorative nickname for McGarvie. "They confirm my sense that he's basically a thug — y'know, rude and crude. Also that he lacks intellectual substance."

"They? You have more than one?"

Leonard, as he scratched an unshaven cheek, looked uncomfortable. "Well, one senior mandarin for sure."

"As long as there's back-up when we get to the fact-checking," Max replied, wondering when Leonard would give him a name. "That bit about the PM joking in a staff meeting that he's slept with five per cent of the women's caucus. . . . We can't print something like that on hearsay."

Leonard arched an eyebrow. "I'll check it out. But there's a limit to how hard I can press. They've taken some risks for me already."

"Anything I should know about?" Max felt uneasy. His friend was being oddly coy. But it would be a mistake to push him.

"Nothing we could go to jail for," Leonard replied with a lopsided grin.

CHAPTER 13

May 4

Twenty-two degrees and full sun. This heat would not last. But it had definitely chased away winter, Sarah thought, as she ran the paint roller up and down the final kitchen wall. The rhythm reminded her of shaving her legs, careful vertical strokes, attending to every centimetre. Today's cream was a light butter hue. Painting a new face, a new chapter. She'd been waiting for the first warm days so she could open all the windows and clear the fumes. Late May, she'd thought. But the first heat had arrived a week ago, and today she'd decided to indulge herself with a day off.

There. All shaved. She wriggled her shoulders to ease her backache. The kitchen table and chairs were gathered in the middle of the room under a sheet, so she took her sandwich out to the deck and sat on one of the wooden steps. The first new leaves were nosing out from the crusty limbs of the gnarled apple tree. Today, she thought, I'd be content to stretch out and watch the trees grow. She lapsed into a spring trance, letting the sun nuzzle her hair and skin. And then roused herself, remembering that she'd promised to visit her mother.

In the bathroom Sarah piled her painting clothes on the stool and stood at the sink. It was unstoppable. She was becoming Eleanor. For several years the face in the mirror had been drawing tiny lines on itself, familiar little wrinkles around her eyes, smile creases — tracing her mother's — around her mouth. It was a slow march: nothing dramatic, no terrorist attacks of baldness or sagging jowls. More like the thickening and curling of a green leaf in August, with all the nicks and dust of summer preserved. She examined the barely perceptible fine white lines now engraved in her black hair. Barely perceptible, that is, unless seen in the mirror under a strong light. Then she thought she looked like a salt-and-pepper-topped bag lady.

Okay, hyperbole. Bag ladies didn't care. They let their faces and their bodies collapse. They couldn't afford to fix their teeth. They couldn't even afford nail clippers. Not for a sane moment did she ever really think . . .

"Nuts!" she blurted, making a mean face at herself. Bag ladies were emotionally dysfunctional. That wasn't at all the same as making some bad decisions.

As she brushed some shape into her hair, a succession of male faces made cameo appearances in her mind. Several of them scowled at her, one eyed her guiltily. It was a parade of the lovers she'd had in the last fifteen years, a reproach to herself for not trying hard enough, or not being accommodating enough, or in one case, for being far too tolerant and wasting a year of her life. Martin hadn't yet become a member of this rogue's gallery, but Sarah had been feeling increasingly that he was about to be. Was there *always* something wrong with them? She skimmed the list and ended where it ended, with Max.

After which came . . . *that delicious thought*. She finished applying her eyeliner and grinned. It wasn't so long ago that she'd been throwing up in this little room — from too much wine and that last toxic dose of him. This spring, she'd begun to feel she'd finally slipped the emotional stranglehold of Max's craziness. Maybe you could never escape altogether from that kind of entanglement. But it was an exhilarating sensation to feel invulnerable when he popped into her head. Not completely free, no, but finally in charge. A feeling that had been enhanced by her current plan.

It had occurred to her that more often than not Max had been the dramaturge of the theatre piece they'd played out together. *He* had always been the director, *he* had always played the lead. And often in outrageously self-centred ways.

Now Sarah felt she had possession of the script. Live by the pen, die by the pen, Maxwell.

She dressed quickly, jeans and a blue cotton sweater, practical clothes in case Eleanor wanted her to do laundry or carry something up from the basement. Her mother lived out in the Beaches in the same two-storey red-brick house she'd occupied since the 1950s, the house Sarah's father had died in when she was two, and the house where Eleanor would almost certainly die herself. Eleanor, who Sarah was sure had never had a bag-lady fantasy in her life. Ornery and critical and sometimes obtuse, but no coward and certainly no slouch.

Driving east along the Danforth to Main Street, Sarah passed the turn-off to Max's place. She chuckled. If she could discuss Max with Eleanor, which she couldn't, Eleanor too would laugh about the plan. Or would she? Her antiquated ideas about courtesy might get in the way.

"I knew my limits," Eleanor would sometimes say, heavy with implication, when the subject of men came up. She disapproved of Sarah's inability or, as Eleanor more likely saw it, her daughter's disinclination, to settle down with a husband. And Eleanor had liked Max. His cock-eyed spontaneity, his good looks, his solicitousness had won her over. But she hadn't had to deal with his dark side — the drinking, the egocentric ranting, the missed dinners, the fucking around.

★ ★ ★

Max was at his desk, trying to finish off some chores before the editorial meeting. He had been working longer hours since Arnold's sudden exit. They were down from six editors to five, and Chaser seemed in no hurry to find a replacement.

Giorgio, the art director, had just swanned into Max's office insisting that a piece Arnold had edited must now be cut by a further twenty-eight lines in order to accommodate a "fabulous picture of George Bernard Shaw." The article was a tart essay on academic archives, written on the occasion of the purchase of a new collection of Shaw's letters by Niagara University. The writer of the article, a professor and an acquaintance of Arnold's who moonlighted as a magazine journalist, had enjoyed himself with Shavian witticisms, lacing them strategically through his piece.

"This is just the right statement to make, don't you think?" Giorgio was referring not to anything in the text but to the wacky picture of Shaw he'd found, a photograph of the famous writer with his eyes closed, his chin down, and his mouth wide open.

"He looks like a buffoon," Max scoffed. "You half expect a pigeon to fly out of his yap. That's not exactly the effect we're looking for."

"Not a buffoon, Max." Giorgio ran a hand back through his long dark hair and gave his shoulders a bounce, lifting his magenta silk shirt, which fell back over his torso like a windless ornamental flag. "Not a buffoon. You do not take this kind of photograph literally. It's like, you know, a metaphor for the offbeat. That's the kind of statement we're trying to establish. You have, like, the very personal thoughts of George Bernard Shaw that I feel this piece presents. We'll use this image to make Shaw into, like, a new-age wise man, like, a hip oracle for, ah . . ." Giorgio was momentarily stumped. He held out his arms for emphasis. "For downtown in the nineties!"

Max looked suspiciously at the art director. Giorgio had flourished in the magazine business because he was a trend junkie. His mind darted from novelty to novelty as nimbly as a bee in a bed of lilies. If it was new, Giorgio had just bought it or had just experienced it or had just been to a party and talked to someone who had flown in from wherever it was.

But Giorgio thought in pictures not words.

"Whatever that means, it's a demotion for Shaw," Max snorted, "and I'm sure the old boy would resent it."

"You have to seduce people into a piece like this," Giorgio replied patiently. "Everyone is not a professor."

"Let's take it up in the editorial meeting," said Max.

Giorgio nodded with his ambiguous smile. "Of course." He slid a page proof onto the desk. "I just need one line shortened there. Otherwise we're okay." Then the art director, whom Max thought of as post-corporeal and cyber-based, weightlessly glided back into his own office.

Max took up the page proof. The note on it said, "PLEASE CUT 7 CHARS." Which meant seven characters had to be removed from the display copy he had written. Ordinarily, this cutting to fit was a task Max didn't mind. You had to substitute a five-letter word for a twelve-letter one, or somehow rejig the caption or knock-out so it had the same meaning with fewer letters. The art department never fretted about meaning. They cared only about how the type looked and whether it was balanced by sufficient white space.

Max's eye followed the arrowed line Giorgio had drawn down the page from his note. The knock-out, drawn from the essay and set in bold type in an oblong space in the middle of the page, read "ASSASSINATION IS THE EXTREME FORM OF CENSORSHIP." It was a Shavian epigram that the writer had used in the body of the article. Giorgio had crossed out the word "ASSASSINATION" and written in "MURDER" with a question mark.

Jesus, Max thought. "To be or not to be" — cut five characters. "To be or not!" Giorgio would prefer that. Ditto for

"Be or don't!" Forced to choose between Shakespeare and David Mamet, Giorgio would prefer Mamet. Because his words left more white space.

Max scrawled beside the change: "Sorry. You can 'murder' my prose anytime — but not Shaw's. Not even the *Berger's* art department can improve on the maxims of GBS." He scribbled the acronym for "set to existing type" and added his initials below.

On his way to the editorial meeting room, Max poured himself another coffee and carried it down the hall. He stood for a moment and contemplated the battered mansard roof on the other side of the street. Only from this level could you see the top of the old house opposite. The Victorian dwelling had years ago been lost behind a series of concrete-and-glass additions, which were now all you could see from the street. In the 1970s, Max remembered, the upstairs had been a body-rub parlour. That was before fax machines and personal computers had replaced sex as the most popular mode of urban communication. In the new era of fatal bodily fluids, the massage business had been replaced by the message business — purveyed by large discount electronics stores that sold cheap phones, answering machines, computer equipment, and faxes, all from Asia. Now, Max thought, the sexiest word in creation, the thing that connected you with other beings and joined all of humanity in a tantric oneness, wasn't the Big O. It was the Big M, the hot node of the nineties. The M spot. Modems.

He took a seat as the others began to drift in for the weekly meeting. *Berger's*, which in some respects had never made it out of the pre-sexual 1950s, fit comfortably into the repressed nineties, except for one awkward fact. The magazine had resisted all nudges into the electronic age. Not only did the editors have no modems, they were still performing all their editorial tasks on old, accident-prone typewriters.

Max's eyes rested unhappily on the empty chair at the far end of the table. The meetings weren't the same with Arnold gone. His ghost still sat down there, making for some queasy moments. Arnold's name still came up as the main liaison with many older writers, and his initials haunted the editorial memo beside stories he had commissioned.

Across the table, stiletto-sharp pencil in hand, Dot Scrivener sat brooding behind the large-lens shades she habitually wore outside her office. With her close-cropped red hair, El Greco fingers, whiskey-deep voice, and rhinestone choker, she had the imperious, resentful air of an expropriated aristocrat. A nit-picking line editor, she covered manuscripts with cavils and rebukes; her unforgiving eye yielded to no journalist's passion. When she wasn't cross-examining on the telephone one of the few writers still willing to work with her, she spent her time obsessively checking word definitions in the larger OED, and inscribing other editors' manuscripts with florid commentaries on obscure grammatical points. Inside the baroque skin of an aggrieved contessa fussed the soul of a pedant.

Beside her sat Giorgio: the spaceman who, Max idly thought, would be the first to fly down for modem-implant surgery at the Mayo clinic. Even without it, Giorgio's brain was living proof of the different planets inhabited by the *Berger's* art and editorial departments. Next to him sat his assistant Celia, then Maureen, the most junior editor, and then Frances, the chief copy editor and director of fact-checking. Frances had spent her entire working life at *Berger's* and had memorized every rule of style used by the magazine. Max thought of her brain as the human equivalent of Pavlov's dog: hundreds of times each week as she pulled her inner lever a comma or semi-colon would roll down the chute and fall into place.

Chaser burst into the room, chatting with Joanne, the entertainment and personality-profiles editor. He took his seat at the head of the table. He was wearing a purple bow tie with white polka dots. Max reflected that Joanne would sit as near to Chaser as she judged advantageous. Too close made her look like his Girl Friday. Too far away and her power lines could get tangled. About two seats away usually seemed just right for her.

And there she was, positioning herself two down from the chief.

"Newsstand circulation is up five per cent!" Chaser exclaimed gleefully as he sat down. "It must be the transvestites that did it. A few old subscribers have cancelled, of course."

"Don't worry. It's only the closet cross-dressers who are cancelling," Dot growled in her feline baritone. "They're afraid we'll put *them* on the cover."

"Let's," said Giorgio. "I had so much fun with the shots for that story."

"Once in every decade may be our quota," Chaser said. "I rather doubt the people down at Janus were thrilled with it."

"How do you know some of *them* don't have secret wardrobes?" Giorgio retorted.

"I vote we leave that one alone," the editor replied, looking down at his notes. "There's some interesting news about the fall line-up, but I'll let Giorgio take us through the schedule for the July issue first. He's promised to help us make our final deadlines."

"Oh boy," groaned Giorgio, with a distaste bordering on hostility. "Basically, folks, we're in fairly deep shit, if I can put it so delicately. Almost everything is at least a week behind, some stuff more like two. Three of the feature stories are still being fact-checked. Some of the essays in the front haven't even been edited yet. One of them I saw today for the first time, so I'm just commissioning the artwork for it now. That'll be extremely tight. It's a nice piece, though. On a weird new thing called virtual reality."

Max found it difficult to concentrate. Giorgio, normally a

loose bundle of sass and irony, was instantly transformed into a tightly scripted bureaucrat when he took charge of the production segment of the meeting. His voice became squeaky and officious, his tone reproachful. Max listened groggily to this accusatory monologue as Giorgio plowed through the July editorial memo, explaining why each article was late. Around the table everyone was doodling or shifting impatiently — everyone, that is, except Dot Scrivener who, with her permanent, world-weary pout, sat as still as a hunting cat, watching Giorgio from behind her big dark glasses.

"You'll have it when it's ready," she purred when the art director asked for an estimated arrival time for one of the July features she was editing. It was a report on violence in high schools.

"That piece needs to be typeset. Then I need to shape it," Giorgio fretted. "I need to book the time."

"Like I said, just as soon as it's ready, it's yours. But I want to take another run through it, and the writer has still to get back to me on a couple of points."

"Could we set a deadline?"

"You can set any deadline you want," she said.

Giorgio looked around in disbelief. "Hey, maybe we should just move all of July into September and have a double issue in the fall! That's where we're heading with this baby if we don't put some speed on." He slammed down his notes and sank back into his chair.

Dot said nothing.

Chaser's face was flushed. "God bless us. Let's all take a deep breath. We don't have to sort this out here and now. I think we should move on. Anything else on production?"

"The Shaw piece is in page proofs," said Giorgio, sitting up. "Thank God *something* is ready. We just need a small cut to accommodate a picture. Maxwell seems to have reservations about this old Shaw photograph. *We* think it's quite fabulous."

Giorgio passed the picture around the table, starting with Joanne.

"It's kind of cute," she said brightly. "He looks like a seventy-five-year-old kid. I think it's charming."

Thanks a lot, Max thought. He scowled down the table.

Joanne glanced at him. "Of course, it's Max's piece, not mine," she added.

"Actually, it's Arnold's piece," Max said with an edge to his voice. "I'm just minding it till we put it in the book."

Silence.

Chaser looked around the table anxiously. "Our phantom limb," he said.

No-one responded.

"Okay," said Chaser. "I know a conversation stopper when I hear one. But he can't edit from the grave. Reminds me of an old folk rhyme at the *Trib*:

> an editor misses a day
> he forfeits a week's pay
> a writer muffs a headline
> he goes on the breadline
> a reporter's late
> he earns the same fate
> but an owner who's incompetent
> always lives high off the rent."

Chaser chuckled. "This business waits for no man, unless he owns the press."

You bastard, thought Max. An image of Arnold on the foot-bridge came crashing into his mind.

"Let's have a look at the Shaw photo," said Chaser.

"Ha!" shrieked Frances when it came to her. "Well, he was a humourist, wasn't he?"

"Not exactly," Max replied. "A wit, yes. But a serious writer."

"Mmmmm." Dot's gravelly voice pulled all eyes in her direction. With two hands, she held the picture out in front of her. "No, this is dead wrong," she declaimed. "I've read the essay. This image makes him look senile. There's an empty innocence about it. The piece, by contrast, is full of Shaw's quite cynical, prickly observations. No." She shook her head and passed the photograph on.

"We like the vulnerability," Giorgio protested. "The simple, human side, the . . ."

"Why not just get a shot of him naked, then?" Max interrupted, sourly. "Maybe a baby picture."

"I think," Chaser said quickly, "that photograph will have to be retired for lack of support. Can we move on to the fall issues and new story ideas?"

Dot slid a folded paper across the table. Max opened it a crack and read: "You owe me one."

"May I just say," Giorgio replied stiffly as he turned in Max's direction, "that I need *something* so I can commission the cover art for August. A first draft? Some notes from the writer? *Something.*"

Chaser looked at Max. "How's Leonard Freeman doing? He seems to be defending his reputation as a defier of deadlines."

"I expect his first draft within a day or two," said Max. "I read about two-thirds of it when I was at his place about a week ago." He paused, choosing his words carefully. "It looked very promising."

"At this point," Giorgio said, "I'd feel a lot better if we had some back-up."

"Why is this a problem?" Chaser asked. "Can't we just use stock shots of the prime minister?"

"Ideally we'd try to set up a photo shoot," Giorgio replied impatiently. "If they won't go for that, then sure, we'd use stock shots. I'd still need to assign a photo researcher, which takes

time. But that's not the big problem." Giorgio paused dramatically. "What you don't seem to understand, Chaser, is that if
the Freeman piece doesn't work, we need to have a good
understudy article waiting in the wings, and I need to know
what it is. I can't come up with alternate cover art on two days'
notice."

"I know, I know," Chaser shot back with a sarcastic grin.
"We're not running a newspaper here."

Joanne straightened her black velvet hair band. "I think we
may have an easy solution," she said. "I've got that long
political essay on Tom Broadfoot, the new Ontario Tory leader.
It's scheduled for the front of the book in September. It's long
enough to be a feature and it's really well done. The writer's
just adding a few things."

"You mean move it into August?" Chaser asked.

"Why not? We could if we had to."

"Tom Broadfoot on the cover?"

"He's young. He's on the radical right. He's good-looking."

"You make him sound like a better cover than McGarvie."

"Maybe he is."

"Whoa!" Dot's deep voice again drew all eyes down the table.
"We have a very adept magazine writer assigned to do a piece
on the most controversial character in the country, Barton
McGarvie. The piece is a little late. Let's not abandon all good
sense because we're panicky about the schedule. Broadfoot's
acceptable as a back-up, okay. But McGarvie's a tastier story."

Chaser looked unconvinced. "Okay. We'll get together a
cover layout for Broadfoot," he said to Giorgio. "And maybe
Max can brief you on the direction Freeman is taking with his
story on the PM, so you can get started with arrangements for
a shoot or an illustration. We'll treat them as alternates for now
and proceed in tandem. That way we're covered."

"Nice try — thanx," Max scribbled on a note which he folded
and passed across to Dot.

Max could see that the discussion about August had ener-gized Chaser. He had always been nervous about Leonard's piece. Now there was an escape hatch. Joanne looked satisfied too.

"Okay," Chaser said cheerily, "on to new story ideas."

"Speaking of the McGarvies," said Joanne. "We were going to look into the stories about Maya. Is Leonard Freeman doing that?"

"No," Max replied quickly. "It's a separate piece. You'd have to go around Ottawa and Montreal and try and interview all her friends. It's a second assignment."

"Too bad. We may be missing some good stuff."

Right, thought Max. And maybe I can drop a banana peel for you as a return favour.

"I think we should commission a story on *her*," Dot growled, "as I've said several times before. The rumours about their marriage being on the fritz don't properly belong in a political piece by Freeman. But they could be tested very nicely in a story about her."

"You've talked about this before," Chaser said. "But I still don't see it. The stories, especially the sensational ones about physical violence, are just rumours. We can't print any of that stuff without it being attributed. Which it never will be."

"Don't be so sure about that," she retorted. "Some of the scuttlebutt is getting very close to home. I've heard, for exam-ple, that Maya was seen around town in March and April wearing dark glasses. This isn't California in July we're talking about. This is Ottawa in late winter. And apparently — or so I've been told via people who share the same opthamologist — there *have* been some black eyes, which account for the shades. A lot of the gossip can be discredited, I grant you. But you can't dismiss a woman's eye doctor."

"Okay," Chaser nodded impatiently. "But what do we *do* with it?"

"Commission a piece."

"To trash the prime minister's wife?"

"To find out if the rumours are true."

Chaser looked around the table.

"I like it," said Max. "I doubt Freeman's piece on McGarvie is going to be well received in the PMO. If we commission a piece on Maya to run, say, this winter, we're in a win-win situation. A sucky profile helps to appease all the readers who may be offended by Leonard's piece. If, on the other hand, we get the goods on her, we'll be a publishing sensation with the best political one-two punch in years."

A hint of a smile loosened Dot Scrivener's pout as she watched Max.

"Interesting analysis," murmured Chaser. He no longer looked at all cheerful. "Unusually Machiavellian for you, Max."

"Thank you."

"Let's keep a watching brief on it. If there's a writer close to the scene, it's probably worth stumping up a bit of research money."

"I'll get on it," Dot said.

"Good," said Chaser, trying to sound upbeat again. But his mouth was twitching and his eyes were small, angry, brown stones. He looked down at his notes. "I have some really excellent news about September. I've pulled in an eccentric feature story that I think is a wonderful sleeper."

"You mean it's already written?" asked Giorgio excitedly.

Chaser nodded. "Written and ready for illustration."

"Hallelujah!"

"It's by the American writer Gardiner Redstone. He edits a prestigious Washington journal, *Global Strategies*. The piece is about the looming North American water shortage. He calls it 'Canada: Reservoir of the North.' It's a very thoughtful analysis. I think we'll put it on the cover. We so rarely get big American names into the magazine."

"Never heard of him," growled Dot.

" 'Reservoir of the North?' " said Joanne incredulously. "We were going to cover Madonna's Toronto concert in June and put a rush on it for the September cover."

"Madonna — now there's a *big* American name," said Dot. "Who is Gardiner Redstone?"

"He's a heavyweight in the policy-wonk community in Washington," Chaser replied. "He publishes in all the important public-policy journals."

"Are you seriously saying we should kick Madonna off the cover in favour of the Great Lakes, or whatever he's on about?" asked Joanne, looking at Chaser strangely. "I thought we were trying to *build* circulation."

Chaser shrugged. "I think you're wrong. Our readers want the magazine to take on difficult issues. They want us out there on the leading edge of public discourse. . . ."

"I've never heard of this Redstone guy either," Joanne replied sourly. "How'd you find him?"

Max watched Joanne with interest. She rarely challenged the editor. But everyone, including Chaser, knew she had already set up the Madonna assignment with one of her best writers.

"After seventeen years in the newspaper business," Chaser said edgily, "I have a few connections. Gardiner Redstone happens to be a respected specialist in Canadian studies. He's edited two collections of papers about us."

"Can he write?"

"It reads well. Trust me. And it's provocative. He takes the position that our water is their water."

Everyone stared at Chaser.

"*Berger's* quenches your thirst for knowledge — with the Great Lakes!" said Max, breaking the silence. "We could have a poster made up. Sell it Stateside."

"Okay, okay," Chaser said, in retreat. "I can see I'll be editing this piece myself. No volunteers?"

"I have the perfect cover line for you, though," Max offered.

"Yes?"

" 'Canada Dry.' "

CHAPTER 14

Memorandum

DATE: May 6
TO: Maria Jonsson, *Canadian Woman*
FROM: Sarah McDermott
SUBJECT: *Mid-thirties, Looking for Mr. Letter Perfect,* by Sarah M.

[*Dear Maria -- Here's my first draft. Let me
know what you think. -- best, Sarah*]

You're thirty-six. Your biological clock is not only ticking loudly;
you're beginning to hear the alarm in your dreams. You've had
boyfriends. You've been in love. Nothing has worked out, at least
not permanently. You'd like to settle down, start a family.

But good men are more difficult than ever to find. Many of
your old friends, male and female, are married. Some are lifelong
singles and comfortable with it. A few are gay.

Where are the single guys who want what you want?

Nowhere.

But that can't be true.

You've taken to reading the personal ads. There are guys
aplenty, if you believe what you read.

But you don't reply to any of them. It's, uh, too *personal.* You
don't know these people. (Your instincts are telling you something that you don't fully grasp.)

Here's what happens. You begin to have fantasies about plac-
ing an ad yourself. Just for the hell of it. What have you got to
lose? None of the ads are very revealing. Just a sentence or two.
You risk nothing. If you get replies, fine. If not, that's fine too.
Maybe, just maybe, it's a way to connect with your future. You've
tried bars, parties, blind dates, friends of friends. Why not try the
newspaper?

And so you place the ad. Here's what mine said: "France,
Alice Munro, irony, risotto, reliability, salt water, intelligence, a
wooden chopping block, a garden spade; attractive female
wordsmith, 36, wishes to be wordsmitten. Tell me who you are."

I thought I was being honest — and clever too. I work in
publishing. I'm interested in books, language, words. If a guy
can't write me a good letter, there's not going to be much hope.
So that's what I asked for.

All companion ads are like telegrams: crisp, abbreviated sum-
maries of who you are and what you want. It's easy to misinter-
pret a telegram. It's also easy to send out false signals when
you're writing one. And telegrams are a peculiar way to get to
know someone — like shouting back and forth down a long tube
and hearing only a few words of what the other person is telling
you. We're all selective in what we show of ourselves to prospec-
tive mates. We all try to put the best foot forward. Companion
ads compress that process a hundredfold.

Let's forget the dozens of letters that were pathetically inept
or clearly inappropriate. (I received forty-two replies within a
week of my ad's appearance in the *Tribune*.) When I look back
on it now, there was really only one response that showed any
real promise. I did go out on a few dates with some of the others.
But in the end none of them were emotionally compelling
enough to continue into a romantic relationship. I'm not talking
sexy here. I'm not talking bright. I met a few men who fit those
descriptions. What I'm talking about is that combination of sex
appeal and emotional rapport we call chemistry.

Let's call him V. (I can't use his name for legal reasons. Hence I'm not using my full name either.) He wrote me a good letter — a bit too forward maybe, but interesting. I remember I put it aside for two or three weeks because I felt he had been too open, too frank. I was a little dismayed, for example, that he mentioned sex right up front in that first communication. Hold on there! We haven't even met! But he was a writer, and he said he wanted to exchange some letters to see if we had anything in common.

So we became pen pals, living in the same city, but not meeting. He was smart. He seemed to have a sense of humour. He didn't take himself too seriously, always a good sign in my books. Certainly he could write one heck of a good letter.

So can I. We outdid ourselves with those missives. (Or should I say undid ourselves?) Seduction by mail is an unusual strategem nowadays. Maybe that was part of the attraction. It was like courting on forbidden ground.

Finally, after a couple of months of, uh, foresay, we met. It was quite delicious, I can tell you. We thought we knew all about each other. And in fact we did know quite a lot.

But not everything.

I know now that by the time we agreed to meet, I was already infatuated. I hate to admit this, but the truth is I had been indulging myself in a variation of the Harlequin romance. I was the dreamy heroine and V was my Mr. Perfect. Except that this was an interactive Harlequin. I wasn't just reading about this lovely fantasy male, I was stepping right into the book and having conversations with him on the page. He was palpable — I had his letters to prove it. On the other hand, I was also making him up. Here's a sample of what he wrote:

> Dear Sarah,
>   Is this getting ridiculous or what? My favourite week-end activity has become the writing of letters to a woman I haven't even met. But I feel strongly that we're onto

something worthwhile. I'm tempted to rush over to your apartment and appear at your door on bended knee with a box of chocolates, but don't worry, I won't spoil this letter thing. It's much too interesting. (Do you like chocolates?)

You say you think you're "both male-wary and a little male-weary too" after some bad experiences. I've got a few love scars myself. But my wariness evaporates whenever I read a letter from you. Your intelligence is bursting out all over the place in what you write. Your letters give me enormous pleasure. Delight, I think, is the right word. I feel, when I get home and there's an envelope from you in the mail that (I'm quoting my Dutch grandfather here) "I've fallen with my nose in the butter." Which means, on top of the world, as good as it gets.

My Harlequin hero had fallen for me.

Finally, after two months, we met for coffee, reverting to the established protocol for first contact following a personals ad. Of course, it wasn't really first contact. We'd been talking through the mail for weeks. And we had exchanged photographs, a practice that until then I'd considered a bit sleazy. This shouldn't be about surfaces, I'd told myself. But after about a month of writing letters, he had sent me a picture of himself, as pen pals sometimes do, and he'd asked for one of me. He'd had one taken specially for me — he was standing in a backyard leaning on a garden spade and smiling mischievously, his mop of curly dark hair brushed back from his broad forehead. When I realized I was more than casually interested in this photograph, I decided I had to send him mine, for the sake of emotional symmetry.

I liked looking at his picture. He said he liked looking at mine. And that first meeting apparently didn't disappoint whatever fantasies we'd both constructed. We laughed about our old-fashioned, epistolary courtship and congratulated ourselves on our slow and cautious exploration of romantic possibilities.

Still, in retrospect, our first face-to-face had aspects of the hothouse atmosphere that all companion-ad meetings inevitably have. You exist in a sealed room together. There's no mystery about why you're both there, no ambiguities. It's an appointment. Both parties have stated their needs. You're negotiating for love, or at least you purport to be. You've skipped a few crucial moves in the mating ritual and you've gone directly to the hot buttons. I'm not talking about jumping into bed. Call it jumping into intimacy. Even with all those letters behind us, it was odd to be talking about a possible shared future with someone I'd just laid eyes on.

Next we had dinner. We met at a restaurant. It was one of the most agreeable dates I've ever had. He asked me about my childhood, my family, my friends. And he expanded on things he'd said about himself in his letters. He told me more about his work, which was writing feature articles for magazines. Since we'd first connected by mail, I had read an article of his about changing sexual mores in the nineties. Naturally I'd been fascinated when I first discovered something written by my new friend and potential love interest; when I read what he'd written, I was relieved to learn he seemed to have some reasonable opinions.

"I'm a sexist," he said light-heartedly at dinner. "That's partly what my article was about. I believe in the ancient courtesies between the sexes. My first premise is that men and women are almost different species. They want different things and behave in different ways. So each has to defer to the other in different ways."

"I thought chivalry was dead," I remember saying sceptically.

"I'm not talking about dropping my scarf in a puddle so your feet won't get wet," he said. "I'm talking about different brain chemistry underpinning different ways of seeing the world. You know: all that gender-difference research I cited in the article. Most women want to nest. That's not all they want, but that's a priority. Lots of men want to nest too, but they mainly want to be able to fly away regularly for adventure."

I asked if he meant sexual adventure. Not necessarily, he said, adding that, "Twenty years ago sexual adventure was in vogue. And I admit guys like me followed the fashion. But that was then."

I found his honesty bracing. A lot of well-educated men I know have become earnest male feminists. They are reassuring, safe, predictable. And most of what they have to say about gender relations is sanitized, boring, and borrowed. V, I thought that night, was genuinely thinking his own way through these things. Yes, he exaggerated, but I felt there was more than bravado in what he said about the gender gap. We are fundamentally different — not altogether, but in some important ways. Studies have shown this again and again. For almost three decades North Americans blindly chased sexual equality. I agreed with him that it was time to relent and acknowledge reality.

Our next date was a party given by one of my friends. V and I had discovered we had a few acquaintances in common, but none of our close friends overlapped. So I felt both proud and nervous when I took him to what was for me an intimate gathering of people I'd known and liked for years. V was a success. He seemed to be a great schmoozer and charmer. In fact, I could see he was a bit of a party animal. He liked to laugh and ham it up. He liked to drink. He liked to talk. Especially, I noticed, to women.

"Definitely an unusual find. But watch out. He'll test your endurance," one of my girlfriends told me after talking to him.

Another female friend told me he had begun to put the make on her. I, of course, did not believe a word of it.

Ah yes, biological differences. By midnight I could see that he was seriously intoxicated. He broke a glass and howled with laughter. "Where's the broom?" he gasped, overcome by the hilarity of it all. I cleaned up the mess, protecting him from his own drunken ineptitude. A symbolic moment.

He insisted on driving me home. We had words on the sidewalk. I said I never drive with drunks. He apologized and took me home in a cab, then went on alone. Later, I heard that he had gone back to the party before picking up his car.

The next morning when I stepped outside to get the paper, I was startled to see a vehicle parked on the front lawn of my building. I recognized it as the car I had driven in on the way to the party the night before. It was V's car. I walked down onto the lawn. V was in the car, asleep on the back seat. He looked extremely dishevelled.

I wrote him a note: "Don't park on the grass." I put it on the windshield before I drove off in my own car to do the Saturday shopping. I was angry. At the same time, a little flattered. I'd obviously been on his mind at the end of the evening.

The car was gone when I got home. He sent flowers to appease me. But there was never any question that I'd ditch him at that point. It was the letters, you see, that had hooked me. Long after we stopped writing and started dating, those letters were still working their black magic.

On the next date, after the unfortunate parking incident, we had dinner again. V was quiet, apologetic, admitted alcohol was occasionally a problem. We talked about books, movies.

And we slept together. I had decided he was worth the commitment. It was also a case — for me — of being seriously in lust.

We had two glorious weeks together. We went underground, saw no-one but each other, did a minimum of work during the day and flew back home at night to go to bed and eat, usually in that order. I thought: Finally, this is IT.

For a few months we seemed to be moving in the right direction. Even though he was sometimes raucous and rowdy at parties, which I didn't like. And once he stood me up — but that was a misunderstanding, we agreed.

Then one evening after work when he was in the shower, I took the messages off his answering machine. (I'd been expecting a call.) The machine malfunctioned. I had to fuss with it to hear the day's tape, and I rewound it farther than I needed to.

It was the electronic equivalent of lipstick on a handkerchief. The message — I haven't forgotten — was from a woman called Karen. "I had a wonderful time last night, Max," she said. But the words that caught my attention were: "It was so good to be with you again." Not "to see you again." Not "to catch up with you." Her tone was intimate and, to me at least, suggestive of more than a drink after work. She apparently knew him well. In what way had they "been together" the night before? By this time I thought I'd been told about all of V's old flames. Who was Karen?

V and I went out to dinner that night. For a couple of hours I managed to suppress my curiosity and dismay. I reasoned that jealousy (or paranoia) would only damage such a young relationship. Maybe I'd be able to sort this out in some quiet, unhurtful way. But as we were finishing our meal he said I seemed preoccupied.

"Who's Karen?" I blurted.

There are moments we all remember, clear particles of time that are inviolably preserved inside us. This is one of them. V was clearly thrown off balance. He sat there slack-jawed for a second or two, then dropped his eyes to his plate and fiddled with his cutlery.

"What Karen are you talking about?" He sounded embarrassed.

"The one who is in your life. Or was last night."

"Oh. That Karen."

"How many are there?"

I still have the letters in which he discussed fidelity. "I believe in loyalty," he wrote, "sexual and otherwise. I can't honestly boast I've never violated that lofty principle, but I do believe it's an essential ingredient in the glue that holds couples together. Without it you're just exposed flesh in the turbulent wash of hormone sharks and sexual jelly fish, the risky love tide that we unattached people swim against every day. All of us have been bitten or stung, most of us more than once. Fidelity, I'm pretty sure, offers the only respite."

Sounded good to me. I thought he meant it. And in a way he did. V, as he said repeatedly, really believed in fidelity as an ideal. When he failed to live up to it, he spoke regretfully of "lapses." He always promised to do better.

Karen was a woman he'd been seeing on and off since before he'd replied to my ad. He said he'd been fond of her, but not fond enough to make a commitment. I said, okay, these are early days for us, I don't have the right nor do I want to manage your life. Do what you feel is best for yourself. Let's not see each other for a month. Then we'll decide. But if we're on again, it's got to be exclusive.

He wrote letters, remorseful appeals in which he itemized my praiseworthy qualities, the good times we'd had, our most memorable table talk. I relented. We began dating again.

Not that I didn't have some misgivings. But my mother liked him. *Some* of my friends liked him. I liked him. And as I've said, the biological clock was ticking loudly. I was willing to make some allowances. So I stayed with it, and after almost a year — and one more fidelity "lapse" — we began to talk of settling down. Oops, I'm projecting. The truth is, *I* began to broach the subject. We spent weekends together. Why not, I reasoned, spend week nights too?

"We already do, sometimes," he'd reply.

"But why pay for two apartments when we almost never use yours?" I'd then ask.

"Speak for yourself!" he'd say. "I *live* there. All my stuff is there. Believe it or not, I actually like that place. I'm happy to keep on paying for it, at least for now."

At least for now. All arrangements, in V's view, were temporary. "*Life* is temporary," he'd say. Well, yes. But I wasn't looking for a philosophical debate.

Why, I wondered, did he need that apartment? "I want my own space," he'd say, with an exasperated, hangdog look. "I need somewhere I can be alone."

Alone alone, I began to wonder? Or alone with someone else? I didn't like those thoughts. But I was having them.

One evening during the week when I'd agreed to cook dinner, he was unusually late. I phoned his office — by this time he'd taken a steady job in the magazine industry. I knew that sometimes work emergencies arose that kept him downtown until six or seven o'clock. No answer at the office, no answer at home. I waited till maybe eight-thirty, then downed my own dinner in a rage. I imagined him on a tear downtown. I imagined him out on a date with someone else. I imagined all kinds of things.

I stayed up till early morning asking myself whether he was worth it. Be calm, I remember telling myself. Don't make a decision in a fit of temper. But I knew that unless things changed dramatically, I'd had enough. As the night dragged on, I moved through quiet resignation back into anger. I reread some of his letters, which now seemed full of outlandishly false promises. "I'm ready for a commitment — looking for one too." And "I'm old enough and experienced enough to know you can't march to your own drummer and expect another person to follow."

We had a scene. I went over to his place at six in the morning, not knowing what I'd find. But I had my suspicions. Now I wonder how I ever let myself be pushed into that psychological corner. Why didn't I just call him up the next day and tell him he'd dropped the last straw on the back of our relationship? The answer is that this kind of man plays relentlessly on my kind of woman's instinct to cater and appease. Haven't we all complained about how often it's the woman who takes emotional responsibility for making a relationship work? It may be wrong, it may be counter-productive, but it's a trap many of us fall into.

He was asleep, alone. I'd never let myself into his place unannounced before. I felt a little ashamed of myself. I was exhausted, I was angry. I shouted insults, made accusations, did whatever I could to make him feel as small as I was feeling.

"Did you really think I'd bring another woman back here knowing you had a key?" he yelled back at me.

"So you do your sleeping around somewhere else," I replied angrily.

"Yes," he hissed back at me. "Damn right I do."

He never really did apologize for standing me up.

I told him to come and collect his things, which were messing up my apartment. It was over.

Of course, there was another letter. It was pulsing with regret, replete with fulsome denials and apologies. In it were some glimpses of the guy I'd fallen in love with. But I'd had enough of the other guy, the real flesh-and-blood one who showed up late every other day and apparently couldn't connect his words to his deeds.

I'm the first to admit that companion ads do work for some people. We all know the stories of contented couples who met through the newspaper. All I can say is: Don't believe what you read. Keep your expectations low. And that first letter, or in my case, stack of letters? Forget it. He's showing you his best profile. And the more adept he is with words, the better it will look. Wait for the full view, in the flesh, before you form a stable impression. The ads, after all, are just an easy way to arrange a blind date.

I like to think that if V and I had met some other way, we'd have been smart enough to save each other a lot trouble.

But that's something I'll never know.

★ ★ ★

Sarah sat at her computer in her bedroom, reading each page of the article as it rolled out of her printer. This isn't too bad, she thought. Maybe the ending needs a little work. Maybe not. She chuckled to herself. Max, you poor bastard. You'll want to crawl into a hole.

She was surprised at her twitch of sympathy. No, she thought. Max can take care of himself. All too well.

She quickly typed a covering letter to Maria Jonsson at *Canadian Woman*, the editor who had bought the idea. "A first-person piece on a disastrous affair that started with a companion ad — with all the gory details included" was how Sarah had pitched it. *Canadian Woman* had been enthusiastic. "We're game for all the emotional gore that's fit to print," the editor had said. "The less you censor, the better."

Sarah walked west along Bloor Street to the photocopy shop where she could fax her freshly minted article downtown to *Canadian Woman*. It had been a sunny May day, but cool now at five o'clock. She had not quite reached her dentist's building — the photocopy shop was just beyond it — when a familiar face appeared walking towards her on the sidewalk. It was Dorothy Scrivener.

"Hello, Dot," Sarah said. "How are you?"

The older woman smiled and greeted Sarah, but in an off-hand and distant way.

"I'm Sarah. You may not remember. Max Vellen's old girl-friend."

"Of course you are!" said Dot, planting a kiss on her cheek. "I knew the face but couldn't put a name to it. It's been months. I was sorry when you and Max broke up. I miss seeing you at *Berger's* parties. Not that we have that many."

"I miss you too."

"We should have lunch one day," Dot added. "Call me. I've got to run back downtown now. I was just up here on an errand." She paused for a rasping smoker's cough. "Some shopping."

Sarah said good-bye and continued down the sidewalk. As she walked on, she felt pleased that she had bumped into feisty old Dot, so out of place — with her up-market tastes and pricey clothes — in this grungy, student neighbourhood. Sarah had talked with Dot at several *Berger's* office parties and had formed an impression of her as an admirably tenacious woman who had dug in for a career in journalism when it was still largely a male trade.

Odd though, that Dot was shopping in this part of town, Sarah thought as she handed the young man at Kwikcopy her typescript along with *Canadian Woman*'s fax number.

CHAPTER 15

May 7

"Very rare indeed," said the bald man in the wrinkled brown suit. "Almost impossible to find now. Hence the value. This New York estate included one of the better American collections. Did I mention I have these on consignment? For sixty days only." He spoke with an English accent.

"Cigar?"

"Thank you, but I won't."

Edward Clubb took one from the wooden box on his desk. He clipped it, moistened the mouth end with his lips, and struck a wooden match.

"You might be interested in an early American lighter I acquired not long ago," said the man.

"Never use a lighter for cigars," said Clubb. "Matches. Lighter gives a bad taste."

"Ah."

"We were discussing the price. If I'm interested at all, I'm interested in acquiring the whole brigade."

"Quite right. I think it should be kept together. They're so difficult to round up for a full parade once they've been broken up. Quite right."

"I'd like to come to a decision. What *is* the price, Mr. Stackhouse? No need to be coy. *Pecunia non olet.*"

"Wot?"

"Money doesn't smell. As I am sure you would agree."

"Ah. Quite. I think I could let you have the whole lot for eighteen thousand Canadian dollars."

"Eighteen thousand!?! You could have outfitted the whole bloody Light Brigade itself and shipped it to the Crimea for that."

"Did the Canadian dollar exist then?"

"But you take my point." Clubb picked up one of the tin soldiers that had been unwrapped on the table in front of him. "They're nothing more than little pieces of painted metal, after all. We're not negotiating for artistic masterworks."

"Perhaps not," the brown-suited man sniffed. "But they are scarce, and scarcity has pushed up the price. They didn't come cheaply in New York, I can assure you."

"I'll give you twelve."

"I'd be able to move it down to sixteen, perhaps. In anticipation of doing further business with you."

"Fourteen?"

"Mmmm. I suppose I could just do it at fifteen. That's getting a little sticky, but I suppose I could manage it."

"Fourteen and a half," countered Clubb with a glint in his eye.

The man shook his head gloomily.

"Done then. Fifteen thousand for the Light Brigade. That would be twenty-five dollars apiece. I doubt I'll be able to display all six hundred. But it will be good to have them in my personal armed forces. Do you have your own army, Mr. Stackhouse?" Clubb asked with a cold smile.

"Can't afford one, to tell the truth. I do have a few representative pieces. Some personal favourites. A bodyguard rather than an army, if you will. Shall I deliver the shipment to this address or to your home?"

Clubb walked the antique dealer out to the elevator. Mrs. Crutchlow waved a pink phone-message slip. He took it and glanced at her familiar scrawl as the dealer pulled the gate closed.

"Prime Minister's Office," the message read. "Please call

Louise Garon for connection." There was an Ottawa number beside the name.

He lumbered back past his secretary's desk. "The Light Brigade won a redeeming victory today, Edith."

She looked up at him quizically.

"We pressed him for better than fifteen per cent off his asking price. In my experience, ten per cent is as good as Nicholas Stackhouse ever gives. Must have been a little desperate."

"The Prime Minister called."

"When was that?"

"About ten minutes ago. But you asked not to be disturbed."

Clubb went into his office, sat at his desk, and, with his cigar clenched between his teeth, punched in the Ottawa number. He was put on hold for a couple of minutes until a familiar baritone voice came on the line.

"Eddie. How ya doin'?"

"Not bad, Prime Minister, not bad. Still enjoying your soft life as a public-sector employee?"

"You're a card, Edward. Make another million this week?"

"Our profits are running about a million a month. I believe my shareholders are satisfied at the moment."

"Since you're your own biggest shareholder, you must be a happy man," the voice shot back. "And I'm glad to find you in a good mood, because I have a favour to ask."

"I stand ready to serve my country," Clubb replied. "But I think I continue to do you a large favour as it is. I mean by never publicly recalling your uncivilized behaviour at our Christmas party in second year."

"That's not a favour. It's a public duty. Like I said, Edward, you're a helluva card. This time I'll owe you one. Your magazine — *Berger's* — is apparently doing a piece on me. Do you know about it?"

"I don't micromanage all my properties, Bart. Couldn't if I wanted to."

"Well, this article is by a guy I don't know — Leonard Freeman's his name. He's not in the press gallery, not one of the regular boys up here. So we don't know him. But my people say that judging by his past performance, he's unlikely to be singing my praises. You know, the usual left-liberal axe to grind. And there's something very hard to figure about the way he's operating. We've offered him an interview. I rarely give any reporter private time these days. It just pisses off all the other boys in the press gallery. But my people figured that for a respectable rag like *Berger's* maybe I should. So I agreed.

"Here's the curious part. He's not biting. He's told my press people that his magazine doesn't want him to see me. Any other reporter in this town would jump if I offered them one-on-one time. Not this guy."

"Sounds odd, I agree."

"I'll say. The word back from your Mr. Freeman is that he's been commissioned to do a meditation on me, not a conventional report. A *meditation*. What the hell's his game, Eddie?"

"A meditation? I've no idea. I think you're doing a fine job up there, but it's difficult for me to conceive of you as the subject of any kind of pious meditation, Prime Minister."

"Yeah, and I'll say a prayer for you too. Lookit, I'd be obliged if you could tell me where this guy is coming from. We'd just like to get our side of the story on the record. I can well imagine what some self-indulgent young hack could do by way of a so-called *meditation* on my government. You might as well print the ravings of open-line radio callers."

"I'll certainly look into it, Bart. I don't approve of the pages of any of my publications being taken over by the lunatic fringe. Or the typically incompetent and uninformed middle, for that matter. Leave it with me, sir. I'll get back to you."

★ ★ ★

Late the same morning Chaser Makepeace had received a call from his publisher's secretary.

"Mr. Clubb would like to see you this afternoon. He says it's urgent and he's going out of town tomorrow."

"Can we do it over the phone? I've got a crowded afternoon as it is."

"He said he wanted you to come down. This afternoon," Mrs. Crutchlow had twittered nervously.

Which was why Chaser Makepeace was walking down Church Street at two-thirty in the afternoon, hurrying from the *Berger's* offices on Richmond Street to the flat-iron building on Wellington.

"Chaser!"

Across Church, by the grounds of the Anglican cathedral, he saw a woman waving. The face was vaguely familiar, someone in the business, someone he instinctively knew he did not much want to talk to. Sheila Moses. A friend, he remembered now, of Arnold's.

She crossed the street. "I've just had the most marvelous lunch at La Maquette," she gushed as she stepped onto the sidewalk beside him. "With Michael Rector. I've been meaning to call you. I saw you at the funeral. That was a lovely reading. But wasn't the whole business awful? I talked to him only a few days before."

"Yeah, dreadful," Chaser nodded gravely. "You don't know what a huge pillar some people are till they're gone. We'll be scrambling a long time to fill the space Arnold left behind at the magazine, God bless him." He looked at his watch, then quickly back to Sheila's inquisitive face. He could smell beer on her breath.

"Tell me, though," she bubbled, "did they ever find a note?"

He shook his head. "No. You knew him very well, didn't you?"

"For years and years."

Chaser's mouth twitched.

"Oh, but we were never intimate," she added quickly. "Nothing like that. Arnold had his ladies, but I wasn't one of them." She paused, her moist eyes widening. "Isn't it strange how we can say things like that. Now that he's gone."

"I knew he liked women," Chaser said.

"Speaking of which," she rushed on, "I've heard a scurrilous tale about his involvement in a sexual harassment *scandale* at your office. Some people are saying that's what pushed him over the edge." She stopped, looked searchingly at Chaser. "Any clues?"

He glanced at his watch again. "My sense of it all is that there's no need to speak ill of the dead. For twenty years he brought credit to *Berger's*. That's how we should remember him. Sorry, Sheila. I have to run. Nice to see you. Call me. You should be writing for us."

"Bloody Arnold," Chaser murmured to himself a few minutes later as he anxiously straightened his yellow-and-blue bow tie in the flat-iron building's elevator.

He approached Mrs. Crutchlow's desk. "You won't have to wait today," she said. "He told me to send you right in."

Chaser opened the baronial door into his employer's office. The chairman was on the telephone, but motioned to the *Berger's* editor to take a chair.

"Tell them Jeremy Glass will freeze in hell before we accept a private letter of apology," Chaser heard him saying. "The whole point is that he's made a public issue of my reputation and my business, and if he's going to unmake anything, he's going to have to do it at length and in public. I'm talking about paid notices in newspapers. Large and expensive ones. I want all that detailed in any settlement proposal. Down to the last dollar."

Edward Clubb banged down the receiver.

"You've come at an opportune moment, Chaser. I've got a few other things to discuss with you, but we can talk about the Glass situation as well."

Chaser took a notepad out of his briefcase.

"Why don't you tell me first exactly what you're proposing to do about this Glass business. I've got my lawyers working on the legal end, as you may have surmised from that call. I'm assuming Glass and *Wellington* will eventually choose to settle. Certainly Glass won't have the funds for a protracted fight in court. But *Berger's* should be doing something on the public-relations front."

The editor was scribbling on his pad: "His nibs' legal fart catchers."

"There *is* the question of editorial independence," Chaser said, looking up from his note. "We made a point of that when I took this job."

"*You* made a point of it," Clubb frowned. "Far too much of a point, in my view."

"I'm just saying it's part of the landscape now," Chaser replied calmly. On his pad, he wrote, "Gen'l Bullmoose dmands fealty of troops."

"Alright. Let's just speculate here, *ianuis clausis*. For our ears only. What happens when you conclude your precious independence has been violated?"

Chaser pondered this for a moment. "Well, I'd have to resign. And sue you for constructive dismissal."

His employer looked at him. "Exactly," he said.

They stared at each other.

"I have been turning the Glass affair over in my mind," Chaser offered meekly. "I may be able to write a piece."

"I'm glad to hear that, Chaser. That's very good news."

"I'll let you know when it's done."

"Good. I'd like to see it as soon as I can."

"Just as a courtesy, of course," the editor added, sticking a finger between his neck and his collar.

Clubb leaned forward. "You know, Chaser, I do own the bloody magazine. A little courtesy, as you put it, is surely my due."

"Of course it is." Chaser scribbled: "Col. Pitbull, hngry for human mtballs."

"Good. By the way, what do you know of *Wellington*? Apart from their article on me?"

"Apart from that, I like it very much. It's a spunky city magazine. Why?"

"Just curious about what sort of animal we're dealing with."

"Did you know it's backed by a small real-estate developer? Emmanuel Rosenfeld. It's a window into a new world for him. I doubt he likes the look of a lawsuit, though. I don't think he bought it to spend money on lawyers."

Clubb looked interested. "Justin said nothing about a developer. He said he doubted they had money."

"That sounds right. Rosenfeld isn't a big hitter, as far as I know. Just a guy with a few spare millions who wanted to do something different."

Clubb nodded.

"Incidentally, Edward, I hope you're satisfied with the arrangements for your . . . Churchill article."

"It could hardly be described as a 'Churchill article,' " Clubb glowered. "An essay on contemporary geopolitics was what I wrote. But yes, I'm satisfied with the arrangements. Very pleasant fellow, Mr. Redstone. I enjoyed my talk with him. He's certainly keen on my essay. We see eye to eye on a number of things."

"I'm also pleased that he's agreed to do a piece for *Berger's*," said Chaser. "Most American writers won't give us the time of day. But he is very interested in Canada."

"Perhaps he feels he owes us a favour. Since I've agreed to let him publish my essay."

"Of course," said Chaser eagerly. "I'm sure you're right."

Clubb nodded. "Now. There's a matter of some urgency that we have to discuss, Chaser. It concerns an article you have apparently commissioned." He glanced at the sheet of paper on the desk in front of him. "By one Leonard Freeman. He does work for you?"

"Occasionally."

"The Prime Minister called me this morning. He sounded quite upset. He says he's agreed to grant a rare interview to your writer. But the writer has declined. Which sounds like the height of incivility to me. Not to mention questionable journalistic practice. . . ."

"We may be cancelling that piece," Chaser cut in quickly. "The writer is very late with it."

"But you may not cancel?"

"It's under review this week."

"What I want to say is, if you publish that piece, your Leonard Freeman has to have the courtesy to go and see McGarvie. And I'd like to make it clear, if I haven't already, that I didn't purchase *Berger's* to underwrite left-wing radicals launching attacks on my old friends. Leonard Freeman, whoever he is, can damn well print up his own repellent pamphlets and pass them out on street corners. It's a democracy. But in *Berger's*, as long as I'm footing the bills, I am not funding intemperate screeds against Barton McGarvie or any other hard-working conservative politicians. I'm glad to see you're taking notes. I regard all of this as of the utmost importance."

Chaser looked up quickly from what he was scribbling. "It may not be quite as simple as you think," he said. His scribble read: "Edouard de Trunkful. Gt hero of late 20th cen N. Amrcn demcrcy. $1=1 vote."

"Why not? It sounds straightforward enough to me."

"Edward, as has been explained to me many times since I took this job, we are not running a newspaper. We publish a magazine almost entirely written by freelancers. To some degree we are beholden to the writing community for our product."

"Beholden? To *the writing community*? My advice to you is to hire more compliant contributors. You do pay them, after all."

"Not all that much. Most of them could be making more doing something else."

"Are you telling me we have to follow the publishing tastes of *writers*?"

"Not entirely. But we don't own them either. They all work freelance. We're obliged to give them some free rein."

"Not on this bloody article we're not."

"Well, no, maybe not on this one."

"I want this rectified, Chaser."

"I'll see what I can do. But I certainly can't let it be known that the Prime Minister has been running editorial interference in an article on himself. We'd be the laughing stock of Canadian publishing."

"Ah. I see. Well, no-one need know about that. It was just a personal call between old friends. I mentioned it to you simply as background. My concern is really larger. If *Berger's* is doing major articles, say on the Prime Minister, we should do them judiciously, with proper journalistic procedures. Don't you agree an interview is the proper way to proceed?"

"Yes, I suppose so."

"Then fix it, for Christ's sake."

★ ★ ★

"Not a word about it, though, not to a soul, please."

"To the grave," replied Dot Scrivener.

"If anyone finds out McGarvie has so much as his pinky finger in our pie, we're toast, God bless us," said Chaser.

"There's no reason anyone should find out. I'm not sure why you're trusting *me* with this information, though."

"I can't fly solo. Never could. And you're the only one in this place who doesn't lust after my job."

"You're right there."

"We make a good team. You know more about running

magazines than I ever will. We can help each other." Chaser stopped, then banged one fist on top of the other. "I just hope Clubb knows enough to keep his big trap shut."

★　★　★

"Giorgio is begging for another page for the Shaw piece," Chaser said. "He desperately wants that photograph. Says he can take a page out of the piece on child abuse. I know the ladies will howl. Especially Dame Dorothy."

Chaser's patter put Max on the *qui vive*. The editor's male-bonding strategy always alerted him. Whenever Chaser wanted something, he would begin to speak in low confidential tones about "Dame Dorothy" and "the ladies," by which he meant the four female editors at the magazine. He would affect a beleaguered-male stance, and there would be a wink in Max's direction which conveyed something like, "You and I, pal, the ladies may have us in a corner, but at least we're in it together."

Balls to that, thought Max. You could fire me tomorrow. I'm just as vulnerable as anyone.

Chaser sat behind his enormous carved desk in his padded swivel chair. As he leaned back, Max could see the editor's legs dangling. They were too short to reach the floor. Chaser at that moment reminded Max of Pinocchio.

"How's the Freeman piece coming?" the editor asked.

"He sent the first half up by courier today. I plan to work on it over the weekend."

"You know, I think we should probably revert to plan B. Go with the article on Ontario politics. Put Tom Broadfoot on the cover."

"Really? The Freeman piece is very close now. I can send part of it to the fact checker Monday. Leonard has promised the rest by early next week."

Chaser raised his eyebrows. "It's getting terribly tight. The ladies are all upset about the schedule, God bless them. I think it may be time to cut our losses."

"To be fair, the schedule disruptions around here aren't just Leonard Freeman's fault," Max remonstrated. "We lost one of the best editors in the country two weeks ago."

"You really think he was that good?"

"Yes."

"There's another problem."

Chaser's intense eyes, compressed to dense brown stones, put Max on the edge of his chair. He sensed that everything Chaser was saying now had been carefully calculated.

"I hear from a source of mine at the *Trib* in Ottawa that McGarvie was open for an interview. You say Freeman hasn't done one. I think that was poor judgment on his part. But it's too late now."

"I don't know about that. The structure of the piece will all be in place by Monday. If it's true that they'll give us time, he could fly up next week and slot in the new material as I edit."

Chaser shook his head. He swung his chair forward and banged his loafers on the carpet. "At this point I think we'd be better off to dump it. I really do. But I guess we have to be fair to the writer. Okay. See if you can get Freeman to Ottawa and keep pushing the piece along as fast as you can for a few more days. But I want you to know that we may have to kill it. We're too stretched as it is."

Goddamn, thought Max. "Incidentally, who's your source at the *Trib*'s Ottawa office?"

Chaser stared at Max. "I wouldn't want to say. They have a pipeline right into the PMO. Very reliable. But all off the record, of course."

"I was just curious."

"See you at the magazine awards tonight." The editor stood up and pushed his door half-closed as Max was about to step into the hall. "The ladies are doing the seating plan for our two tables tonight," Chaser added in a confidential whisper. "Maybe you should have a look and defend your interests."

Max walked straight into his office and phoned Leonard. "Helloo," said the recorded greeting. "This is Leonard Freeman. Your electronic echo will reach me later, if you leave a message after the beep."

"Leonard, we should talk. A.S.A.P. I'm being told the PMO *will* give you an interview after all. We need to see if we can set it up and get you on a plane. Fast. We also need to have a first draft in this office by Monday. I suggest you and I meet for a marathon editing session on Sunday. Call me."

Goddamn liar, Max thought, as he put down the phone.

CHAPTER 16

It was worse even than going home for Christmas. Magazine Awards night was Max's least favourite box on the calendar. This was the night when freelancers, who all year long had fought desperately to beat each other out for plum assignments, assembled in one big ballroom and smiled on one another; the night when editors, who for twelve months had been badmouthing their competitors to advertisers and anyone else who would listen, were suddenly all over each other with praise; the night when winners went home knowing that this year's juries had been exceptionally right-minded and sensitive to the rigours of the craft; and the night when losers went home confirmed in their career-long suspicions that the whole process was corrupt, rigged in favour of the same old hacks whose friends sat on all the jury panels.

Max circulated warily in the lobby outside the ballroom where the dinner tables were set. Once it was time to go inside, he'd be okay. He had looked at the seating plans of the two *Berger's* tables that afternoon. At the dinner all you had to do was be civil to your seat mates, listen to the patter of the guest host, and hope that you or one of the writers you had edited won a prize. But circulating out in the lobby was another matter. Every writer whose ideas you had ever rejected was likely to accost you reproachfully. Even the ones you had collaborated with successfully were eager to buttonhole you and sell you another idea. Thinking about it at home as he dressed in his old blue suit, Max had felt glum.

Now he was quickly downing his third ale, determined to enjoy himself. He surveyed the crowded lobby adjoining the awards dinner ballroom. Across the floor he saw Chaser wearing a red bow tie and matching red cummerbund. Giorgio, tall and sleek, stood in a corner, wearing no tie at all. He sported a formal white Russian shirt with silver studs. There were a few celebrities on view too. The novelist Mordechai Wexler had flown up from Montreal. His hair was tousled and his tie was askew; he held an amber-filled snifter in one hand and a cigarillo in the other. Max wandered past him, hoping to scoop up any trenchant literary opinions his favourite novelist might be offering. "Naw," Max heard Wexler's nasal voice insist, "it'll be the Blue Jays this year. Not the Expos. Their pitching is drek. The only thing they'd know how to throw would be the game."

Dot Scrivener had parked herself near the bar. She was an apparition from half a century ago, with her long black dress, her black cigarette holder, and her hair in a close-fitting cloche hat. She was talking to a writer Max wanted to avoid, Liam E. O'Chancre. His original name, Paul Green, had been discarded when he had moved to Canada from Britain in the late eighties as a young writer on the make.

"What does your middle initial 'E' stand for?" Max had asked the only time they had met. O'Chancre had cold-called him and invited Max to lunch only a few months after he had been installed as an editor at *Berger's*.

"Need it stand for anything?" O'Chancre had replied grandly. "I suppose it stands for notoriety, just as the rest of the name does. 'Paul Green' was hopeless. A writer must be noticed. So I adopted the principle of brand-name advertising. And it works. No-one will ever forget a by-line like O'Chancre."

He had wanted an assignment from Max. But Max had been unconvinced. O'Chancre had come to Canada armed with a degree from a red-brick university and one thin volume of literary scholarship, a mediocre biography of Rudyard Kipling. Max felt these were not compelling credentials on which to base a career writing for Canadian magazines. O'Chancre, with his large girth, prematurely balding head, and slight lisp, struck Max as nearly as ugly as his assumed name. Never mind that, though. He was bursting with bravado and hauteur, good signs in a writer. The problem, as Max intimated at their lunch, was that O'Chancre knew almost nothing about Canada.

"You can just fuck off!" O'Chancre had shouted after Max had said that maybe young Liam, who was only twenty-eight, might spend a couple of years earning himself a pair of Canadian eyes before he leapt into the kind of social and literary commentary he was proposing. The obese young man had stood up abruptly, pushed the table away from himself — jamming Max in the ribs — and had stormed out of the restaurant, leaving *Berger's* to foot the bill.

O'Chancre's eye caught Max's across the room now as he was remembering their unpleasant lunch. They had not spoken since then — about a year ago. O'Chancre briefly raised a middle finger in Max's direction.

I love you too, Max thought.

There had been repercussions. Max had grown more adept at stroking writers' elephantine eggshell egos. Too late for O'Chancre, but a lesson well learned all the same. For his part, O'Chancre had taken his grievance to *Poop* magazine, the only publication in town that would give him work at the time. Max had heard that O'Chancre was responsible for the series of vicious attacks against him that *Poop* had started running not long after their lunch. And O'Chancre had been in demand at *Poop* ever since. The *Poop* editors warmed to his snide British-style humour and had even given him his own column.

But as Max observed every time he bought a copy, *Poop* itself was modelled on the snide, *schadenfreude* British humour of *Private Eye*, so there was no surprise in O'Chancre's finding a perch there.

Max could still remember, word for word, the first item about him they had printed: "Anyone seen Maxwell Vellen's by-line these past few months? Maxwell Who? You might well ask. Vellen is a washed-up freelancer who has been having trouble making his car payments now that every editor in town is wise to his overly moist ways at lunch and dinner — breakfast too for all we know. But *Berger's* has provided a halfway house for the unsteady futureless hack. They have actually hired Vellen to help do their editorial ironing. Someone at the magazine better be making some strong coffee."

It had been Max's first sting by a gossip sheet, the first time he understood how gossip writing, with a small lie here and a shift in emphasis there, could transform someone's personal triumph into a rout. For several months he had congratulated himself for landing the job at *Berger's*. He'd told all his friends, "I haven't felt this upwardly mobile since I left college." But the *Poop* item, and others that followed, had flattened him. Max had never forgiven Liam O'Chancre.

Cutting a wide arc around Dot and her new friend, Max made his way to the bar, where he bought another cheap beer. Bruce Guilman, the dean of Toronto editors, was there talking to the dean of CBC radio hosts, Pierre Stankiewicz. A large inflatable happy clown, Max thought, talking to a gravelly voice with a muskrat face. Max had met both of these older media celebrities — once — but neither seemed to recognize him as he nodded and murmured a hopeful hello. He brushed past and stood next to them, hoping to overhear something tradable. He regarded them as the two most savvy commentators in the room.

"Mr. Vellen!"

Max wheeled around, ready to confront an angry scribe whose thin skin he had somehow pierced over the last year. Instead it was tall, teddy-bearish Gamie Goodfellow, a friend who had got his nickname at some point in a long lifetime of taking goofy risks, which included having paddled up remote tributaries of the Brazilian Amazon with another innocent Canadian writer, and on another trip inadvertently wandering into embargoed territory in Castro's Cuba. The first had put him in hospital, the second in jail.

"How's the article? Halfway done yet?" Max laughed. Gamie had been working on a magazine piece about his Cuban escapades for over a year, since Max had commissioned it. Max now expected the story would still be a work in progress the day he left his job at *Berger's*, whenever that might be. Gamie wrote novels. His wife was a successful author. Magazine assignments were a diversion for him, not a living.

"It's coming along nicely. I'll have a draft for you soon." Gamie stroked one of his Victorian mutton-chop sideburns. He was wearing granny glasses and, instead of a cummerbund, a low-cut vest under a wide-lapelled dinner jacket.

"Do you know why Barton McGarvie's necktie is so often touching the floor?"

Max shook his head. "Of course I don't. You inevitably know first." Gamie was always ready with the newest lame joke.

"Because his head is so often between George Bush's legs."

A typical Goodfellow joke. With the paranoia about American power thrown in — a fear Max did not share. But he grinned obligingly. Gamie was twelve years older than Max and a diehard Canadian nationalist. Gamie had been convinced, for example, that the buying up of small Ontario cheese factories by large American firms in the 1970s had been a part of Canada's continuing economic capitulation, an insidious piecemeal invasion probably engineered by the CIA. Max, on the other hand, thought it was simply a big cheese factory swallowing a smaller one. But he admired Gamie's dedication to his ideas.

"You up for an award?" Gamie asked, puffing on his long Benjamin Franklin pipe.

"Actually, yes," Max nodded. "I did a profile of Robertson Davies about two years ago, but it wasn't published in *Berger's* till January of last year. So it was eligible and it's made it to the finals. Seems like another life now, writing articles for a living." Over Gamie's shoulder he noticed O'Chancre watching him talk. Their eyes made another hostile connection. A future *Poop* item darted into Max's mind: "Maxwell Vellen, the booze-rotted journalist who is masquerading as an assistant speller at *Berger's* was seen at this year's pre-magazine-awards cocktail party in deep conversation with sixties throwback Gamie Goodfellow, the boring drivelist known chiefly for his silly first name and his Masterpiece Theatre sideburns. Goodfellow once wrote that there was nothing wrong with Canadian culture that a hefty tax on American TV sitcoms and films could not cure. Is he seriously hoping to peddle these addle-brained ravings in Edward Clubb's mass-market magazine?"

Max quickly drained his bottle of beer and ordered another. "You up for anything yourself?"

Gamie nodded. "First time I've ever been a finalist for a magazine award. I did a piece on toxic effluents in the Great Lakes, and the effect they are having on Canadian birds. It was set mostly out near our cottage at Point Pelee, and . . ."

"Gamie," Max cut in. "What is a *Canadian* bird?"

"That's easy. I ascribe citizenship to birds same way we do to people. A Canadian bird is one hatched in Canada."

"Ah ha. I guess I think of birds as more pan-national than that. Anyhow, I vaguely remember the piece now."

Gamie went on enthusiastically describing how American industrial waste was killing off the Canadian bird population

by corroding reproductive systems in some species and inflict-
ing nerve damage in others. Max was trying to pay attention.
He was beginning to feel light-headed, and he could never
bring himself to quite believe in the insidious malign forces
that Gamie habitually identified as a threat to Canada's survival.
He could hear Gamie's voice saying "poisons" and "Canadian
nesting grounds" and "vicious American sewage," but his mind
was drifting and his eyes were wandering through the crowd.

Suddenly his throat felt cramped and dry. About ten feet
away, he spotted an attractive and familiar face. Jill Kavanaugh,
Sarah's best friend, was talking to a younger woman Max did
not know.

"I had a nice title for the piece," Gamie was saying. " 'Toxic
America: The Last Bird Call.' But the editor didn't like that.
She called it 'Crying Fowl: Why Your Sky May Be Empty.'
Which was okay. Although it didn't quite get across the point
about how the Americans . . ."

"Gamie," interrupted Max. "I hope you win a prize. I see
someone I have to talk to before we get called in to dinner."

Would she hector him? Two hours ago, maybe even two
minutes ago, he would have edged around the crowded room
to avoid Jill. But something about Gamie's long disquisition
on chemical death propelled Max in the direction of the two
pretty women, one of whom he had strong reason to believe
disliked him.

"Hello, Jill."

"Max. He*llo*. You're looking unusually sheepish tonight. It's
okay. I won't bite you."

Okay, thought Max, have your piece of flesh. I can take it.

"No, not really. Haven't seen you for months, stranger. That's
all."

"Uh huh."

"Are you here with a magazine person, Jill?" He turned to the
younger woman, who was wearing a décolleté black dress that

showed a cleavage Max involuntarily found himself staring at.

Embarrassed, he jerked his head up and put a finger on one of his eyelids.

"Speck in my eye," he said as he rubbed the lid gently and looked down again at the naked cleavage with the other half of his vision. "My name's Max Vellen."

"Betsy Cerniak." Her gleaming, poppy-red mouth smiled.

"Should have introduced you," said Jill. "I thought you might know each other. Betsy has been at *Wellington* magazine since last fall. I know her from a seminar I taught at the Ryerson J-school."

"Really?" Max said, sounding surprised. "When was that?" He turned back to the younger woman and looked again at her bright green eyes.

"Two years ago," she said.

"No kidding," he said without thinking. "You don't look like a recent J-school grad."

"What are we supposed to look like?"

"Oh, I dunno. Younger maybe."

"Are you asking me how old I am?"

Max thought for a moment. "That seems to be what I'm doing."

"I'm twenty-six."

"I'd have thought older."

"You're at *Berger's*, aren't you?"

"How did you know that?"

"Every Ryerson grad who wants to work in magazines knows exactly who works at every magazine in Toronto. Or if they don't, they should."

Ambition, thought Max. Part of the brightness in the eyes. "Networking," he said.

"Of course."

"Somehow I don't think I'm needed here," said Jill. "I came with Jeremy Glass, since you asked."

"What do you want to go out with that fop-around-town for?" scoffed Max. "Anyway, I thought he lived with someone."

"Sure he does. It's not a date. I'm doing a piece on him for the *Herald*. I got very interested in his libel problems. Ask your owner about that."

"Hey," Max snapped back, "don't expect me to apologize for anything Edward Clubb does. I just work there."

"See ya." Jill smirked at him and turned to Betsy. "Watch this guy. He can be a little dangerous."

"What was that all about?" Betsy asked when Jill was gone.

"I think Jill maybe has a warped view of my essentially virtuous personality. I went out with her best friend for a year or so."

"And?"

"Let's just say it ended badly."

"How did it start?"

"With a companion ad in the *Tribune*."

"Oh? I've never done that."

"You will, if you stay single long enough. You are single?"

"At this moment, yes."

Max couldn't tell whether she was tempting him or drawing a boundary line. "Forget Jill's unflattering comment," he said. "There's nothing to it."

"Too bad. We should all have some danger in our lives."

"Oh, sure. But with me it's never daredevil stuff. Nothing heroic. It's all inadvertent."

"I like spontaneity," she said with a friendly smile. They could hear an announcer asking people to find their tables and take their seats.

"Really? How about spontaneously coming out with me for a drink after this?" Max felt himself staring at her glistening lips longer than he should.

"That might work. Let's wait and see how late it finishes."

★ ★ ★

Berger's had bought two large round tables — the editor's and the publisher's. Max had arranged to sit with the publisher so he would not have to listen to any Chaser Makepeace stories for the fourth time. The nominated writers were divided evenly between the two groups. Chaser had made sure the better known nominees were sitting with him. "Otherwise," he had said grandly, "they'd be insulted."

Graham Nutley presided at Max's table. Dot Scrivener was placed two seats away. On Max's right sat Jan Kertesz, the brilliant Hungarian-Canadian writer who had been nominated for his article on legalizing prostitution. The piece — and the writer — had been Max's idea, and he could still remember the first line, which had read, "When I first came to Canada after the Hungarian Revolution in 1956, I was regularly a client of several prostitutes, to no-one's lasting detriment, as far as I could tell."

Max felt uneasy, given the subject of the article, that Jan had insisted *Berger's* include his Taiwanese girlfriend at the awards dinner. She was seated on Max's left.

But he was glad to be safely ensconced at the table, away from the bear pit of the cocktail party.

"Marilyn." Jan leaned over Max's place setting to get his girlfriend's attention. "I vant you to meet my edidor, Maaax Vellen." With his accent and basso-profundo voice, Jan sounded a lot like Henry Kissinger.

"Hello there," giggled the tiny woman. Max guessed there must be about a thirty-year age difference between Jan and his young partner.

Since the Hungarian's conversation was usually studded with references to the likes of Kant, Hegel, Milton Friedman, and Karl Popper, Max had been looking forward to an intellectually stimulating dinner. But the pretty young nominee on Jan's right immediately caught the writer's attention, leaving Max with Marilyn and, on the other side of her, Dot.

Jan's girlfriend picked at her salad and said nothing. "What did you think when you read Jan's article?" Max ventured after a long silence.

"What did I think? I thought Holt Renfrew's," giggled the tiny woman.

"Sorry? You mean the clothing store?"

"I buy all my clothes there. When Jan gives me the money." She giggled again. Max noticed she was wearing what looked like a silk pajama suit.

"I see," he lied, and drank half the glass of wine that had just been poured by a waiter. "And, um, when you read the article, Holt Renfrew's came to mind? Is that a sociological observation on the moonlighting habits of the sales personnel at Holt's?"

"Could you speak more slowly?" she replied. "I don't think I understand you."

"You think Holt Renfrew's has a lot of whores on staff?" Max heard himself shout. A few heads turned. He tried to grin disarmingly.

The tiny woman seemed to be dismayed. "What are you talking about? I shop there. For *clothes*."

"Yes. Right. But you said Holt's came to mind when you read Jan's article, and I was wondering . . ."

"Oh, I never *read* anything Jan writes. I am always very happy when he sells a magazine article. He says magazine money is fun money, because he doesn't really need it. More money, more shopping. I love shopping. I could shop every day."

"Ah," said Max, finishing his wine. "So you separate yourself entirely from Jan's work?"

"I guess so," she giggled. "Whenever I pass his room in the condo, he's busy, busy, busy. Always writing. I think that must be boring. But he says not."

"What do *you* do?" Max asked.

"Like I told you, I mostly shop." She frowned at him as if to question his intelligence.

"I like your outfit, Marilyn," Dot broke in. She had been watching with her amused half pout, half smile.

They began talking about clothes and shops. Max felt excluded. Sensing he'd been inept, he silently ate his slab of beef along with the watery cauliflower and leathery roasted potatoes. As he drained his wine, he remembered Betsy Cerniak, and decided he had better remain passably sober. He was already experiencing a very pleasant fuzziness from all the beer.

Well, maybe one more glass of wine, he thought. What the hell.

Dessert arrived and the lights dimmed. Max looked at the awards program to see the order of the prizes. Dot leaned across to get his attention. "I had a word with Liam O'Chancre before dinner," she said. "He's nominated for travel. I think it's time we got him into *Berger's*, don't you?"

"Hell yes," blurted Max. "I think he should have a regular column. We could call it" — he attempted a British accent — 'Nasal Notes from the Old Country.' Or even better, 'Everything I Don't Know About Canada.'"

"He's *very* smart," Dot retorted. "And remarkably savvy. He told me he was invited to a neo-conservative party that Edward Clubb is giving next week."

"Interesting," said Max, trying not to show any sign of the alarm he felt. "I didn't know O'Chancre was that much of a free-marketeer."

"Maybe not," replied Dot. "But he's definitely socially ambitious."

The master of ceremonies for the awards, the radio personality Arthur Swartz, was beginning his patter up on the stage.

"Good evening, my name is Arthur Swartz, and I'm the guy

who's giving out the money tonight. We have cheques for the winners and possibly a free drink and a bear hug for the runners up. But please be a sport and come up here for your second-prize certificates anyway.

"I envy all you magazine writers out there. Okay, your words aren't etched in stone, but they are etched on paper at least. People buy them and carry them around all week or all month and even send them to their mothers.

"In the electronic media, our words disappear into cyber-space as soon as they leave our lips. You can't reread a radio show. You don't find radio shows in the pocket in front of your Air Canada seat. You don't find radio shows in your dentist's waiting room. . . ."

"Your radio show *is* a dentist's waiting room," yelled a drunken guest from one of the front tables. Someone else threw a bun.

"You don't find old radio shows from last summer waiting for you on a shelf at the cottage when you open it up on the twenty-fourth of May." Another bun flew over Arthur Swartz's head.

"Come to think of it, you can't throw a bun at a radio show either." There was a ripple of laughter. He went back to his text. "You can't use a radio show as a beer coaster. You can't rip it up in frustration. You can't use it to swat flies. And you can't use radio when you run out of toilet paper.

"I think I'll stick with radio."

Another bun flew high above the M.C.'s head.

"I was warned that this can be a tough crowd," he said. "Didn't anyone here eat their bread at dinner?"

Two more buns sailed into the curtain behind the podium.

"I think we'd better get started, folks, while everyone is still conscious."

As Swartz read the lists of nominees and then opened the envelopes with the winning names, Max grew drowsy. It was a monotonous litany — five nominees in each category, a first and a second prize, perfunctory applause. There were more than forty awards in all for editorial and art, and winners were asked to keep their acknowledging remarks down to less than a minute.

Max roused himself when he heard Swartz announce the winner for business writing. "Jeremy Glass for his article in *Business Connection*, 'Canuck Capital Flies South of the Border.'"

Glass strode confidently up to the podium and shook the M.C.'s hand. He appeared entirely at ease at the microphone where he cut a striking figure with his long, shoulder-length blond curls, broad forehead, and trim athletic build.

"I'd like to thank the judges for this generous award. It will help defray some unusual expenses that I'm about to shoulder." Some tittering and applause. "As you may know, I am being sued for libel by one of this country's most powerful press barons, Edward Clubb. More than that, on the advice of my lawyers, I cannot say publicly. But I will tell you this. The support of my colleagues is vital to me and so this award is even more welcome. We intend to fight this case to the best of our ability for as long as we reasonably can." As Glass left the platform, loud applause broke out. People at the front tables quickly stood; a few seconds later almost everyone in the ballroom was standing.

Max leapt unsteadily to his feet; his chair crashed to the floor behind him. He was clapping wildly with his arms above his head when he looked down and realized that he was the only one at the *Berger's* tables who had joined the standing ovation. Graham Nutley was eyeing him reproachfully, apparently wondering which UFO this errant employee had just disembarked from. Max picked up his chair and sat down.

"Freedom of expression," he shouted at Nutley over the noise. "Very important principle." This seemed to compound the error. Nutley gave him a stony look.

Several awards later, Max applauded as Gamie Goodfellow walked up to collect second prize in the science category. Next came culture. The nominees were read out. Swartz tore open the envelope. "And the winner is . . . Arnold Sturgess for 'The Merry Wives of Stratford' in *Berger's* magazine."

It was as if a giant vacuum had sucked all the noise out of the ballroom.

The din bubbled up again as Chaser Makepeace made his way to the microphone. "On behalf of the magazine, thanks for this honour. Arnold Sturgess's passing is still fresh in our minds and it will be a long time before *Berger's* absorbs his absence. But Arnold, bless you, wherever you are, you deserved this."

The applause was louder than usual. Max watched Chaser walk back down the aisle to his table. He looked oddly disconcerted.

Swartz was now reading the names of the nominees in the cultural essay category. Max pricked up his ears. "And this year's winner is . . ." The host fumbled with the envelope. "The winner is Maxwell Vellen for 'Robertson Davies: Canada's Literary Magus.' " Applause greeted Max as he propelled himself in a less than straight line up the carpeted aisle. He stopped at the steps and peered down to take their measure in the dim light. Five. He counted them off as he climbed up to shake hands. His face felt flushed with alcohol but he knew no-one could see very well in the darkened room. He thanked Arthur Swartz and, holding the certificate, swung around to say his few words.

Reaching for the microphone with his left hand, he banged its sharp metal casing with his knuckle and drew a drop of blood. He glanced at the glistening red dot on his skin as the microphone arced slowly over and fell to the floor. A bun hit him on the shoulder.

Shit.

"Your minute is up," someone hooted.

Max bent down and grabbed the micophone tightly. "I'd like to thank my grade-eleven English teacher, who was so bad she saved me from being an English major at college, which in turn allowed me to maintain my enthusiasm for reading — and maybe sometimes writing — clear English sentences. My thanks to the former *Berger's* editor for publishing this piece. I've never won an award before. . . ."

"Never again," someone shouted.

"But it's a great moment and I'd like to thank the judges. . . ."

"Don't forget your mother," a voice up front yelled.

"My mother is dead," said Max, annoyed with the voice. He noticed the room fell silent. Then he realized that half the audience might not have heard the heckler.

"But of course I'd like to thank her too," he added quickly. Mild tittering. "And I'll now try to get out of here without any permanent damage to the facilities."

"Congradulashons," said Jan Kertesz when Max sat down at his table again. "I've won four timz. Vonz I sanked zuh wrong magazeen edidor. Just for laffs. Apparently only two people nodiced. Zis iz alwayz a bad crowd."

Swartz was nearing the end of the long roster of nominees. The last of the editorial prizes was for travel. Max pricked up his ear when he heard the category announced.

"And the runner-up . . . Liam E. O'Chancre."

Oops.

Arthur Swartz signed off; people began to leave their seats and mill around the dance floor. Max was standing a few feet from the *Berger's* tables. He was trying to find Betsy Cerniak's face in the crowd. Instead, Liam O'Chancre's hove into view. He came up and, with his jaw jutting out, looked nastily at Max. He was taller than Max by a couple of inches.

O'Chancre leaned very close. Max could see the black hairs growing out of his nose.

"Vellen. I have now won a Canadian national magazine award for an article in the Air Canada magazine. I write a column in *Poop*, one of Canada's national journals of opinion. And I am a regular book reviewer for *The Bay Street Journal*." He jabbed Max's chest with his forefinger. "I trust I am now sufficiently Canadian even for an inbred Canuck Wasp such as yourself."

"Don't touch me," Max barked, batting away O'Chancre's outstretched finger. "And leave my ancestors out of this, you fat fuckhead. I'm half Dutch, it so happens."

"What did you call me?" O'Chancre shouted. He grabbed Max's lapel.

Max lifted his knee quickly into the larger man's groin.

"Congratulations!" he yelled as O'Chancre let go and doubled over. "On your fucking award!" A crowd of people had turned to watch the scene.

O'Chancre, still in a semi-crouch, swayed for a moment, then slowly straightened and, halfway up, let fly his right hand.

Max saw a large solid object coming at him and jerked his head away. O'Chancre's closed fist landed on the right side of Max's face and knocked him off balance. He staggered back, then lurched forward and swung wildly, missing.

O'Chancre spat angrily on the floor, and approached with both hands closed.

"Excuse me, Liam," said a female voice.

Betsy Cerniak stepped between the two men. "I have a date with Max, Liam. Do you think you two could settle this another time?"

"You know him?" Max exclaimed.

"Mmhm," she nodded.

O'Chancre backed away. "Only for you, Betsy. Anyhow, this might not be quite the place to cripple someone for life."

"Don't count on your own continuing good health," Max snapped.

"Any time you say," O'Chancre snorted as he walked away. "But next time come without protection."

"Ugly customer," muttered Max as he and Betsy turned away. The music started playing for the dancing.

"Congratulations on your award," Betsy said. "I'm impressed."

"He a friend of yours?"

"No, no. Liam's doing a little piece for us at *Wellington*. I'm his editor."

"Obviously my life would have been simpler if I'd just given him an assignment," Max said, and told the story of his first encounter with O'Chancre. "And what's with the all the attitude — the fabricated name, the mannered column in *Poop*, the literary airs he puts on? Who does he think he is?"

"He's inventing a public personality for himself," she replied. "Maybe that's what you have to do to make it in this business."

"I have enough trouble running my private personality without trying to start up a whole new public one," Max reflected. "Anyway, thanks for arbitrating. How about that drink? Or would you like to dance?"

"I think maybe we should get out of here," she said. "Are you badly hurt?"

"Just a scratch." He could feel his eye was puffy. "But apart from a basically vicious nature, Liam O'Chancre is ten years younger than I am and about fifty pounds heavier. He could probably have done some damage if we'd really gone at it."

"How old are you?"

"Thirty-eight. Soon I'll be forty. Soon after that I guess I'll be dead. I think that's how it works."

"You're *old*," she laughed.

"Please," he objected. "I'm the only one who's allowed to say that."

"We'll go somewhere for a drink and you can tell me all about *Berger's*," she murmured, taking him by the arm.

★ ★ ★

They talked in a hotel bar two floors down from the awards ballroom. She wanted to know everything he could tell her about *Berger's*.

"Are there any jobs opening up?" she asked finally. "I mean, with Arnold Sturgess out of the picture."

"There might be," Max lied. He knew the magazine had no immediate plans to hire anyone. "Why? You looking?"

"Sure. Always. I'm stuck at the bottom at *Wellington*. I'd like to do better. *Berger's* is where everyone wants to be."

Max laughed. "Until they actually get there. But yeah — go for it. I'll find out what I can."

Betsy insisted on paying the bar bill. At the front door of the hotel, she told the doorman she wanted a cab, then turned to Max. "Come back to my place for one last drink?"

When they were in her flat on Major Street, she made herbal tea.

"It always tastes like camel's piss," he complained, leaning against the kitchen counter while she watched the kettle.

"So have a double scotch," she said drily. "It can only kill you."

They took their mugs into her living room.

"Do you still look at companion ads?" she wanted to know.

Max wondered drunkenly how he should answer this. He had the feeling there was only one right response, but as he searched his mind, all the possible replies blurred together.

"Ah, sure," he shrugged. "They have some entertainment value." Which seemed disingenuous to him as he said it. But it also seemed like the right move. The truth was that occasionally he still scanned the ads and thought about Sarah, or about finding someone like her. "They don't work the way the uninitial, the un . . . achh!" He took a sip of herbal tea. "The way," he said slowly, "the uninitiated think they do. They promise moonlight and romance. What they usually deliver is a blind date over coffee in a deli with someone whose company you can't wait to escape."

"Why did you do it?"

He struggled to think of the right answer. "Why? Not that I was desperate." He looked at her to see if she might think he was desperate. Her green eyes were watching him closely. She had folded her legs half under her and her hand was tucking a strand of black hair behind one of her perfect little ears.

"Ah, I don't even remember now, not exactly." No, he could see that was wrong. Not true, either. He began again. "When you've lived here as long as I have, Toronto begins to feel like a small town," he said. "Companion ads give you the illusion of going somewhere else."

She nodded. "I came from Montreal to go to school here. I like this city. Doesn't seem small to me. Not yet, anyway. Have you ever been married?"

Max wondered for a moment if he should somehow decorate the truth. Or maybe not. He jumped in without a plan. "Some of my friends went looking for marriage, and found it. Some of them made horrible mistakes. Now they're single again, part-time fathers, financially strapped. I figure, wait till the situation feels right, and then see if it happens. What I mean is, I'm not against it. I'm also hoping to avoid a disaster."

She looked sceptical.

"I mean I'm all for it," he added quickly. "I'd like to have it. But one that works."

"Yes," she agreed. "That's the important thing. I don't want to be divorced in five years. Do you ever reply to ads anymore?"

"No."

"You said the last one came to a bad end."

"Did I? Well, yeah. That's true. But it wasn't the companion-ad part that was the problem. At the beginning we hit it off. Like one of those personal-ad success stories you read about.

You know, 'We met through the newspaper, and now look at our four beautiful children.'"

She smiled. "So what was the problem?"

"Do *you* have a past?" he said. Suddenly he could see Sarah's face, the little lines around her mouth, the big brown eyes.

"Of course I do. But I've never been married, never lived with anyone," she said matter-of-factly. "And I've *never*," she added, her voice rising with what Max thought was an overtone of disgust, "placed an ad." She went on: "I lost my virginity when I was seventeen and left my last boyfriend a year ago. My parents are both alive. I don't hate them."

Max felt a twinge of dismay as she finished this uninhibited recitation. "The problem," he said slowly, "was that we had different ideas about gender." He looked at her for a reaction. Betsy nodded. "She disapproved of my independence. Wanted us to be in the same boat all the time. I like rowing my own boat." Betsy was nodding again. Apparently she understood.

"Yeah!" he said excitedly. "That's it. I wanted to share the dock where we'd both tie up. She wanted more than that. She wanted us to share a boat. I wanted my own boat."

"That doesn't sound so bad. As long as there wasn't anyone else in your boat."

"No, no. There were a few other things. But that was the main sticking point. I believe in primal biological differences between the sexes. She believed in . . . I dunno . . . she said she agreed with me. But she didn't really."

"I'm post-feminist myself," said Betsy. "I don't want to hear about the downtrodden victims of patriarchy. I mean, get a life. It's not just women who are unemployed and underpaid. But primal biological differences, sure. That's exactly how I look at it."

"Really?" said Max, feeling immensely pleased. "I'm glad to hear that."

CHAPTER 17

May 8

Max opened his eyes. He was in a room he had never seen before. A gang of construction workers seemed to be hammering nails into his temples and eyeballs. He tried to estimate the number of drinks he had consumed, but that made his head worse. He ran his hand down under the sheet and found a used condom.

On the other side of the bed Betsy was still asleep. The strange soft scent that lay in his nostrils was hers. He could see one silky white breast uncovered by the rumpled sheet. He remembered they had gone to a bar and talked about magazines and then had come back here to her apartment in the Annex and talked about relationships until two in the morning.

I got lucky, he thought.

Gingerly, he lifted himself out of the big bed and groped his bleary-eyed way down the hall to the bathroom. In the cupboard behind the mirror over the sink he found a vial of Tylenol. He washed down three tablets with a handful of water.

"Fucking Liam O'Chancre," he groaned, squinting at the unmistakeable black eye in the mirror.

He padded down to the end of the hallway and into Betsy's small kitchen, opened the cupboards over the counter, and turned on the cold water faucet. He groggily drank and drank, emptying a glass three times. A woman, he suddenly noticed, was looking at him from the next building over. He covered his groin with one hand and raised his glass at her with the other.

"Cheers," he croaked.

Sitting at the kitchen table and massaging his temples, he could see Betsy's cat calendar on the back of the kitchen door and on the fridge pictures of her with friends. A bright, attractive young woman. But somehow disconcerting. Sarah was more . . . more easy-going. Less wilful. Sarah had some immutable notions about men, but she wasn't always trying to push life where she wanted it to go. She took it as it came. She would never have acted as Betsy did last night. From the moment Betsy had stopped the fight with O'Chancre, she had orchestrated the evening. She had chosen the pub, she had steered their discussion about magazines, she had said it was time to go, she had invited him back to her place, she had said he could sleep with her, she had provided the condom.

I might as well have had a ring in my nose, thought Max. Maybe this is how it is when you're thirty-eight and she's twenty-six.

When I was twenty-six, she was fourteen, he thought uneasily as he heard a rustling in the hallway and looked up.

"It's ten after nine," she said. "I'm going to have to hustle and get out of here. I have an exercise class at ten." She looked down at his nakedness on the chair. "There are bath towels in the hall closet if you want something to wrap around yourself."

Max grunted his assent. His head was still pounding. In her white bathrobe, without lipstick, without any make-up, Betsy was still unusually attractive, and looking at her pristine face made his own disgusting morning-after condition feel worse.

"I have to get moving too," he said. "I'm supposed to be working this weekend."

"Good luck," she said doubtfully. "You look like you could use an ambulance." She turned to go back down the hall. He walked after her and touched her shoulder as she reached the bathroom. She looked around.

"Last night was great. I mean, everything that happened after I got pasted in the eye."

"Yeah," she said lightly. "It was good." She turned as he tried to kiss her. His lips brushed her ear clumsily as she stepped away.

"I have to get into the shower," she called out from behind the bathroom door. "Make sure you pull the latch so it locks when you leave."

Am I falling in love? Max asked himself as he walked down Major Street to the subway.

★ ★ ★

Max picked up the Saturday *Tribune* from his doorstep and carried it inside with the *Herald*, which he had bought at the subway. He dropped the papers on the kitchen table, drank a glass of orange juice, and checked his answering machine by the living room couch. The red light was winking. He punched the LISTEN button.

"Max, this is Leonard. What's the crisis? I suppose I could go up to Ottawa this week, except that I'm still getting the message McGarvie won't see me. And anyway, I've almost finished the piece. Don't think we really need an interview. You want to come over on Sunday and do a read through? You're on. Call and confirm."

There was a second message, a reminder from the cable TV company that his bill was four months overdue. They would be cutting him off unless he showed up at their storefront office with money by Tuesday.

He poured another glass of juice and pushed away the dirty dishes left on the kitchen table from Thursday night's meal. When he spread the *Herald*, a corner of one page fell into the congealed fat on his unwashed plate. He snapped the paper open, but it fell into the fat again, so he carried the juice and papers into the living-dining area.

His table was cluttered with unopened mail and the week's copies of the *Tribune*. As he dumped the old papers on the floor and shuffled all the mail together into one pile, little clouds of dust were raised. Some of the dust got up his nose. He coughed violently. But his head was pounding more gently now.

"You never dust," he trilled, trying to imitate Sarah's voice. "I'm not sleeping there again until you dust." Well, okay, she had allergies that she claimed the dust exacerbated. But still. Dust? With what — a feather duster?

"Why?" he had asked. "Dusting only moves it from the tables onto the floor."

"Normally," she had replied, "people also vacuum the floor."

He coughed again, looked at all the mail he had been meaning to open. But not right now. He took a slug of orange juice and flipped through some of the letters: what looked like appeals from the Canadian National Institute for the Blind, the Cancer Society, the Liver Foundation, Oxfam; the phone bill; magazine subscription renewals; what looked like a book club offer; bank statements and a credit card bill. This last one he plucked from the pile along with an unidentified hand-written envelope that had come this week. Picking a letter off the floor at night, or opening one as he was doing now with the envelope addressed in longhand, could still stir memories of his pen-pal days with Sarah.

"Ain't no way," he croaked to himself. "History I am and history I'll be." Then he thought of Betsy and dropped the letter onto the pine table. He fished in his pocket for her number, which he had scribbled on a scrap of paper before leaving the apartment. She was out, as she'd said she would be. He left a message asking if she would have dinner with him.

The credit card bill he left in the kitchen to remind himself to pay it, and then he returned to the letter. The note inside was hand-printed on business stationery. The letterhead announced it was from AAA Afghan Towing. "Please to come for sign papers for car. We leave many messages your phone number have no person answer. You must sign paper or we put car on street. Thank you."

"Okay, okay," Max grumbled. He remembered several messages on his machine from Afghan Towing. But he had not found time since Arnold's death to go back to the yard.

He sat down at the pine table and flipped through the *Herald*, looking for any mention of the magazine awards. In the entertainment section, he saw a short article, along with a picture of Jeremy Glass.

CELEBRATED WRITER FLAYS PUBLISHER, read the headline. "*Berger's* magazine once again led at the annual magazine awards Friday night, winning eleven gold medals and eight silvers. But the most memorable moment of the evening came when author and magazine writer Jeremy Glass publicly excoriated millionaire publisher Edward Clubb.

"Glass was accepting first prize for business-writing. His promise to fight the libel suit Clubb has brought against him was greeted with cheering and loud applause.

"James Goodfellow, a past chairman of the Writers' League who won the silver medal in the science writing category, told the *Herald*, 'It's about time someone stood up to the outrageous Edward Clubb and defended freedom of expression in this country. Writers are the first to blow the whistle on corruption and corporate bullying of all kinds, and so they are the first to be muzzled. But libel chill freezes the free speech of every Canadian.' Goodfellow added that he thought the Writers' League should consider supporting Glass's defence."

Max was relieved to see that the reporter had not mentioned any fisticuffs at the end of the evening.

He leafed through the front section of the paper. On the national news page a large photo featured the Prime Minister in formal dress. The picture accompanied a short article on a charity ball for the Canadian Red Cross that Barton McGarvie had attended the night before.

PM PRAISES PRIVATE GIVING, read the headline. "In his short after-dinner speech, Prime Minister McGarvie extolled the virtues of private-sector charitable fundraising and . . ." Blah, blah, blah, thought Max, not bothering to finish the report. He looked at the picture, which showed the grinning politician dancing with his wife; several other white-tied dignitaries were also grinning in a semi-circle around him. Behind them could be seen some unidentified faces, and Max saw now that one of those other faces belonged unmistakeably to Leonard Freeman.

"Leonard baby!" Max shouted. "You're on the case!"

CHAPTER 18

May 9

Max lay in bed on Sunday morning thinking of Betsy — her crisp matter-of-factness, her soft white skin.

He had fallen asleep Saturday afternoon and missed her call. Her message had said she was busy Saturday and Sunday nights, but she could see him during the week.

He thought of Sarah, of the nights her still form had slept beside him here. She had left such a palpable imprint in this bed and on this room that he had considered moving just to be rid of it. She'd had some cock-eyed paranoid ideas. Imagining him a duplicitous womanizer. That last morning she'd shouted at him, stood by the curtains and yelled furiously at six a.m., she'd been wrong. He'd been guilty of a few lapses, that was all. Accidents, really.

And now she probably imagined him, if she thought of him at all, on a wild carnal rampage, erasing her memory. The aggressive male brute, impervious to feelings of all kinds. Did Sarah really think that? Maybe not. But that's how she'd often sounded.

He had tried with Karen one more time after Sarah's final blow-up. And then he had been alone. Karen had been a consolation, but he'd never loved her. Which he later realized had been part of the attraction. She had left a large part of him untouched. Safe.

"Men have feelings too. Boo hoo hoo," he lamented to himself, yawning.

And now Betsy.

Peculiar she's busy all weekend, he reflected, unable to pin down exactly why. But it felt wrong. He'd never done it this way before. A one-night stand was one thing. A mutual fling, or a mistake; it happened. But if you were both really interested, you went underground, spent a few days together, got to know the possibilities.

"I need to think it through," was all she had said before going to sleep.

Like waiting for a decision from a job interview, Max reflected.

He jumped out of bed. There are other jobs. Today's the day I finally get Leonard's article up and running.

★ ★ ★

Max took the subway into the Annex to have a late breakfast and, after two cups of coffee, he strolled up Leonard's street. It was a breezy, sunny May morning. They had agreed on noon. Max was a few minutes early. He rang the bell.

Leonard opened the door unshaven and dressed in a bathrobe. "You're early, Max. You're usually late."

"I'm still on a high from Friday night. It's the early delirium of true love." He talked about Betsy as they walked through the sandblasted-brick living room and into the kitchen.

Leonard scooped coffee grains into a filter. "Where did you acquire the serious black eye?"

"Magazine awards. Helluva party."

"I guess. I read you won something."

"That was easily the least exciting moment of my evening."

"So it's true love, eh? Tell me what you mean by that."

"You know. The male-female thing. You meet this ravishingly

beautiful young woman, you talk, you touch, you fall in love."

"Something tells me if you were drunk enough to get into a fist fight with three hundred people watching, you were probably too drunk to fall in love."

"We had a wonderful time together," Max said defensively.

"You mean you enjoyed bonking her. That's not love. That's sex. The male conquest thing."

"No. No conquest. It just happened."

"Right. Like with fish."

"Well, yeah. We talked and talked. And then she asked me to bed."

"Let me put it this way. Did you fall in love before you went to bed with her or after?"

"After, I think."

"I rest my case," chuckled Leonard.

Max heard the bathroom door close and light footsteps going into Leonard's bedroom.

"Got company?"

"Yeah, but she's leaving," Leonard answered with an edge to his voice. "I said I had to work this afternoon."

"Who she?"

"A new friend."

The doorbell rang. Leonard walked into the living room, padded across the thick carpet, and looked out the front window.

"Danielle," he called. "Your cab is here." He came back into the kitchen and looked nervously towards the bedroom.

She came out carrying an overnight bag. Max thought she looked familiar.

"My friend Max. Max, Danielle."

"Hello, Max." She extended her hand and smiled. "I enjoy *Berger's* very much, so I know your name well. Sorry I have to rush off. But Leonard says you've stolen his afternoon."

"Really? I thought he was making a voluntary donation.

Anyhow, I'm glad you like the magazine." Max remembered where he had seen her before. Here, that day when he had come up to prod Leonard, she had been the woman who had stepped into his cab.

"Have a good flight, and call me later," Leonard murmured as he saw her to the door. He came back into the kitchen looking pleased with himself.

"Catching a plane?"

"Yeah. She's from out of town." He handed Max a mug of coffee.

"Quebec accent, sounded like."

"Yeah. She's from Montreal originally. That's where she's flying today." Leonard was standing in the kitchen doorway. "I'll give you my piece. I'm still working on an ending. Maybe I can do that while you're here." He came back with a pile of typescript and dropped it on the table in front of Max. "Give me a minute to get dressed," he said, disappearing again.

Max read it through. Leonard had done some footwork over the past two weeks. There was now some hard data in the article to anchor his windy polemics. Gracefully trimmed, it could work. Just. And an interview with the PM was bound to spin out at least a few quotable quotes that could be slotted in. He pencilled long lines beside passages that were tangled or fulsome.

Leonard reappeared. "What do you think?"

"I think it's magnificent," Max replied. "Just a little fine tuning needed. Could I do it here on your machine? Maybe you could work on the ending in longhand."

"I guess so."

"Sorry," said Max. "But we're really down to the wire. It's now or never. And I have to get you to Ottawa in the next few days."

"That's the part I fail utterly to comprehend. Who gives a fuck what McGarvie says to me in a formal interview? Besides which, they're still telling me he won't sit still for it."

"Really? When I saw your face in the *Herald* on Saturday, I thought you must've gotten lucky."

"Eh?"

"The Red Cross Ball. Picture of McGarvie. With you in the background."

"Oh, the Ball." Leonard looked confused for a moment. "No. I was there . . ." He hesitated. "For something else. My picture was in the *Herald*?"

"I saw it and my spirits lifted. I thought you were on the case."

Leonard shook his head. "A coincidence. I was there with . . . a friend."

"So when did you last try to see him?"

"About a week ago. I talked to his people. Nothing doing."

"Apparently they've had a change of heart."

"You haven't told me why it matters."

"It's matters to us because it matters to Chaser Makepeace."

Leonard shrugged. "It's a waste of time. McGarvie'll blow a lot of hot air my way, that's all."

"Makepeace thinks it's bad journalism not to do an interview when your subject is willing. And his sources in Ottawa say McGarvie is up for it."

"Why don't we just defy Chaser? What can he do?"

"He'll deep-six this piece faster than you can blink. He'd love us to give him an excuse to do that. He knows roughly what your take on McGarvie is going to be, and he's not looking forward to having to defend a hatchet job."

"I didn't think my views were that predictable," Leonard sniffed.

"Your politics are no big secret. Chaser knows there are going to be a lot of irate McGarvie fans when this piece appears."

"Who says he has a lot of fans?"

"The ones he has make a lot of noise."

"Tell your boss to take a valium."

"Leonard, this ain't gamesmanship anymore. If we're not ready tomorrow, we may be passed in the stretch. People at the magazine are already sniffing around for another cover story. We have to deliver yours tomorrow. We can fill in some quotes from McGarvie later in the week."

"So what's the competition?" Leonard asked sourly.

"A profile of Tom Broadfoot. It's written and ready to go."

"That dweeb? You can't be serious. He's barely worth a page of print. All he knows is how to fart through polyester."

"The production people were going bananas this week. There's no more give in the schedule."

"So postpone it for a month."

Max shook his head. "No chance. September's filled with a piece that Makepeace wants in. After that all bets are off. Maybe we could use your piece later, maybe not. No guarantees."

Leonard drank a cup of coffee in silence. Then he said, "Y'know, I hate working under pressure."

Max told himself to stay calm. "Meaning?"

"I'm half-inclined to tell Makepeace to go fuck himself."

"I'm glad it's only half of you that's so inclined. I'm still willing to work with the other half — all afternoon if we have to."

"Yeah, well, I could use the money."

Max went into Leonard's tiny office, copied the article onto a disk, and began rejigging the sections he wanted to cut. Leonard wrote on a notepad in the kitchen. After four hours, Max emerged from the office.

"I'm done," he said. "Time for a beer."

Leonard had already opened a bottle for himself. He was sitting at the table looking at the current issue of *Esquire*. "The ending's there." He nodded at his notepad. "I just need to key it in. Then that's it."

"Not quite," Max replied, taking a slug of beer. "You still have to go to Ottawa."

The phone rang. Leonard went into the bedroom to answer it.

"It was great to see you too," Max could hear Leonard saying. "Looks like I'm going to have to fly to Ottawa some time in the next few days. If you're still . . ." Leonard's low voice faded out. Curious, Max moved closer to the doorway to listen. "After Tuesday we could connect." There was a pause. "Well, they're insisting I . . ." Max lost the middle of the sentence. " . . . uh, your boss. Yeah, he must know about it. No big deal. A little awkward the way we've been playing it." Another pause. "Okay, Andre Thibault. Yeah, I got it. But it has to be this week. If it's . . ." Max lost the rest. Hearing his friend ring off, Max moved back to his chair.

"Where were we?" Leonard asked when he reappeared.

"You're going to Ottawa."

"Yeah, I can try my channels again first thing in the morning."

"Or I could probably arrange it for you."

"No," Leonard said definitely. "I'll do it. It's better for me to stay on side with the people I know there."

"Incidentally," said Max. "Your new friend. She's quite the babe. A beautiful woman."

Leonard looked away. "Yeah, she is."

"What'd you say her name was?"

"Danielle."

"Last name?"

Leonard looked over at Max sharply. "Why?"

"No reason. Just curious."

Leonard looked out at the deck again, took another swig of beer. "Choquette," he said, after a long hesitation.

"Is it serious?" Max asked.

"Yes and no," said Leonard. "It's been happening on and off for a couple of months. It's different when it's a long-distance thing."

"A Toronto-Montreal thing."

"Yeah. Well, a Toronto-Ottawa thing actually."

"She's from Ottawa?"

"From Montreal. Lives in Ottawa."

"Ah."

"I don't know where it's going, but it's great while it lasts."

"More or less how I feel about my prospects with Betsy. But that may be a simpler situation. I get the sense yours is a little complicated."

"Yeah," said Leonard, avoiding eye contact.

"The long-distance thing," Max added.

"Yeah."

CHAPTER 19

May 10

"My name is Maxwell Vellen. I'm a journalist here in Toronto and I'm preparing an article on how the executive branch operates in the federal government. Could you send me a list of everyone who is employed in the Prime Minister's Office?"

Max listened to a surprised voice in the PMO's press office.

"Oh, yeah," he said confidently. "Our readers are *very* interested in that sort of thing. Fascinating subject when you get into it. Do you think you could fax me a list?" He gave the fax number.

It was just after eight o'clock Monday morning. He had come in early because he wanted to use Giorgio's computer — the only one the magazine owned. He took Leonard's disk into Giorgio's light-filled room, switched on the machine, printed out the article, and wrote "URGENT — READ NOW" on the title page. Then he made photocopies; he left one on Giorgio's table, and then did the circuit, dropping a copy on each editor's desk.

He could hear the fax machine spitting out pages in Martha's cubicle. When he went to see if it was the PMO responding, he saw Joanne going into her office with her briefcase and the morning *Trib*. She turned in her doorway.

"Wow. What happened to your eye?"

"Got hit by some heavy neo-conservative horsepower," he said, hoping she wouldn't ask any more questions.

But Joanne seemed to be very interested in his condition. She walked over to have a closer look. "I heard you got into a shouting match after the awards on Friday."

"Well, yeah. More than shouting, as you can see. But the other guy had to go in for groin surgery."

"Liam O'Chancre I heard? I don't know him."

"You will. That's his mission in life. To be known. And if possible admired. And if you don't admire him, he slugs you."

"I guess you won't be giving him any assignments soon."

"Oh, I have an open mind. I was thinking of sending him to cover the war in Bosnia. Without a flak jacket."

"That's not really the kind of article we would run," she said flatly, immune, as always, to his sense of irony.

"No, not really. But it's the kind of thing he deserves. He's always sabre-rattling in his columns. They amaze me, these guys in their twenties who are itching to volunteer for World War II, half a century after the fact. They should have their own theme park. O'Chancre could put out the local paper, and write thundering editorials denouncing Hitler."

"Why is he so obsessed with the war?" Max could see she was genuinely interested. Possibly something she's never noticed, he thought. But her survival instinct as a magazine editor keeps her alert to any usable trend.

"I think it's a generational thing," he said. "They hate us because we're the generation ahead of them. We've got the jobs and the numbers and we've dictated the social agenda ever since they were born. We'd probably hate baby boomers too if we were twenty years younger. So what do they do? They jump back a generation — at least the intellectuals in their cohort do — and they adopt a pre-sixties conservatism. That puts them much more in sync with the war generation than with ours."

"Yes, but they're also into computers and cyberspace and lots of other stuff that didn't exist fifty years ago."

"Oh sure. So call them cyber-Tories. Computers are perfect for them. The PC is the great new emblem of laissez-faire capitalism. Everyone who wants to can suddenly have the illusion of being an independent entrepreneur. That plugs right into the kind of neo-conservatism young puppies like O'Chancre embrace. Of course the O'Chancres don't sit in the veal-fattening pens of huge corporations, staring at spreadsheets on a screen all day."

Max stopped and thought, Hey, maybe I should save some of this for a meeting. He could imagine Joanne shaping it into a story idea for one of her writers and then unfurling it deftly at the weekly editorial meeting and sounding very smart.

"Interesting," she said, and turned to go back to her office.

"By the way," he added, "I left Freeman's piece on the PM in your office. We have to decide what's going on the July cover."

"The Broadfoot piece is quite good, you know," she called over her shoulder. "But I'll have a look."

Max saw the fax was from the PMO. He took it into his office, closed the door, and saw by his clock it was 8:45. There was a call he had to make. He pulled out the yellow pages, looked up the number for AAA Afghan Towing, and phoned the yard.

"I'm sorry. You've had my Pontiac for a few weeks. Max Vellen. There was a fire in the engine. I haven't been able to . . ."

"Yes, yes," said the voice at the other end of the line. "I recognize your name. My cousin has been trying to reach you." This one, thought Max, is the one I didn't deal with before. This one speaks much better English.

"Yeah. I haven't been able to get down there. It looks like I'm going to have trouble this week too."

The man at the yard asked Max where he worked.

"It's not a problem for me. I'm coming downtown every Monday to my bank. I'll pass by your office with the paper."

Max hung up and started going through the fax pages. There

were a lot of bodies keeping the PMO warm, he noted. Enough to put out six or seven monthly magazines. Maybe eight or nine if you added up all their salaries, which were much higher, he knew, than what most of the people at *Berger's* made. He ran down the columns carefully with his pen. Nothing on page one.

Bingo.

There it was, halfway down the second page. Assistant Director of Media Relations — Danielle Choquette.

Leonard, you idiot, Max thought. You flaming jerk.

He folded up the fax and stuck it in his bottom drawer, then stood up and looked out the window. The situation was awkward. But not, he estimated, unsalvageable.

He sat back down at his desk to read the paper while he waited for the others to pronounce on Leonard's article. A headline in the *Tribune* arts section caught his eye: BONANZA FOR LOCAL WRITER.

"A Toronto writer has won France's richest literary prize.

"The 500,000 franc Prix Lafleur, sponsored by the Lafleur Tire company, was awarded on Saturday to the Canadian author Jeremy Glass for his post-Cold War thriller *The Plutonium Fraternity.*

"The Prix Lafleur, awarded to the year's most distinguished political novel published in French, has been dubbed the Prix Gonfleur by France's cultural commentators. *Gonfleur*, which means tire pump, is a French *jeu de mots* that refers both to the award's pumped-up purse and to its relatively frugal parallel prize, the prestigious Prix Goncourt.

"Contacted in Toronto after the announcement, Glass said, 'I'm surprised and delighted. The French are not easy to please, particularly where politics are concerned.'

"Glass, who also won a national magazine award on Friday night, has promised to fight a libel suit brought against him by publishing baron Edward Clubb. Asked if the approximately

$100,000 purse from the Prix Lafleur would help with his legal fees, Glass replied: 'I've been very fortunate to be offered some legal support on a *pro bono* basis, but yes, this prize certainly enlarges our war chest. I think I can now say with some confidence that we're prepared to fight the case all the way to the Supreme Court.'

"The *Tribune* also sought a reaction to Glass's good fortune from Edward Clubb, but the publisher was unavailable for comment."

Max swung his chair around to look out the window. MAX VELLEN WINS PUMPED-UP PRIZE was the headline in his mind, as he slid into his most delicious daydream — the writing of a bestselling book.

"*Max Vellen, asked what he plans to do with the substantial literary prize he has just won, declared that he would be immediately resigning from his editor's job at* Berger's *magazine. 'Magazines are all dictatorships,' he lamented, 'and my soul hungers for democracy. What the publishing world needs . . .'*"

"Max, old trout."

Max swung his chair back around to his desk. Chaser was standing in the doorway. He stepped into the office and said, "We need to talk about this piece on McGarvie." He looked Max in the eye. "Boy, that's quite a shiner you got. I heard young Liam O'Chancre and you did a round or two."

"It was self-defence," said Max.

"Writers are all a pain, I know," Chaser went on. "But I've never hit one yet. Bad editorial policy."

"Being half a writer myself, I agree," said Max. "But I didn't have time to check my policy manual."

"I also heard you had a date after." Chaser was gloating with a characteristic know-it-all expression.

Max resented the intrusion. "Sure. It's the one good thing about awards night. You meet new people."

Chaser waited for him to elaborate. Max stared at the wall.

"Well," the editor began again, "I've just read Leonard Freeman's piece. So has Joanne. She doesn't like it much, and I have my own reservations. It's more a polemic than balanced reportage. Who are these sources in the PMO who are painting such a sour picture of their boss?"

"The sources are solid, I'm told. Naturally they don't want their quotes attributed."

Chaser had the article in his hand. He looked down to read from it. Max could see the editor had flagged passages with a pen.

Chaser read: "One PMO staffer recalls a meeting when McGarvie was fuming about a disloyal party faction, 'They're either with us or they're against us. And if they're against us, we'll take them out on the sidewalk and crack their skulls.' McGarvie is apparently unaware that language has meaning and that it might be ill-advised for a head of government in a democracy even semi-publicly to use words that more appropriately cross the lips of small-time hoods in sleazy, run-down bars." Chaser looked up. "That's heavy stuff, and I'd say more than a little over the top."

Max shrugged. "It's strong. But it's Leonard's voice. Readers aren't obliged to agree."

Chaser shook his head. "This isn't a debate. Print is a monologue. There are other passages that worry me. The piece still needs a lot of work. I think we'll go with Tom Broadfoot in the August issue. It's cleaner, it's more conventional, and it's ready. Sorry Max. But that's my decision. Joanne has another story ready that can fit into the front where Broadfoot was slotted. So we're fine for August."

"You're killing the Freeman?"

"Keep working on it. Do the Ottawa interview. We'll put the piece on the shelf. Maybe use it in the fall. No promises. But you never know what's going to happen in this business."

Chaser went out and closed Max's door. Max stared at the

typescript that ten minutes ago had been the August cover story. He thought of all the sweat and anxiety he'd put into it, wheedling and cajoling Leonard, putting himself on the line at editorial meetings, reassuring Chaser, begging for more time from Giorgio.

Now it was a pile of ashes on his desk. Worst of all, he would have to lie to Leonard and act as if the assignment were still alive. Leonard would never go to Ottawa to interview McGarvie if he knew Chaser had just stabbed his piece in the back. Quite the contrary, in fact. Leonard might come into the office and loudly tell Chaser exactly what he thought. Leonard enjoyed burning his bridges.

"What a ridiculous business," Max grumbled to himself. He opened the phone book and wrote down the number for *Wellington* magazine. To console himself he called and asked for Betsy Cerniak's line.

"Hi, Max. So early Monday morning. What's up." She didn't sound as eager as he had hoped.

"It's already been an action-packed day and I just got here," he replied. "Feels like five o'clock already. How about meeting after work?"

"Can't tonight. I have a busy week actually. Are you free Thursday?"

"Thursday. Hang on. Let me check my book." He went through the motions of opening his diary and looking at the week's engagements. As he already knew, he was free Monday, Tuesday, Wednesday, Thursday, and Friday nights. And the weekend too. "Hey, yes, it so happens I *am* free Thursday night. That's great. I'll see you then. We'll have dinner."

How come, he thought after hanging up, young Betsy with the entrance-level job is going out every day between now and Thursday? Whereas I, a slightly used but indisputably worthy older goat, have only myself for company?

The phone rang. It was Leonard.

"I'm on a five o'clock flight this afternoon. He's giving me forty-five minutes tomorrow morning. You were right. Suddenly they're gung-ho for an interview."

What a whopper.

Max saw his intercom light winking. "That's great," he bubbled, hiding the gloom he felt. "Get back as soon as you can and do the transcript. We'll work on the rewrite Wednesday. Call me as soon as you're back. Gotta run."

He pressed the intercom button and was told someone was waiting for him at reception. Chaser was in the corridor with his briefcase. He looked like he was leaving for an appointment. They walked together out to the reception area.

"Chazer!"

"Fared!"

In front of the reception desk, Max saw a dark, stocky man dressed in work clothes and wearing a black beard, his face alive with a surprised smile at the sight of the *Berger's* editor.

"This is your workplace?" the man asked Chaser as they shook hands warmly.

"Yes," said Chaser, beaming. "This is my magazine. I've been meaning to get in touch since I got back to Canada. How did you track me down?"

"No, it is only by chance. An accident. I didn't know I will find you here today."

"Oh," said Chaser, apparently crestfallen. "Why are you here?"

"I come to do some business with a Mr. . . ." He looked down at the piece of paper in his hand. "Mr. Mox Villain."

"Oh. This is Max right here. Max, meet my old friend Fared. He was my interpreter for a while in Kabul when I was covering the war in Afghanistan."

Max shook hands with the man from AAA Afghan Towing.

"I greased a few wheels at this end so Fared's family could resettle in Canada," Chaser continued. "How is your family? Are you all well?"

"We have our own business," Fared said proudly. "I am in business with my cousin. Towing and scrapyard." He turned to Max. "This man is great hero to me. Helped many pipple in my country. A great man."

Chaser basked in the light from the huge halo Fared had just crowned him with.

Chaser a hero? wondered Max in amazed silence. He knew Chaser and his wife were involved with a church charity that helped immigrants. But a hero?

"Bless you, Fared, great to see you," Chaser said. "I have to go to a meeting. Here's my card. Call me and we'll arrange a get-together." He rushed out the glass door to catch an elevator.

"Chazer Mockpiss is your friend?" Fared asked after Chaser had left.

"He's my boss," said Max. "He runs this place."

"He's what you call 'a goot guy,' I think?" said Fared, showing Max where to sign on the contract.

"I guess you could say he's a complicated guy," Max replied.

★ ★ ★

As Edward Clubb and Justin Carrier stepped out of Clubb's chauffeured limousine that morning onto the Wellington Street sidewalk, they were greeted by a shout from the middle of the small crowd that was milling around the entrance to the flat-iron building.

"There he is! There's Clubb!"

The crowd began to chant:

"Rubba dub dub
Don't Join That Clubb
Freedom of Expression
Clubb is for Suppression"

"We're from the Writers' League, Mr Clubb," a tall man wearing granny glasses shouted into his megaphone as Clubb stopped to survey the scene. "We demand that you drop your suit against Jeremy Glass." Some people in the little throng were waving placards. They had slogans painted on them: FREE SPEECH and STOP CLUBBING WRITERS and YOU CAN'T BUY SILENCE and LIBEL LAW = CENSORSHIP.

Clubb drew a bead on the man with the megaphone. "I am exercising my rights as an ordinary citizen in a democracy. I have been libelled and I am seeking the legal redress available to anyone under the laws of this land. Not on your life will I drop my suit, not until such time as a full and detailed apology has been issued by Mr. Glass and the publication in question."

He turned abruptly and went into the building. Justin Carrier followed him.

"Pathetic no-account rabble," said Clubb inside the antique elevator.

"Ha!" exclaimed the lawyer, as if his client had just said something extremely funny.

"Bunch of layabouts and nogoodnicks. Probably all on welfare."

"Ha, ha, ha," guffawed the lawyer.

"I'd sue them all if I could."

"Ha. Goddamn right," said the lawyer in what sounded like a fake locker-room voice. "Let's hope they say something intemperate in print."

"Can we have them removed?"

"Ha! Not unless they damage property. I don't think so. I'll look into it."

On the top floor, as they walked past the secretary's desk, Clubb said, "Mrs. Crutchlow, phone our friends at Intelliguard and have security personnel posted down at the front door and up here too if they think it's advisable. And tell Graham Nutley we're ready to meet. And get me the price of Janus on the TSE this morning."

From below they could hear the chanting. "Freedom of expression; Clubb is for suppression; freedom of expression; Clubb is for suppression."

"Beatnik shit-disturbers," Clubb fumed to his lawyer. "I've half a mind to go down there again and give them a verbal reaming."

"Not worth the risk," said the lawyer.

Graham Nutley slipped quietly into the room and took the other chair in front of his employer's broad wooden desk.

"No it's not. I don't have a fly swatter big enough for all of them."

"Har, har, har, har," Justin Carrier brayed. He laughed with his mouth wide open, as if it were a performance he expected other people to enjoy. He was a heavy-set, silver-haired man with the polished self-presentation of a seasoned advocate.

Clubb's antique intercom buzzed.

"Janus is trading at eight dollars and one-eighth this morning."

"Holding our own," said Clubb.

"Yrrrm," Nutley assented in a neutral voice.

Clubb turned to his lawyer. "The Glass case. What we require is a sharply defined strategy. How best to force an unconditional withdrawal — a full and public recanting of all of that tiresome little amoeba's malicious falsifications."

"At this point, Edward, I'd have to say it's very doubtful that we'll get an apology. Glass's counsel Bruno Cayly tells me they're ready to see us in court. Cayly loves these underdog fights. He's the champion of the little guy. David and Goliath. Har, ha. . . ." The lawyer met his client's steely gaze. "I've heard Bruno's even prepared to donate time to it."

"That's preposterous. Why would he do such a thing?"

The lawyer shrugged. "High profile case. His name'll be in the press for months. Who knows, maybe he believes in the cause. He does a lot of *pro bono* work."

"What cause?" Clubb snarled.

"Ha! Exactly."

"Exactly," said Nutley.

"So you're saying we will be obliged to meet them in court. Have we any reason to believe they can pay the freight?"

"You probably saw the *Trib* today," Nutley cut in. "Glass has $100,000 now that he didn't have on Friday."

"Glass is determined to go to the wall on this," said the lawyer. "That much we know. Cayly maintains there's absolutely no inclination to fold. We're less certain about the publisher."

The intercom buzzed again. "Chaser Makepeace is here."

"Send him in."

Chaser appeared in the large doorway. "Sorry," he said. "I've been delayed."

"Yes. I can see that," said Clubb. "Take a chair. Did you get bitten by any of those horseflies downstairs?"

"I actually know most of them," said Chaser. "It was an awkward moment. I told Gamie Goodfellow, the one with the megaphone, that we're still hoping for an amicable solution."

"You WHAT? BLOODY HELL we are."

"I have to deal with these people, Edward. Let me handle it my way."

"I'm not sure how much use you're going to be at this meeting," Clubb snapped. "Where were we?"

"Going to court," said Carrier.

"Right. And how much is that going to cost me if it does go all the way to the Supreme Court?"

"I can only speculate. As you know, there are many stages to this kind of litigation. It's really not possible to know how the other side is going to play every one of them."

"I'm not asking for a signed estimate. Just give me a rough idea."

"Half a million, give or take twenty per cent. That's just a ballpark figure."

"And you're confident we would win it?"

"I'd never make that undertaking. No libel case similar to this has ever been pursued up to the highest court. I'd say our chances are excellent. But I can't make any promises."

"Hold on a minute. Half a million, maybe more, and you're informing me that the action might be *unsuccessful?* I am not inclined to support an outlay of that magnitude unless it leads to a favourable judgment. And I am not running the Toronto Attorneys' Benevolent Society here."

"Har, har, har. That's a good one, Edward. Attorneys' Benevolent Society. Ha, ha, ha."

"It's a lot of money," Graham Nutley said.

"Maybe we could attempt some sort of compromise," Chaser blurted.

"A compromise? Such as?"

"Well, *Berger's* could publish a spirited rebuttal to the charges made in *Wellington.*"

"It was my understanding that you were already engaged in doing precisely that. This discussion is about an *apology.*" The Janus chairman enunciated it syllable by syllable, as if he were talking to an eight-year-old.

"Then we'll have to fight," Carrier said.

Clubb shook his head. "We are not going to hurl ourselves into court *ab irato.* For half a million dollars, I have a better idea."

CHAPTER 20

May 11

As soon as he had entered the westbound train at Greenwood, Max found a seat. He'd missed the rush. It was nine-thirty and he was late, but he felt no urgency about the work on his desk at the magazine. He could not see the point of doing another minute's work on Leonard's article. It was dead, and any distant carrot Chaser was holding out for fall publication was a phantom. Chaser always said the thing he thought would make you feel better, even if it was a bald lie.

Max snapped open the *Tribune*. His eye drifted to a short news story running down the far right column.

"TORY LEADER CRITICALLY INJURED"

"Tom Broadfoot, leader of the Ontario Progressive Conservative Party, sustained life-threatening injuries Monday night when the car he was driving was struck by a tractor-trailer on the 401 highway.

"Broadfoot was rushed to the emergency facilities of North York General Hospital, where he remained in a coma early this morning.

"Broadfoot's injuries, according to information circulating informally at the hospital last night, include several broken bones, and the possible severance of his spinal-cord. The hospital will make no statement until later today.

"Asked about Broadfoot's condition last night, the resident

neurologist, Dr. Simon Wong, would say only that, 'The injuries at this point in time appear to be serious and we will be doing everything we can to assess and restore the patient's impaired neurological functions.'

"Tom Broadfoot is the youngest MPP ever to be elected a party leader in Ontario. Recent polls suggest that if an election were called this spring, he would become Ontario's youngest premier."

Stunned, Max reread each paragraph. Tom Broadfoot was a good ten years younger than he was. The *Trib* story suggested he had been banged up very badly and maybe irreparably. Max envisaged himself in traction on a hospital bed, then pictured wheeling himself down a hospital corridor in a wheelchair. He felt queasy.

When he reached the magazine, all the other editors were in their offices including, he assumed, Joanne, whose door was closed. There was a note from Chaser on his desk. "Need to talk, ASAP," it said. Max walked into the editor's office.

"I now have a crippled pol on my August cover," Chaser said. "According to my sources at the *Trib*, he came out of the coma about an hour ago. But he's got a bad head injury and a spinal-cord rupture. They say he won't walk again. Broadfoot has just become No-foot." He grinned and his small brown eyes danced at his own witticism.

"I'd call that a lame joke, Chaser."

The editor laughed and burbled on, unrepentant. "Reminds me of my young days as a reporter doing the blood-and-guts stories on the night shift at old *Mercury*."

"It's pretty sickening," said Max. "Not that I liked the guy's politics. But still . . ."

"Oh yeah, it's too bad," said Chaser. "Completely skews our editorial line-up. Joanne is in a snit. She thinks we could still somehow finesse the Broadfoot piece into a compelling cover story. But there's no way. I'm going to have to dump it. We'd look like ghouls putting him on the cover now. The story is all about what a fine young student and athlete he was, and how all the young neo-cons look up to him. He may be hospitalized for months. And he's probably finished as leader. It's a downer. I wouldn't touch it."

"I guess I know what the alternative is."

"I've just reread the Freeman piece. There's nothing else in that issue that has the weight of a cover story, and nothing else is anywhere close to being ready. Just tone down some of the passages where Leonard's ego soars into outer space, if you would. It'll make my life easier."

Back in his office, Max felt the anger rush up in his body like an attack of vomiting. And what about tomorrow? Would the article suddenly be dead again? No, that was unlikely. Chaser had relented only because he was in a tight corner. He had been looking for a way to kill the piece all along. But in the end he was obliged to fill pages and get the magazine out.

Now, Max knew, he had a problem of his own. He wondered how much potential mayhem Leonard had sown, and what, if anything, should be done about it.

★ ★ ★

"Good morning, Prime Minister."

"Good morning, Mr. Freeman. Are we ready? Both recorders on?"

"Mine is rolling."

"I believe ours is operating too. My staff insists on it. Just a back-up. For your sake as well as ours."

"First of all, can you tell me why you went into politics."

"Eh? That's easy. To get elected."

"Yes. But to get elected for what?"

"I wanted to serve my party and to serve my country to the best of my ability, to bring this fractured and disaffected land together in the great common cause of providing a better life for our children and grandchildren, and . . ."

"How?"

"Eh?

"How did you, do you, intend to do that?"

"We have brought on stream a number of initiatives, as you know, to stimulate job creation and economic prosperity by cutting government spending and giving this country confidence in itself again at a time in our history as a nation when we should be the envy of the world, and let me say this: we will be again. My government intends to preside over a renewal of Canadian prosperity the likes of which has not been seen for several decades. We know what has to be done. And we've got the will to do it."

"Your spending cuts have not been popular."

"That's a matter of perception, and if I may so, the press has taken a lot of liberties with public opinion on this very issue. It's my view that when the options are properly explained, the people of this country, the voters, are behind us. I can show you polls to prove it."

"Please do."

"My people will get you all the material you need after. Let me say this: the Liberal Party of Canada is not the fount of all wisdom on these matters. The press has too many times acted as the Liberals' mouthpiece on economic issues, and has distorted out of all recognition the government's coherent and compassionate policies on such matters and . . ."

"I wasn't aware that many people had accused your government of compassion."

"There you go! Says who? That, if I may say so, Mr Freeman, is just the sort of bias and distortion I am talking about. Have you done a survey? No. Your opinion, with all due respect to your professional accomplishments, which I'm told are many, your opinion in this case is just plain unfounded."

"Maybe it is. But I'd think even you would probably have to admit, sir, that there has been tremendous opposition both in and out of parliament to your spending cuts and the general direction of some of your more aggressive policies."

"Baloney."

"You don't agree."

"I think the question is loaded. Opposition in parliament? Sure. That's what the opposition members are paid to do, to oppose. Outside of parliament? There was a hardly a bleeding-heart interest group in the country that wasn't receiving some pork from the previous Liberal government. Some of those groups do worthwhile work. Others, in our opinion, do not. Of course people howl when you cut them off. What do you expect, a torrential downpour of thank-you notes? But all that noise comes from relatively few mouths."

"Would you care to identify a few."

"They know who they are. You do too. There's no need to rub salt in anyone's wounds. And speaking of wounds, it's obvious to me that we've healed far more wounds than we've opened since we came into office. Why doesn't the press ever choose to adopt a more positive approach to these matters? Lookit, I could tell you a thing or two about healing wounds in this country. When I came into office, Quebec's disaffection with the constitution was about to come to a boil and the West was yelling blue murder at central Canada and I believe I can fairly say that I have in a balanced fashion dealt with . . ."

Leonard flicked off his tape recorder. "He goes on and on like that. The guy is an unstoppable drivel machine. It's just like I said it would be. More or less useless."

"You made a transcript?"

"Of that shit? You must be joking. I've got better things to do." He took a swig from his bottle of beer.

Max frowned. "You're wrong. The bit about pork and bleeding hearts is good stuff. He'll regret that, I promise you. We'll find a way to work it in. Why don't I take the tape and go over it at home tonight? See what I can pull out of it. You've done all the heavy lifting already."

Leonard shrugged. "It's all yours."

"There's one other thing. About the fact checking."

"What's that?"

"Your source in the PMO is going to have to back up the quotes."

"No problem. I did a deal." Leonard smiled coyly. "My source talks to the checker, no-one else. My source wants to remain anonymous. No name in the article, no gossip around town. Unless of course there's a lawsuit or something and then the source backs us. But that won't happen. McGreedy's got enough trouble without making more for himself."

"Can we cut the bullshit for a minute?"

"What?" Leonard looked surprised.

"I have a pretty good idea who your source is."

"Oh yeah?"

"I don't know what her motivations are, but I presume she's got it in for McGreedy for some reason. Which is okay."

Leonard stared at Max resentfully.

"What's maybe not okay for you and for me is if it becomes widely known that you've been putting it to her."

"You're presuming a lot."

"I'll apologize if I've got it wrong. But I don't, do I?"

"It's just one of those things," Leonard protested. "I met her on a research trip to Ottawa a couple of months ago. She liked me. I liked her."

"Who knows about it?"

"We've been discreet. We've never been out in public in Ottawa."

"Here?"

"Once or twice here. No-one knows her in Toronto."

"Don't count on that. Some rogue columnist will make

mincemeat of you if they get wind of it. Ordinarily it wouldn't matter. But this piece is going to get a lot of heat. McGreedy's gang will do whatever they can to take the sting out of it. And they know how to stick a finger in your eye."

Leonard laughed derisively. "I'll keep my eyes closed then."

"You bastard," Max fumed. "You damn well keep them wide open."

CHAPTER 21

May 12

A few minutes after seven o'clock in the evening, Max finished reworking Leonard Freeman's article on the Prime Minister. The quotes from the interview were neatly tucked into the piece now, and Max had shaved off all the rough edges from the insertions. He would send a fresh copy to the fact checker and give one to Giorgio for a page estimate. And Chaser always wanted a copy.

He walked from the photocopy machine to Chaser's office, passing the advertising department, the art department, and all the editorial rooms. Even Dot, who habitually worked into the early evening, had gone home. He was the last one in the office.

He laid a copy of the article on Chaser's desk. Tired after a long day, he plopped himself down in the editor's chair and flipped through the piece to make sure he had collated the pages properly. Then he stretched back, yawned, and put his feet up on the editor's ample antique desk.

He looked around the room. This place had startled him a year ago when he had first seen it. Part of one wall was devoted to framed photographs of the editor. There was Chaser with Prime Minister Botha of South Africa, Chaser shaking hands with Margaret Thatcher, Chaser standing beside Valerie Giscard D'Estaing, Chaser walking on Parliament Hill with Prime Minister Trudeau, Chaser with the Canadian ambassador to

Moscow in Red Square, and Chaser being introduced to Henry Kissinger. Hanging together, the photos gave the impression that this greying page boy with the mischievous grin and the wire-rimmed glasses was either a global powerbroker like the others or some kind of diabolical courier doing the bidding of world leaders. For each photo opportunity Chaser had puffed himself up in an attempt to look statesmanlike, but all Max could see was the impish power-groupie he had come to know at *Berger's*.

There were also photographs of Chaser holding up the national newspaper awards he had won over the years. There were eight of them, an unusually large number, and he had framed all eight separately and hung them in a cluster. Inflated ego aside, there could be no doubt that Chaser had been a crack daily news reporter.

Along another wall a floor-to-ceiling mahogany bookcase had been built with the editor's Janus Corporation expense account. The shelves, dense with books on Canadian and British history and politics, also housed a collection of Victorian first editions. Max's eyes coursed enviously along the spines of a complete set of original Trollope novels, a handsomely rebound first printing of Hardy's *The Mayor of Casterbridge*, and copies of early titles by Carlyle and Macauley. Set above these volumes, on a top shelf, were Chaser's treasured Derby-ware figurines, family heirlooms — as he told every new visitor to his office — left him by his grandmother Makepeace. They were late eighteenth-century and early nineteenth-century likenesses of the actor David Garrick dressed for a variety of Shakespearean roles. Max thought they were dreadful kitsch and had made the mistake of telling Chaser that he should get rid of them in a garage sale. The editor had replied testily that English china figurines were part of a respectable arts-and-crafts tradition, and that his eight pieces had been valued at more than $12,000.

Max leaned back and contemplated how he would change the decor if Chaser were hit by a truck tomorrow and it fell to him to step into the editor's chair. And then a picture of Arnold, dressed for the opera and swinging lightly in the April breeze, burst into his mind.

That's how it started. One day, many years ago, Arnold sat in a chair like this and thought to himself: if and when I am installed here for real, I'll hire, fire, advance my ideas, take no more crap, reinvent myself.

Chaser's enormous desk was filled with the usual chaotic heaps of manuscripts and unanswered letters. On top of one pile lay copies of some current magazines. Max picked up *The New Yorker* and thumbed idly through it. He looked at the cartoons and then at the classified ads. One he lingered over: "Small house in the south of France, village near Arles, suit couple, fully equipped, splendid view, privacy, $600 per week."

This year, he reflected, something like that would be affordable. Maybe even desirable. He thought of Sarah, of how they had been planning to go away together on holiday, which they had never done, and of her French-villa fantasy, which she had never made real.

Sheepishly, he remembered saying to her: "A house in France? Chateau Sarah? Isn't that getting a little pretentious?"

"Better than holidaying at Chez Max," she had shot back, "where you eat beans for dinner and choke to death on dust balls."

He pictured Betsy's hazel eyes and her small white ears, strands of black hair curled behind each one. What had been keeping her busy last night? And tonight?

At home, he remembered, there was nothing in his fridge.

And he heard Sarah's voice. "Why do you want to keep that place?"

He felt thirsty and tired. Too late to go out for a drink. By the time he got home it would be eight-thirty or nine.

Then he remembered that Chaser kept some bottles in his

office somewhere. He liked to offer his more valued guests a drink.

Max stood up. "Wouldchew lyaack a gloss of sherreehh?" he announced loudly to the empty room in a nasal O'Chancresque accent.

"Don't mind if I doooo," he crooned, opening up all the doors in sight, and finally laying his hands on a bottle of port and a bottle of sherry. They stood in a small, hip-high cabinet across by the window. Half a dozen dainty glasses were lined up neatly on a shelf above the bottles.

He held one of the glasses up to the light. "Frig. A goddamn thimble." He took it and the bottle of sherry back over to Chaser's desk.

I know, I know, Chaser. You're actually in the office late somewhere I haven't seen and you're about to burst in on me. Max downed the small vessel of sherry and poured another. "Well, cheers, old boy. Here's to the August issue. You're up a creek without Leonard's article." He chuckled. "And possibly up a creek with it as well. Let's hope so." He drank and poured again.

He contemplated the pile of mail in a folder on the desk, and then his eye wandered down to the ornate brass handles beside him. The bottom left-hand drawer, a deep file-keeper, was open half an inch.

"A good journalist is a good snoop," he heard himself say, smiling. They were Chaser's words. Max had first heard them the day he had walked into his own office and found Chaser standing over his desk reading his letters.

Max glanced at the open doorway.

What the hell.

He bent down and quietly pulled the drawer open. Then he gently tried the other drawers. They were all locked — all except this one that Chaser had apparently overlooked.

The drawer was full of file folders, all neatly labelled. It

183

appeared to be Chaser's personal storage space. The labels were variously marked MORTGAGE, BANKING, WILLS, COTTAGE, HOUSE REPAIRS, RRSP, MOTHER'S ESTATE, UTILITIES, EXPENSE ACCOUNT, OPERATION OUT, SPEECHES, and FREQUENT FLYER POINTS.

Max eased the drawer closed, downed another glass of sherry, wiped it out with a kleenex, and returned bottle and glass to their cabinet. He left Chaser's room and walked past every office in the magazine. He was sure now that he was alone except for the cleaners, who were still in advertising. He had, he guessed, about twenty minutes before they reached editorial. He hurried back to Chaser's desk and pulled open the drawer.

He looked again at all the labels. "Hell of a way to earn your living," he said to himself, as if to appease the twinge of guilt he was feeling. MORTGAGE? BANKING? EXPENSE ACCOUNT? He couldn't decide. OPERATION OUT seemed to beckon.

What the hell can that be?

He pulled the thin file folder out of the drawer and opened it. This is a firing offense, Vellen.

There was a memo on Janus Corporation stationery. It was addressed to Chaser and signed by Edward Clubb.

To: Chaser Makepeace

I attach a copy of a letter sent to me by Archibald Biddle, Chairman of the Carnegie Bank in New York. As you may know, Archie Biddle is a member of the Trilaterial Commission and is one of America's most distinguished financiers.

I have seldom been more pleased to receive a note of commendation.

It is a vindication of some of what I have been saying publicly about Canada's political future. As you know, in a perfect world, I am in favour of an independent Canada. But as I've said in articles for the business press, I am a realist. We cannot continue indefinitely to mollify Quebec at the expense of our own prosperity. As you can see, Archie Biddle agrees with my private analysis that some political integration between English Canada and the U.S. might soon be desirable. Of course, I have not gone that far publicly, and in the current climate I would deny contemplating such an initiative. The appalling ignorance and prejudice of the Canadian media on the subject of American culture – the champion of freedom in a dark world – mean that Canadians will have to be led gently by the hand into this new area of cross-border co-operation. Anything you can do at <u>Berger's</u> to open up these horizons will be appreciated.

The copy of Archibald Biddle's comments is, I hardly need add, for your eyes only. Please dispose of it once you've had a look.

E.O. Clubb

Chaser had underlined several sentences and scrawled in light pencil beside them, "Doesn't realize what he's said here! Sedition! Media field day!"

Also in the file folder Max found a photocopy of a brief letter on Carnegie Bank stationery underneath Clubb's note.

Dear Edward:

I enjoyed our discussion last week at the conference here in New York, and I appreciate your having sent me a draft copy of your proposed article on North American political integration.

These ideas on the possibility of continental

nationhood strike me as very sound. This is a
medium-term political eventuality we should all
be aware of, and possibly work towards, and Canada
is fortunate to have as its standard-bearer in
these matters as prescient and influential a
business executive as yourself.

With my kindest regards,
Archibald R. Biddle

Max experienced an odd, light-headed sensation, as if he had just witnessed a historical event, though he knew he hadn't. But it was a potential event alright; Chaser was not wrong about that.

TRANS-BORDER TYCOONS CONSPIRE TO WIPE CANADA OFF MAP. That's approximately what the headline would read if the letters were leaked. Edward Clubb would be assaulted by a voracious media feeding frenzy if it was ever revealed he had been huddled in intimate discussions with the billionaire Biddle family over the wholesale selling-out of Canada to the American capitalist class. Clubb would look like an unprincipled and traitorous huckster. It would take years to mend his image.

Chaser, it appeared, had the goods on his boss.

Not a bad idea, Max thought.

He looked outside Chaser's office door. The cleaners were now in the art department. He took the file folder to the photocopy machine, copied the contents, walked quickly back to Chaser's office, and slipped the folder back into the drawer, leaving it open exactly half an inch.

Should really have made two copies, Max reflected, and walked back to the copier. A cleaner was now moving his vacuum into the alcove where the machine stood.

Do another one early in the a.m., Max decided, slipping the photocopied pages into his briefcase.

CHAPTER 22

May 13

As Chaser scurried up Yonge Street from the magazine shop, he leafed quickly through the latest issue of *Poop*, and read the "I say . . . What are they up to now?" column while waiting at a stoplight. The column was written under the pen name of Dr. Jekyll, though it was widely known that Dr. Jekyll was in fact Liam O'Chancre.

"THIS JUST IN — As we go to press I am deeply distressed to learn of a civil disturbance at the prestigious corporate corner of Church and Wellington Streets in downtown Toronto.

"A rag-tag group of unemployed writers has been seen parading with rude signs outside the flat-iron building, headquarters of one of this city's most respected business enterprises, the Janus Corporation.

"Insulting slogans appeared on many of the placards. Where are the local constabulary when we need them? Gateau-guerrilla and unread novelist James 'Gamie' Goodfellow, a local *bon vivant* who champions Guatemalan leftists when he is not consuming bottles of Chateau Mouton-Rothschild in his faux-Tudor library, was seen in the rowdy throng. For shame! This group of shaggy-haired predators are apparently all members of the Writers' League, a group whose sole mission, I know full well, is to suck ever more voraciously on the public teat.

The assembled literary derelicts were inflamed because of a current court case involving one of Toronto's most distinguished personalities, Edward O. Clubb, publishing baron and philanthropist.

"'STOP CLUBBING WRITERS' and 'FREE SPEECH' were painted on some of the signs. I have been told that other, more creative placards were discarded after a lively argument in the finely appointed Annex home where the demonstration was organized. Slogans such as 'WADDLE SOFTLY AND CARRY A BIG CLUBB' and 'KING KONG OF PUBLISHERS MUST BE TOPPLED' were not used in the event. Asked about this as we went to press, Bruce Iversen, chairman of the Writers' League, replied solemnly, 'It's not true, and even if there were some truth to it, our group would never knowingly practice any kind of weightism.'

"Now, what I want to know is this: How can a group that purports to be against every possible bias known to mankind seriously expect the government to exercise a bias in its favour? How can the Writers' League, fearless crusader for social equality, justifiably single itself out for special treatment and continue to demand a large annual public grant for its operating expenses? And what, pray tell, does any of this have to do with the creation of literature?"

Chaser crossed the street and skimmed the rest of O'Chancre's piece, which was devoted to a scathing assault on the pretensions of mainstream feminism in general, and in particular the moral corruption of NEW, National Equity for Women.

Chaser flipped to the "Toronto Tattler" page and scanned it for items relevant to himself.

"Bruno T. Cayly, Q.C., trained legalist and insatiable publicity hound, has signed an unorthodox contract with the thriller drivelist Jeremy Glass. The two will split the proceeds of Glass's next book in exchange for Cayly's defence of the libel action brought by Edward 'Say-it-My-Way' Clubb. *Poop* has been told that Cayly, not known for courteous behaviour with clients, blew a gasket when he learned, after signing the deal, that Glass's next book will be a volume of children's poetry.

" '*And this little piggy had none.*'

"Sorry, Bruno. But don't be sore. You might get lucky. Rhyming schlockster Neil Sneed (an egghead poet in his other life) makes a pile from his kids' books. And Glass might get teary-eyed and give you a piece of the Lafleur Tire Company mega-prize he won last week. (It's known in Paris as the Prix Gonfleur, or Tire Pump Award, which fits nicely with the inflated ego of this year's recipient.)

"Somehow, Bruno, we feel you'll be appeased. After all, who wants to be defended grudgingly by a half-hearted shyster?"

Chaser flipped manically to the "Mediocracy" section.

"Last week's National Magazine Awards — the annual yawn-fest at which the country's most boring and long-winded drivelists can all be seen with their faces upside down kissing each other's bums — had a few (very few) noteworthy moments.

"Arthur Swartz, host of the CBC weekend radio show which, amazingly enough, is broadcast nation-wide, was the awards MC. Black was assaulted by an airborne squadron of baked goods as he attempted to deliver one of his puerile trademark lectures on the mystical differences between magazines and radio. A number of slobbering young hacks from *Wireworks!* magazine who had been reduced to mental defectives by the subsidized cash bar were responsible for launching these missiles, all sadly off target.

"The ballroom full of bumkissers was shocked into silence when the name of ancient mag hack Arnold Sturgess was announced. Sturgess's, uh, spectral presence appeared to distress the old geezer's former employer, Chaser Makepeace, valet-in-residence to Edward Clubb, and in his spare time top edit-boy at *Berger's* magazine.

"Sturgess won first prize in the culture category for three of his sleepifying thumbsuckers lamenting the plight of that near-extinct sub-species, the highbrow Canuck."

Chaser smiled happily as he read on.

"Sturgess, of course, put himself permanently to sleep only a few weeks ago with the help of a nylon cord tied to a Rosedale foot-bridge. Rumours are circulating to the effect that his employer, the aforementioned Chaser On-The-Makepeace, may have been about to come down hard on the old hetero-sexualist for his aggressive-though-never-reciprocated, uh, friendships with young *Berger's* workers of the fairer sex. But we digress.

"Also a prizewinner at the awards was Liam 'Chubby' O'Chancre, noted badboy and bigmouth of the Toronto literary scene. So enthusiastic was Chubby about his own good fortune that he insisted on celebrating after the awards by decking one of his least favourite editors, the ever-moist Maxwell Vellen, a spell-checker at *Berger's*.

"Mr. Vellen disappeared quickly after the incident and was unavailable for comment. O'Chancre, however, was more than willing to clarify matters. 'Hit him? No. Certainly not. He was obviously out of his mind with drink and attempted to butt me. He got the worst of it, that's all. Who cares? The man is not worth spitting at.'

"Vellen got a round of applause earlier when he almost impaled himself on a microphone as he accepted first prize in the Essay category. Seems Maxwell's silver hammer needs a new handle."

Chaser was grinning until another brief item caught his eye. He stopped on the sidewalk and read it carefully.

"We hear there have been unsolicited phone calls to *Berger's* magazine from the Prime Minister's Office in Ottawa. The PM's flak-catchers are said to be pissed about an upcoming article on Himself and want to be given equal time to rebut the falsehoods they believe will be retailed. Can this possibly be true? And will *Berger's* buckle?"

"Fuck," Chaser murmured as he walked slowly towards his office building.

With the gossip magazine rolled tightly into a tube in his hand, he brooded on who his new enemies might be.

★ ★ ★

Later that morning, Dot Scrivener said to Chaser, "I learned a long time ago that any magazine is a sieve. We're in the secrets business, alright, though not in the business of keeping them. But I'm not your leak. I have not spoken a word to anyone about McGarvie's intercession with Mr. Clubb. You can see *Poop* got it wrong, anyway, as they so often do. I wouldn't worry about it."

"They came within a whisker of the truth, though. Would have been simpler if we'd killed the piece as I'd intended."

"Oh? If you're worried about *Poop*, imagine the hay they could have made of *that*. The PMO would probably like nothing better than to see it buried."

"Sure. But that's something we could have finessed. Kill it internally, but tell everyone it's still in the works. First you pay off Freeman and tell him it may be used later on in the year. Then you recommission it, and this time ride herd on the writer, making sure the profile goes where you want it to."

"And where is that?" asked Dot, her eyes widening with dismay.

"I don't mean dictating what can be said. I just mean a degree of steering. Finding some common ground between the magazine and the writer."

Dot bristled. "That's not precisely what comes to mind when I think of gutsy journalism."

"Maybe not. But it's survival journalism. And that comes first."

"By the way," she said with exasperation in her voice, "what is all the scuttlebutt about Arnold and the sweet young things in this office. I never saw him lay a finger on a soul."

"No?"

"Certainly not!"

"No, no. Neither did I. I have no idea where all that came from. We should put a lid on it somehow."

★ ★ ★

Later that day, Sarah sat in her kitchen with a magazine and a cup of tea. In the background she could hear the rat-tat-tat-tat-tat-tat of her printer banging out pages. She was looking at the May issue of *Canadian Woman*, the magazine in which she would soon appear. An article on dolphins had caught her fancy. It was a short, quirky piece on the Vancouver-based dolphin expert who believed sonic pulses she picked up on tape from her dolphins should be beamed up to telecommunications satellites and relayed into deep space.

Sarah sipped her tea and pictured hundreds of extraterrestrial dolphins entering the earth's atmosphere. Instead of self-immolating, they all miraculously plunged unharmed into Lake Ontario. The sky was blue with dolphins, a mammalian shower from heaven. To the rescue! they all seemed to be chanting as they hit the water.

She was feeling content, centred, at peace. She had done a good day's work, first at the office, then here on her computer.

The article, Sarah noticed as her reverie faded, was written by one Martin Davis. A dark reminder of the other Martin and the harsh way she had ended things with him. He had been hurt, a mess of her making. She had not seen any way to extricate herself gently. The fault had been in getting involved with him at all.

Arrrrgh! I didn't need a relationship, she reflected. I needed a good long sexual sabbatical.

She reread the fax that Maria Jonsson at *Canadian Woman* had sent to the office in the morning.

"We love your piece. It needs very little work. We'd like a few changes and additions, which I'm listing on a separate sheet. That's the good news.

"The bad news is: we need the changes right away. We've had two pieces drop out of our July issue for reasons too complicated to explain here. We want to typeset your article and rush it through. We've already commissioned some illustrations. Can you do the rewriting in the next day or two? We'll need to typeset and shape next week. Let me know asap. Thanks. Maria"

Sarah had come home early and worked on the piece for several hours.

Her printer stopped clacking. She went into the bedroom and collected the pages. It was four-thirty, still time, if she hurried, to fax it to the magazine. She scribbled a note on page one, flung on her jacket, and headed out to Bloor Street and Kwikcopy.

On the sidewalk, not far from her dentist's office, she was stopped by a voice.

"Ms. McDermott."

Recognizing the face, she took a couple of moments to place it: Max's boss. "Oh hello, Chaser. Long time no see. For obvious reasons."

"Yes. I was sorry about that."

"Don't be sorry. It's all in the past. Seems like an ice age ago."

"I'll remind him he's a dinosaur tomorrow." Chaser grinned.

"He's already been told," Sarah said, with a tight smile. "You know, this is peculiar. I saw Dot Scrivener here, almost in the exact same place, a few days ago. Are you guys opening a branch office in my neighbourhood?"

"Dot was up here, was she? I was just . . ." He glanced over her shoulder, as if scanning for familiar faces at a party. "Uh . . . just doing some shopping."

"No kidding! So was she. Though I can't imagine what for around here."

★ ★ ★

On his way to dinner, Max stopped at Lichtman's on Yonge Street to check out the latest copy of *Poop*. He turned to the "Mediocracy" page and read the magazine-awards item gleefully until he saw O'Chancre's name linked with his. When he realized the editors of *Poop* had given him another public raspberry, he felt a helpless burning sensation in his skull.

What did the silver-hammer comment mean, anyway? Apart from the reference to an old Beatles' song? Was it a no-lead-in-your-pencil slur? O'Chancre had his hands all over the little gossip rag these days. Probably it was another clumsy insult from him.

For a moment Max stood paralyzed, thinking of *Poop* followers cackling derisively when they read of his Friday-night banana peels. He slid the little magazine back onto the rack. Deciding not to buy it made him feel slightly better.

He was taking Betsy to a French restaurant down on Front Street near the flat-iron building, a small place he hoped would be warm and friendly and put them in a good mood.

He walked over to Church Street and down it to Wellington and crossed to the triangular piece of land where the flat-iron stood. Rush hour was long past. A sleek, polished Lincoln idled by the curb as the last of the homebound traffic rolled out of the downtown. Max stopped to admire the old brick building. A few yards away from him a heavy-set man in a rumpled blue suit appeared in the doorway and looked in his direction. Max recognized the man as Edward Clubb. Clubb seemed to recognize him too.

Sometimes Max thought of the owner of *Berger's* as a cartoon capitalist: the watch chain, the top hat, the big cigars. He was amused that Clubb really did smoke them in public. Max did not despise the flamboyant publisher as some of his friends did. He considered it admirable that Clubb had rescued *Berger's* and was pumping money into it. When he thought of Clubb at all, he thought of him as a clever, headstrong deal-maker who occasionally made life miserable for Chaser Makepeace — which was definitely a point in the publisher's favour.

"Mr. Clubb."

The Janus chairman seemed uncertain for a moment. He peered suspiciously as Max drew closer and proffered his right hand. It was only last Christmas, thought Max, that they had met and talked, albeit briefly, at the *Berger's* Christmas party.

Clubb looked disgustedly at the outstretched hand.

"You're not one of those writers, are you?"

Peculiar thing to say, thought Max. "Well . . . uh . . . yes. I guess I am. Still am, I mean," he sputtered.

As he looked around to see whether Max was accompanied, the publisher said in a menacing voice, "If you think that I am going to put up indefinitely with the likes of you *polluting* the sidewalk outside my office, you inflate your worth above the trash that you and your friends clearly are." He moved brusquely past Max towards his limo.

"I think there's a mistake here," Max tried to say, but the publisher's voice rang louder.

"I will not stand for catcalls, nor for public threats," he snarled. "You are walking on thin ice, my friend. And there's a lakeful of very cold water waiting to swallow you."

Max walked after him, but Clubb had stepped into the car and slammed the door before Max reached the edge of the sidewalk. Max put his hand on the car door handle.

The publisher lowered his window. "Hold it," Max heard him say to the driver. "Yes?" he said, fixing Max with a hostile eye.

"If I'm garbage, you're a trash can," Max began with a broad smile, "because . . ."

"I don't need to listen to your sophomoric insults," snapped the publisher as the window rolled up.

"No, no," said Max, as the car engine started. He felt annoyed Edward Clubb had missed his employer-employee witticism. He was still contemplating how to rectify the misunderstanding when Clubb's chauffeur stepped out of the driver's door. He looked like an ex-boxer.

"You gotta problem?" The chauffeur glared at Max. "Mr. Clubb doesn't like you guys bothering him."

"*You* guys? What you guys? Do you see anyone else here?" Max spread his arms and looked dramatically left and right.

"You know what I mean. Stop the harassment." The driver folded his bulky frame back down into his seat and slammed the door. The car started to roll.

"Hey," Max shouted. "Fuck you, you slimeball."

The car cruised away down Wellington.

Max looked at his watch: ten minutes before his date. He walked over to the benches in the concrete parkette just west of the flat-iron building and sat down. He could see the restaurant from here, maybe would see Betsy coming to dinner. His heart was thumping and he wanted to continue yelling at someone. The last time he had felt this ill-used was when Sarah had given him the heave-ho.

Remembering the photocopied letters in his top drawer, Max thought in headlines.

BULLY-BOY PUBLISHER STABS CANADA IN BACK

SLOB MILLIONAIRE CONSPIRES AGAINST
HOME-AND-NATIVE LAND

TRAITOR CANUCK CONSORTS
WITH YANKEE ROBBER BARON

He settled on:

TYCOON PUTS MATCH TO CANADA

But he knew the letters were much too good to waste on a fit of pique.

He caught sight of Betsy, strolling along the south side of Front Street. Looking at the stores and cafes, she was trying to find the restaurant, which she had said she didn't know. He watched her come to it and walk in. From this distance, with her short flowered skirt and tight black top, she looked disconcertingly like a girl about eighteen.

A young pussycat with nine lives, Max considered, as he stood and walked towards the restaurant. Whereas I've already used up five, maybe six of mine, at least a couple of them with Sarah.

As he walked in, he saw that the tables in the restaurant each had snugged to one side a single long-stem red rose in a clear vase. It was either a dreadful cliche or an especially favourable omen, and when he saw the flower against Betsy's tightly fitted black sweater and short black hair he was inclined to the more optimistic sign.

"You're looking very lovely," he said, kissing her on the cheek that was diffidently offered.

"Thank you. How are you?"

"All stirred up." He explained what had happened by the flat-iron building a few minutes earlier.

"I think he's really neat, though," she said when Max had finished.

"Who? Edward Clubb?"

She nodded.

"I can't see what he was so exercised about."

"For a journalist, you don't get out enough," she chided good-naturedly. "Didn't you hear about the demos at his office this week?"

Max looked puzzled. "My nose has been buried in an editing emergency since Monday. Tell me."

"Don't you read *Poop*?"

"Well, ah, yes," he replied nervously. "Why?"

"There's a mention of it in the new issue, in the Dr. Jekyll column. The Writers' League put a gang of its members out on the pavement by Edward Clubb's front door. They were chanting and waving signs. They're trying to embarrass him into backing off from his libel suit against Jeremy Glass and our magazine."

"My guess is he's not a guy who embarrasses easily."

"Oh, no. I agree. They're wasting their breath."

"You think he took me for one of the protesters."

"He must have. From what he blasted you with, I'd say he's leaving the office these days loaded for bear. Besides, you *look* like a writer."

"I do?" said Max, taken aback. "What do you mean by that?" Her smile was sympathetic, but he thought he could see a note of condescension in it too.

"Number one, you're not wearing a suit. Number two, you are wearing jeans. Number three, your mauve neck-tie is probably sending out an angry-making subliminal message to a guy like Clubb. Number four, your hair is a bit long and a bit tousled."

"You make me sound like I just crawled out of a dumpster," Max replied self-consciously. He looked down at his tie, which had stylized pairs of dice and decks of cards printed on it. "You don't like my tie?"

"*I* like it fine," she said, touching his hand across the table. "I think you look great. Not the picture of a guy who's going to make corporate vice-president one day, that's all."

A waiter appeared to recite the specials and take their orders.

"Are you drinking?" Max asked.

"Not really. But I'll keep you company." She paused. "Up to a point."

"We'll have a bottle of the house red then," he told the waiter and then, turning back to her, said, "Last Friday, I outpaced myself."

"Which part of the evening are we talking about?" Her smile, he thought, was brittle.

"The whole thing. I mean, except after we went back to your place. I was soaking it up like a dry lawn that night. All those egos knocking against each other at such close quarters. I tend to belt down a few too many under that kind of pressure."

"It was the first awards night I've been to. I liked it. It made me feel I was part of something bigger."

"Bigger?"

"You know, bigger than *Wellington*."

"I'm trying to remember how I felt the first time I went," he reflected. "Seems like a long time ago. It *was* a long time ago. I think I was exactly your age."

"That would make it twelve years ago."

His eyebrows shot up. "You were fourteen. It was still the seventies. I figured I had the world by the tail. I was writing a best-seller. The film rights were going to be optioned for big bucks. I thought I'd be buying a house." He stopped himself. "Very Toronto, that. Big dreams. Home ownership!" He laughed and shook his head.

"No-one my age dreams of buying a house anymore," she

said. "Sometimes I get the impression your cohort didn't know how good you had it."

"You're so right. We didn't. But I still don't own a house."

"Finish your story."

Max turned the ends of his mouth down. "It doesn't have a great ending. I spent half a year researching the biggest real-estate scam in Canadian history. I signed with a publisher for $30,000 and they gave me ten up front. For the first time in my life, I felt prosperous.

"Soon after that they went belly up. I worked on it for another few months, thinking I could find someone else to buy in. It was a great story. So good, in fact, that by the time I was cut loose by my bankrupt publisher, another writer was working on it and had signed with another house. All I could find was a small press willing to give me a $2000 advance. By then I was subsidizing myself heavily. Eventually I abandoned it and went back to magazine writing full-time."

Listening to himself relate this old story, Max felt alarmed. "Why am I telling you this?"

"You're showing me your scars."

"I know. But why?"

"You're trying to bridge the age gap." She sounded distant, almost reproachful.

He felt an unpleasant tension. It was as though having slept with her counted for nothing. They were on a first date, her signals seemed to say. No history, no commitments.

Unable to think of the right words, his mind filled with a picture of Edward Clubb's chauffeur barking at him on the sidewalk. His eyes rested on Betsy's green eyes and her full lips, painted the same glossy red as last Friday night.

"Cheers," he said happily, raising his wine glass.

"Yes," she replied quietly, and took a sip.

The waiter brought their main courses and Max watched Betsy take a bite of her pepper steak.

"Good," she said. Max waited for her to say something else, but she didn't. Instead she gave him what seemed to be a patient smile.

The silence threatened to become awkward.

He circled back. "Optimism notwithstanding, are you at all worried about Edward Clubb's libel suit? Personally, I mean. I hear people saying that a long legal fight could cripple *Wellington*. Your job could be on the line."

"I don't intend to stay where I am for long. As I told you," she said.

Max nodded. "I asked a few leading questions," he lied, "about the job outlook at our place. It'll be a while before it's resolved. But I can grease some wheels for you when the time comes." They talked again of the other magazines around town, where the opportunities were, where the professional land mines were buried. Then she fell silent.

Max tried again. "Anyone at *Wellington* ready to throw a rock through Edward Clubb's window?"

"My editor is upset. She thinks the libel laws should be taken off the books. I'm sure she'd like Edward Clubb to die very soon of a massive heart attack. And our owner, Manny Rosenfeld, is apparently very annoyed. But I don't pretend to be a player, Max. I'm just an amused spectator, really. I think it's all good entertainment for the rest of us. Don't you?"

"I wouldn't want to be Jeremy Glass right now."

"No? I disagree. I think all writers should pray for his luck. Thanks to Clubb, he's become a cultural martyr. Plus he just won that fat French prize."

"And how about Edward Clubb? You say you like him."

"Well, I don't mean that I know him. But I like a lot of what he says. I agree with some of his conservative politics and I admire the way he says whatever he wants and to hell with public opinion."

"When you're that rich, public opinion doesn't matter."

"You could be wrong about that," she said firmly. "The PR industry works for an awful lot of wealthy clients who care deeply about their image."

Max sensed a steeliness underneath the pretty face, an opinion-tempered toughness that he had not counted on. They ate in silence for a couple of minutes.

"Alright," he began again. "Tell me what it is about Clubb's politics you find so attractive."

"He's against big government. Business bail-outs. Public funding for interest groups. Government hand-outs of all kinds. That's a position I admire." She said it quickly and easily, he thought, as if she had said it many times.

"You sound like one of those neo-conservative think tanks," he said, immediately regretting the sharpness of the remark.

"Well, I'm no think tank, believe me," she said testily. "But neo-conservative? Maybe in some ways. What's wrong with that?"

Jesus, thought Max, what have we opened up here? "Nothing wrong with it at all. Who knows, I might even agree with you if I thought it through. Which I almost certainly won't. I'm much too comfortable with all the old liberal verities I picked up in the sixties. All of which boil down to a suspicion of the overdog."

She wrinkled her nose.

"But maybe that's just too easy now."

"Maybe. The paradox is that while I spout all this wishy-washy liberalism, for years I was one of the last of the independent, self-reliant craftsmen — the original small businessman. That's what a freelance writer is. You sit at home fashioning your one-off product all by yourself, and then you sell it in the marketplace. What could be more free-enterprise than that? They should put a few of us in a museum and label us direct descendants of Adam Smith. Edward Clubb really ought to love us. We're kindred spirits."

Betsy smiled. "You can bet he doesn't see that gang of malcontents outside his office as kindred spirits."

"I wonder where the hell *he* was in the sixties?"

"He must have been lonely." She laughed.

"Actually I guess he was already over thirty and therefore not to be trusted even then." Max stirred his coffee. "Anyhow, the sixties weren't all roses. The drug culture took a lot of casualties."

"Self-inflicted." She shrugged.

He laughed. "I'm not gonna take that bait. You make me feel like I'm defending some ancient, decadent civilization we've only read about, like maybe the late Roman Empire."

"Pooey," she said with a mischievous glint in her eye. "There you boomers go being self-important again. That decade will *not* be remembered in 2000 years. You can bet on it."

"Good odds either way. At least in terms of paying up."

"Speaking of which," she said, lifting the bill off its small plastic tray, "let's split this."

"Why? I invited you."

"It's not my policy to be taken out to dinner by strange men."

"Strange men? How strange is a guy who you've already spent the night with?"

"We hardly know each other," she said firmly.

Max was not encouraged. He felt she was drawing a line beyond which certain transactions were not welcome. Exactly which ones he couldn't tell. Somehow the dinner hadn't helped.

As they walked out on the sidewalk she turned to him. "Let's not talk about politics again for a while."

He felt relieved. "Okay. Let's talk about how sexy and intelligent you are."

"That'll be a short conversation," she said looking away, but he sensed that she didn't dislike the remark.

"Will you come back to my place?"

She stopped walking and looked at him without saying anything for a moment.

"Yes," she said finally. "But not for long. I have to be at work early tomorrow."

CHAPTER 23

May 17

Edward Clubb walked towards Yonge along Bloor Street to the Simcoe Club, where Mrs. Crutchlow had booked a table for two. The club occupied an antique mansion on a small street east of Yonge in what was once the southernmost pocket of Rosedale. He opened the heavy oak door, climbed the carpeted steps into the club's lobby, and handed the porter his umbrella. The dark-haired man with his coat still on, who was looking around the hall restlessly, was almost certainly the expected guest.

"Emmanuel Rosenfeld?" Clubb said, walking over and extending his hand.

"Call me Manny," the man said cheerfully. "All my friends do."

"I'm glad you were able to come. Let's go right upstairs to the dining room and find our table."

The real-estate developer slipped off his damp rain gear, and dug into his pocket. He pulled two dollars from a billfold and handed it with his coat to the porter. The porter took the coat.

"That's very kind of you, ah, Manny, but we don't allow tipping in the club."

"No, eh? You should. Good service should be recognized."

"We try to," said Clubb as he signed the guest register. Beside "Edward Clubb" he wrote "Manfred Reed."

The Janus chairman began climbing the grand staircase. Rosenfeld bounced up the purple-carpeted stairs beside him. "Nice place ya got here. Who's this?" he asked, jerking his thumb in the direction of a full-length oil portait that dominated the spacious halfway landing.

"That's Sir Anthony Crowell, founder of the Simcoe Club."

"Sir, yet! Very classy place. I gotta tell ya, though, Sir Whatsisface looks like an unhappy man. Don't you think so? Kinda sour. Or frustrated in some way."

"Sir Anthony's emotional state is something I wouldn't know anything about." Clubb looked up to the top of the stairs to see if anyone was watching them.

"Not saying you should," replied Rosenfeld. They climbed the second half of the stairs. "Boy, this is some pile. Any idea how old it is?"

"It was put up about seventy-five years ago. When such places were affordable," Clubb replied, looking at his guest warily.

"Not by my people they weren't. Not in the shtetl."

"Mmmm."

"You know what I'm saying? The shtetl — that's what we called our villages in the old country. The whole shtetl could have fit into this place. With a room left over for Sir Whatsisface." He chuckled.

"In point of fact, ah, Manny, I do know what a *shtetl* is."

The head steward inclined his head as they stepped into the dining room. "Good afternoon, Mr. Clubb. Your table is over by the window."

"Amazing," said Rosenfeld looking around at the uniformed waiters as he sat down. "Just like the butler in 'Upstairs Downstairs.'"

"Well, Manny, the Simcoe Club was here first."

"Sure it was. You're probably all aristocrats too."

"They're hard to come by in Canada."

"You think so? You're one yourself, I'd say. I'll bet your grandfather had money."

"Comfortable, yes. An aristocrat, I'm afraid not."

"But you come from a wealthy background. Unlike myself. My father ran a small building-supply store all his life. What did he want to be? An architect. He was even talented. His father was a small storekeeper until he escaped from Europe. Here he worked in a factory. Now you tell me, your grandfathers, where were they born?"

Clubb was tapping the table impatiently with a finger. "The one who started the family business was born here in Ontario. His parents came out to Canada in the 1880s from Yorkshire."

"He was a lucky guy."

"I don't know about luck. He worked prodigiously hard by all accounts. And he was a prescient businessman. He started a small-town newspaper, sold it, came to Toronto, started some trade papers, eventually bought some others. When my father took over we already owned eleven publications, I think. Most of them have prospered." He paused, then said, "I've expanded, as you may know."

"I respect your success. But you've got deep business roots here, Ed — you don't mind if I call you Ed? When I started my development company I had nothing but a mortgage and personal covenants up to my ass."

"I'm told you've done very well."

"I'm feeding my family. And I'm still enjoying myself. But I don't do a lot of high living. For sure no fencie-shmencie old clubs like this. Not that I could, even if I wanted."

"Well, maybe someday."

"Are you kidding? The day this place takes me as a member is the day the window sashes're rotten and the roof's falling in because you Wasp bluebloods have all gone offshore." He grinned.

Clubb cleared his throat. "You sound like a realist, Manny.

That's good. So am I. It occurred to me that we might get along. Which is why I thought we should try a meeting without lawyers."

"Suits me. I'm willing to look at whatever you put on the table."

"I don't propose to do any hard negotiating today. Just a friendly discussion. Strictly speaking, we don't do business in the club."

"Is that so? On second thought, I won't join, even when you're desperate."

"I should also mention my lawyer advised me against this meeting. So let's begin by saying if the case goes to court, none of what I'm proposing applies or has any relevance. In fact, this lunch didn't happen."

"We'll see. It hasn't happened yet anyway."

Clubb wrote on the order pad what they wanted to eat and drink. Then he leaned back in his chair. "Manny, do you know what it costs to bring, or in your case to fight, a libel action?"

"Ed, if you think you can threaten me into caving, you can forget this whole dog-and-pony show. I didn't write that article about you, and I didn't even agree with a lot of what it said, but I'm not selling my side down the river. I enjoy owning *Wellington*. And I like the people I've hired to run it. And you'll never nail me personally with any of this. All my assets are well protected. The most I can lose is the magazine itself. You better know that. You're not going to cause me any pain that I'm not willing to suffer."

"I have no intention of trying to discommode you personally. My quarrel is with your editor and your writer. But you're the one paying the bills."

"The magazine's bills, yes. Glass has his own attorney."

"In any case, your defence is his defence in large part. And it's going to be very costly. For both of us."

"It wasn't my idea."

"Well, there may be a better idea. Depending on how you see it. I'm told we could be looking at half a million in legal fees. Each. A million all told. Is it really worth it?"

"That's a lot of green stuff. No argument from me there."

"What if — I'm just speculating now — instead of fighting with high-priced lawyers, what if you and I were to become partners?"

"Clubb and Rosenfeld? Sounds like some kind of comedy team. Or a sandwich you don't want to eat."

"I'm not trying to pull your leg. I'm being perfectly serious."

"What kind of partners?"

"I'm coming to that. You could forfeit half a million to the lawyers. My best legal advice says you stand an excellent chance of losing the case too."

"That's not what my guys are telling me," said the developer, shaking his head.

"Let's not try to settle it here. You'll concede, as a reasonable man, that there's *a chance* you could lose. Say the settlement is for $100,000. You'd be out $600,000."

"You're asking me if I want to lose six hundred big ones, maybe more? The answer is no."

"How'd you like, instead of that kind of blood-letting, to end this whole business *ahead* by half a million?"

"I'm listening."

"This is just blue-sky stuff today. But say Janus was interested in buying a half-interest in *Wellington*. Naturally if we did that the suit couldn't proceed. The magazine would have to print an apology before the deal went through. Then you and I could own *Wellington* together. I'd be a more or less passive investor. I don't want to have my hands in the details."

"You want to buy an apology from me?" exclaimed Rosenfeld, astonished.

"Not at all. I'm told *Wellington* is good value. And that's precisely what I like spending my money on. I don't like giving it to lawyers. Of course, I'd want to look at your books."

"Did you say half a million?"

"Plus some shares in Janus. Precise terms to be worked out. Depending on what your books tell us."

"And you'd want us to publicly apologize," the developer said doubtfully.

"The magazine and that termite Glass."

"I can't speak for him."

"Alright. Leave him out of it for the moment."

"I'm not leaving him out of it. I'm just saying I can't make him apologize. And I won't try. A writer should write what he thinks. You're not talking business now. You're talking culture. Freedom of the press."

"Freedom of the press? *Absolute* freedom? Would you like to have been publicly skewered by that kind of article?"

"No way. But like I said, I didn't write it."

"I hope you'll give these ideas some thought, Manny."

"You bet I will, Ed. How many shares of Janus did you have in mind? Just give me a ballpark estimate."

"We're talking about a centrefold apology, Manny. A big spread that no-one who reads *Wellington* could possibly miss."

"Yeah? Let's not forget who owns the magazine and who wants to buy a piece."

★ ★ ★

When Max came back from his lunch, he found one of Chaser's handwritten messages on a yellow sticky note pasted to his desk: "Please see me when you get back, CM."

As he sifted through his pink phone messages, Max tried to think what might be on the boss's mind. The article on McGreedy had gone into production. Giorgio was working on putting together the artwork. He was now talking of an illustrated cover instead of a photograph. It all seemed to be going well, and it was all off Max's desk until the fact checker called with the changes.

He wandered down to Chaser's office. The editor was bent over in his chair, working on a notepad. Dwarfed by his huge desk, he looked like a small frog hunched on the edge of a dock. He saw Max in the doorway and waved him in.

"Max, old trout. We need to talk."

As soon as he heard "old trout," Max grew wary. Chaser had a habit of trying to reel people in with intimacy just before he planted his little fangs in their flesh.

"Hiya, Chaser."

"Max. I happened to be looking through your office for the McGarvie transcript while you were at lunch. I looked in your desk, in fact."

Sweet Jesus!

"I found some papers which quite disturbed me, Max. I probably shouldn't have been in your desk, I know. But I've been in this business too long to care about anyone's privacy."

Holy Jumping, Max swore silently to himself. Had he left the Archibald Biddle letter in his desk? He'd taken both copies home, hadn't he? He suddenly felt uncertain. He could feel his stomach tensing and his throat going dry.

Good-bye *Berger's*. Good-bye salary. Hello sidewalk.

Chaser picked up the papers that had been lying upside down by his notepad.

"It's not easy to explain," said Max softly.

"Mmm hmm," the editor replied, glancing at the papers. "I wonder how much of a problem it really is."

"How much?" Max was puzzled. His mind raced through the possibilities. At that moment it seemed to him that the problem was approaching monumental proportions.

"Yeah. I wonder how well they really know each other. I mean, are they sleeping together?"

"What?" Edward Clubb and Archibald Biddle! "I had no

idea," he sputtered, wondering if there was some remote chance this might mean a reprieve for him. His heart was pounding wildly.

"I'm glad to know that," the editor replied. "I only met her myself about a week ago. But I didn't realize there was a connection."

"Eh? I'm not sure I follow you entirely."

"Oh. Well, you know me. I always look at everything. When I came across this fax from the PMO in your desk, naturally I was curious. And when I saw you had circled Danielle Choquette's name, I suddenly remembered that she was who Leonard Freeman introduced me to at the Red Cross Ball. Of course he didn't say she worked for the PMO. She was draped all over him. She's quite a dish."

"I didn't know you'd gone to that," said Max.

"Yeah. I met my wife there after the magazine awards. She's on some Red Cross committee, bless her, so I had to show my face. Anyhow, putting it all together, I assume this woman is also Freeman's main source for the McGarvie piece."

Max wondered for a second or two if he could finesse it. But Chaser already had the goods. Danielle Choquette — and Leonard — would have to take their chances.

"She won't admit it publicly," Max said. "I only found out myself a few days ago that they're an item. But I don't think it's a major disaster. Nobody knows they're involved. It's only an accident that I know. Likewise you."

Chaser shook his head fretfully. "It looks very bad. We have an insider who's giving us McGarvie's guts on a platter, and then people find out our writer is doing her! *Poop* would blow a hole through us a mile wide if they got hold of it. It looks tremendously sleazy. We're supposed to be practising reasonably high-minded journalism here. This is barnyard stuff."

"All I can say, and what I did say to myself, was that no-one has to know about the relationship. I doubt it's the first time a journalist ever crossed this line."

"I'm sure you're right. I just wish it hadn't washed up on my doorstep."

"I still think it's a good piece," Max said, feeling bolder. "What did you want the transcript for?"

"Just to make sure Freeman had given the PM a fair shake. It's still an extraordinarily scathing piece."

"I went through the tape myself," Max replied. "The final version has everything that's usable, minus all McGreedy's trademark guff."

Chaser, still looking concerned, shook his head. "Clubb is going to have a conniption. I'm going to be on rocky terms with him for quite a while." Chaser paused thoughtfully. "You are too."

"Me? He doesn't even know I exist."

"Don't be too sure of that. He has sharp eyes."

"He hasn't mentioned my name lately, has he?"

"No. Why would he?"

"No reason," Max replied. He felt relieved. It was true — Clubb probably hadn't recognized him on the sidewalk.

When he returned to his office Max closed the door and searched his desk. As he thought, he had taken the Biddle-Clubb letters home.

★ ★ ★

Max had slept fitfully on Thursday night, with dreams about Betsy that he could not remember. They had had a drink back at his apartment after their awkward dinner. She had been curious about his rooms and his things, and he had had the odd sensation of being a tour guide to his littered life. She had asked a lot of questions again, as she had that first night they had spent together. She had seemed hungry to know his *details*, as if she were engaged in painting a precise picture.

They had joked about their dinner conversation, then they'd made love. He had been allowing himself to feel wildly optimistic when suddenly she had announced she would have to dress and go home. Would she not stay the night? No, she had insisted, it was better not to.

And that was the last he had seen of her. As on the previous weekend, she'd been unavailable Saturday and Sunday. They had agreed to talk, but had missed each other. She had left him two messages.

On Friday morning, he had felt exhilarated. But on the weekend his apartment had felt empty and oppressive. He had escaped to a sports bar on the Danforth in the afternoons.

Now, just after three on Monday, he was trying to reach her again.

"Betsy's in a meeting," the *Wellington* receptionist told him.

"I left a message this morning," he said. "Max Vellen. Do you know if she got it?"

"She's picked up all her messages."

He went back to proof-reading pages for the July issue. Half an hour later the phone rang.

"You have a delivery, Max." It was Dee, the young receptionist.

At the front desk he retrieved a small cheque-sized envelope from his mail slot. It had arrived by courier. He gave Dee a knowing wink, and she giggled. He had told her last week that he had heard a rumour Arnold had put the make on her some time in the past winter. She had looked astonished. "Him? Absolutely harmless. Never even winked at me."

Max took the letter back to his office and opened it. The envelope had been addressed by hand.

Dear Max,

I need to tell you this before another day passes, and I don't think I can do it well on the phone. I've liked knowing you and enjoyed your company, even though we're far apart on so many things! I don't think it's going to work and I'd rather stop now before it could get messy. I can't really explain it, except to say I think there are too many differences — in age, and otherwise. Sorry to have to shut the door in a letter, but I'm busy all this week, and it's unfair for you not to know what my heart has decided. We can talk later if you want.

X O

Betsy

Max read the handwritten note over and over. "'Before it could get messy?'" he said aloud. "What makes you think you're being so goddamn neat and tidy?" He examined every phrase and nuance. "Liked knowing you and enjoyed your company" seemed tepid. "Far apart on so many things" sounded like a fabrication. Far apart on what? On neo-conservatism and the sixties? Who cares?

"What my heart has decided."

What about *my* heart? Max grumbled to himself.

"I'd rather stop now."

Not me, I wouldn't, black-haired Betsy with the hazel eyes and the sassy mouth.

And with you I was on my best behaviour. Almost.

He felt like a refugee suddenly barred from a place he'd thought he might be settling in.

"Shit," he said, covering his face with his hands.

The phone rang. It was Dee again. "There's another delivery for you out here."

I knew it, he thought. She's relenting. Dear Max, I'm terribly sorry, how could I have got it so wrong? Dear Max, I'm sorry, I was confused this morning, I can't believe I sent you that ridiculous note. Dear Max, please forgive me, it wasn't until I wrote you that note that I realized what you mean to me. Dear Max, excuse the note, I panicked, can I take it all back, can we start this day over? Dear Max, I'm confused, I decided to run away from what was happening to us, big mistake. Dear Max, can you overlook my bad judgment in sending you that pathetic little Dear John letter? Dear dear Max, I really do love you . . . .

Dee handed him a long, legal-size brown envelope, which he tore open manically as he walked back down the hall to his office.

Dear Max:

I don't have the heart to spring this on you in public. I've just received these page proofs from my editor. The article is coming out in the July issue of <u>Canadian Woman</u>. You'll understand, I hope, how therapeutic it was for me to write this. Now that it's done I feel better. I suppose I did want to humiliate you just a little bit. And so I'm also feeling guilty. It seems like a good idea to soften the blow and give you a preview.

It was signed with her initials: SM.

He quickly read the pages, then reread the note. Never, he thought, were those initials more appropriate.

He stood and stared out the window. Sarah had me all wrong, he reflected numbly.

But I'm still on her mind.

CHAPTER 24

May 25

Sarah ran into Dot Scrivener as they were both leaving the Spadina subway station. It was a few minutes before five on this Tuesday after the long weekend. She was stopping at the dentist on her way home. The gold crown he had set on her molar in April had been hampering her bite. She thought it needed to be filed down.

As they walked out of the station together, Sarah laughed. "This is becoming melodramatic. Bumping into you around here, I mean. I know. You're starting a new magazine and you're having secret meetings about it up here."

"I meet the best people on this part of Bloor Street," the older woman replied. From behind Dot's tinted glasses, Sarah caught a look she thought was pregnant with guile.

"What is it with my neighbourhood these days? You *Berger's* people are all over the place. Next it'll be Max Vellen, God forbid." They walked on.

"Who else has been up this way?"

"I saw Chaser Makepeace just last week."

"Really? I wonder what Chaser was doing up here?"

"He said he was shopping."

"Ah."

They stopped in front the dentist's door. "This is me," said Sarah.

"Your dentist is in this building?" Dot seemed surprised.

"Yeah. Not very elegant, I know. But he's good."

"We were going to have lunch," said Dot. "Let's remember to do that."

"I'll call you."

Dot gave a coy little wave and strolled on.

Sarah climbed the stairs to the second floor. As she was closing the door to the waiting room she caught a glimpse of someone coming down from the floor above. She recognized the Easter Island scowl of Jerome Segal, the same face she had seen downstairs on another visit.

Back out in the hallway, her crown filed, she looked curiously at the narrow staircase. She climbed up. There were two doors with opaque nubbled glass: Suite 3A and Suite 3B. 3A had neither a painted sign nor a plaque to identify its tenant. 3B had a piece of stencilled cardboard artlessly taped to the wood:

POOP MAGAZINE

As she was walking back down Bloor Street, it occurred to her that Dot Scrivener's and Chaser Makepeace's peculiar appearances in the neighbourhood might easily have been covert visits to the third floor of her dentist's building. Or not. But she knew contact with *Poop* was seldom acknowledged by mainstream journalists. She was amused as she thought of these clandestine manoeuvres, if that's what they were, and mildly flattered that anyone would think her worth deceiving.

At home she picked up her mail inside the front door, carried it into the kitchen, dumped her purse on the table, and poured herself a glass of the cold *vino verde* that was corked in the fridge. She opened her *New Yorker* to look at the contents page. Then she looked at the rest of her mail.

There was an envelope with Max's return address on it. She

had thought he might call the afternoon that she'd sent him the page proofs. But after a couple of days of no word, she hadn't thought of him again.

As she read the letter she felt none of the old anger. Max was misguided about women. He made unreasonable demands and wanted to strike inequitable bargains. But no, he wasn't a war criminal. There were even moments, she could now admit — untethered, irrational, dreamy moments — when she found herself remembering a gesture or a word. And maybe even missing him a little.

```
Dear Sarah:
    I really got up your nose, didn't I? I was
furiously angry when I read your article yester-
day. But then yesterday was a bad day for other
reasons. I've read it a couple of times since. I
can't say I like it. In fact, I think it's trash.
More than that, I think there are things that
happen between people that shouldn't be the
subject of public confession. I guess in the age
of Oprah and Phil Donahue and Shirley that makes
me a dinosaur.
    But what the hell, if it makes you feel better,
I'm more than willing to pay the price of my own
outrage and humiliation (I'm grateful you didn't
use my name!). You and I had some exceptionally
bad moments together, I know. I didn't always hold
my end up, I know. But when I read how you see it
all in retrospect, I can only say that you got me
wrong. For one thing, there weren't a lot of other
women, as you seem to imply/suspect. A few lapses,
okay. But I was not systematically betraying you.
I liked having my own apartment. Is that a war
crime? I think you overdemonize me in your
```

article, to say the least. I'd like to talk to
you about it sometime. I still care about you.

Max
P.S. Do I get a royalty cheque?

CHAPTER 25

May 27

Chaser fumed. He knocked on his desk with his knuckle. He swore under his breath. And he picked up *Poop* again to reread the offending item. He had bought the magazine on Yonge Street an hour earlier and had been in a state of high anxiety ever since he'd read two squibs about *Berger's* on the "Mediocracy" page.

"Rumblings around *Berger's* tell us that Arnold Sturgess, who flamboyantly offed himself in a Rosedale ravine not long ago, was not in fact about to be hauled onto the carpet for sexual harrassment in the workplace. *Poop's* crack investigative team has taken the trouble this week to call every female employee on the *Berger's* masthead to ask if anyone had a case pending against the aging heterosexualist. Our poll, accurate twenty times out of twenty, identified zero complainants. Seems a disinformation campaign may have been set in motion to cover the real reason for the ancient gasbag's hasty retreat. And what was that reason? Nobody's saying. But who could know more than Chaser Makepeace, Edward Clubb's establishment stenographer and personal valet? Makepeace is apparently sticking by the sexual harrassment theory. Why?"

The second item was equally disastrous. "It's come to our attention that the PMO in Ottawa has become deeply distressed about, and deeply involved in, a story that is in the *Berger's* pipeline. Calls have been made to the magazine, deals have been struck, and the piece, we are told, has been altered to satisfy many of Ottawa's demands. We look forward to this pull-all-your-punches profile in the fearless monthly journal owned by one of Barton McGreedy's college pals."

Chaser turned to the P's in his personal phone directory. Under "Poop" was the name of the editor, Bichet E. Malador, a transplanted European of imprecise ancestry who had shown up in Toronto in the mid-eighties by way of Buenos Aires, where he had been an editor on the city's small English daily. Chaser dialled Malador's number.

"Bichet? This is Chaser Makepeace. I've just seen your new issue."

"Hello, Chaser," the *Poop* editor replied languidly. He pronounced the name more like Chase-air than like eraser. There was a hint of a Spanish accent. "Do you like it?"

"Like it? Well, I'm feeling a little perplexed, frankly. I thought we had agreed on a mutually beneficial arrangement."

"We certainly have. I very much value your collaboration."

"Yeah, but if I'm going to feed you juicy stuff from my plate, you have to do something for *me*. I'm appalled by these two items today. They're going to do a lot of damage."

"Really? I don't think we ever do much damage. It's only an elaborate game, you know."

"Boy, have you got that wrong. You're playing with reputations. That's all the capital most of us have."

"I hear the distress in your voice, Chaser. But you know, we just print what our sources tell us. We don't make it up."

"In this case I can assure you your sources are wrong. The PMO has forced absolutely no changes on our story. It's true they've been in touch. That's not unusual. But not one word has been modified. You can check that with the writer, Leonard Freeman. And you'll see when you read the piece that it's anything but flattering to his nibs."

"I guess we've been given, uh, a bum steer."

"Yes, you have. And I wish you could have warned me about calling my staff. I started to hear about it only yesterday."

"But when we had the idea here, it seemed so obviously a good one. To confirm what we were hearing."

"Bichet, your survey is worthless. The young woman in question has told me she doesn't want to speak of the problem ever again. As she said to me, it died with Arnold. She's not going to recant and start talking about it just because one of your researchers gives her a cold call."

"That's an interesting explanation," drawled the *Poop* editor. "I had not thought of that possibility."

"Whoever is feeding you stuff from here isn't giving you the goods," said Chaser.

"Ah ha. It seems maybe so."

"Can you tell me who it is?"

"Oh, we never do that. Why bite the hand that feeds us?"

"If it's feeding you poison, there's a good reason."

"You could be right there."

"I can give you all kinds of great stuff. No-one in this town is better positioned than I am. I've still got lines into the *Tribune*. I know every media type who's worth knowing in Toronto. Trust me. I can help you."

"Is this a carrot you are dangling before my big frothy lips?"

"Let's just say I'm happier with a *quid pro quo* than without one."

"You have an older woman on your staff," Malador murmured. "She seems quite eager to leave a few razor blades in your path. That's all I can tell you."

CHAPTER 26

June 3

At ten to eight in the morning Max had already been in the office for an hour and was drinking his second cup of coffee. There was a fat stack of work on his desk: manuscripts for the fall issues, some pieces that Arnold had been editing and that were still in various stages of production, and as of yesterday a piece of Dot's that he'd been given temporarily because she was away this week with a mysterious ailment.

Max was not happy. He had taken a piece of foolscap and had printed at the top REASONS TO QUIT. Underneath he had written a list which he was now staring at:

1. Overworked
2. Chaser not to be trusted
3. No sign of a replacement for Arnold
4. No time to find a life outside the office
5. No recognition for work accomplished

Looking at his five reasons, he felt they inadequately reflected his frustration. He penned another.

6. Lethal toxicity of anything happening within ten feet of C. Makepeace

Then he wrote REASONS TO STAY.

1. Money
2. Some interesting moments
3. Money

He crumpled up the sheet of paper, flicked it into the waste basket, and took Dot's piece from the top of his pile. Before this, she had not booked off sick once in twenty years, but she had been away for four days now with an unidentified illness. Chaser had said only that "it might be serious." Max had replied that they were understaffed as it was. "I'm working on it," Chaser had said cheerily. Max didn't believe him.

He began reading the piece Dot had been editing, making notes as he went. He was not far into it when he realized that, unless she was in an oxygen tent or had a tube down her throat, he would need to confer with her about the instructions to this writer. He waited until after nine, then punched in Dot's home number.

"I'm afraid I'm still under the weather," she said.

"I'm sorry to hear that. Is it serious?"

"I guess you could call it an occupational hazard," she said, coughing loudly. He knew that was her smoker's cough. But then he suddenly thought — lung cancer.

"Dot, if you can't do it, just say so. But I'm wondering if I could come out to your place for a quick discussion of Andrea Sherman's piece."

There was a long pause. "I'm sure I owe it to her — and you — to make the transition smooth."

His ear picked up a lugubrious undertone that suggested the worst. He thought: the big C.

"We're all hoping you'll be back here soon."

"Come out this morning, then," she went on, ignoring, as she always did, any hint of sentimentality. "I'll be here."

Max took a cab to her sprawling old house in the West End

near the Humber River. A thick lion's-head knocker hung in the middle of the wooden door. He hammered with the lion, then watched through the pane of glass as Dot walked down the honey-toned hallway, a cigarette burning in her mouth. He thought she looked quite spry. But when she opened the door and greeted him quietly, he could see there had been a change. She led him into a spacious oblong living room with a grand piano by the windows at one end. Inuit prints hung on the walls. It occurred to Max that some significant part of Dot did not inhabit the grubby freelance and editing world that had been his whole life for years.

"How are you feeling?" he asked. She seemed somehow more vulnerable, possibly in pain, though she was still smoking furiously.

She blew a stream of smoke into the air as she considered this question. After all the smoke had dispersed, she kept her lips in a tense little o. Then she stared at Max — an amoral, animal stare — long enough to make him uncomfortable.

"How am I feeling? I see no reason at this point why I can't be candid with you. I'm feeling enormously pissed off."

Max nodded stupidly. He couldn't think of anything inoffensive to say except "Yes."

She stared at him again, this time a little curiously. "You do know something about what's happened, don't you?"

"I don't know what's ailing you, if that's what you mean."

"Max, my dear, nothing's ailing me except the unwelcome prospect of early retirement. But as you can see, there are worse situations into which to retire. Alex and I can travel, of course." Alex, Max knew, was Dot's husband, a well-heeled corporate lawyer.

"You mean you're not sick?"

"Sick of Chaser Makepeace is all," she said in an exasperated voice.

"That's not a unique condition," Max smiled. "Why are you staying home?"

"You mean he hasn't let on? I'm surprised. I'd thought he'd be busy doing spin control on me. He wants me out of there. Wants a graceful departure. We had a vicious dispute last Friday. If I don't jump, he's threatened to push me with a bargepole. I said I'd take a week to mull it over."

Max was aghast. "I had no idea. . . ."

"I'll spare you the details. But I've been feeling quite disgusted since I began hearing rumours of Arnold's sexual escapades in the office. I knew Arnold for years. He was no leering bum-pincher. Chaser encouraged those rumours. I have that on good authority. Why is anyone's guess. But it looks to me as if he wanted to leave a cloud over Arnold's suicide. Which he may know more about than he's willing to say."

"Jesus," murmured Max.

"I feel quite powerless," Dot said in a small voice. "I guess it's probably time to go. I'm sixty-seven. I've had a good run at it. But I do resent that evil little gnome's fashioning my exit lines. It's doubly humiliating, in a way. He managed to write his own script over Arnold's exit too, which he had no right to do."

Max thought for a moment, then made a decision. What he had in a drawer at home could be shared. "There just may be a way out of this."

"How could there possibly be any way out? He's got his nasty little hands on all the levers."

"I suppose it depends on your own ethical sense, this idea of mine."

"How so?"

"I have something that Chaser wouldn't want me to have. Something you might find useful. I couldn't tell you what to do with it. But I can tell you that if it was leaked, and if the leak was managed the right way, Chaser's life at *Berger's* wouldn't be worth a nickel."

"Tell me more," Dot said in her gravelly voice. She cocked her head, lit another cigarette, and took a long drag.

CHAPTER 27

June 4

Max had made a copy of the letters at his neighbourhood copy shop, and then had called a courier from his house to have the envelope delivered to Dot. She would have the weekend to plan her strategy. Chaser had flown to Ottawa for his induction into the Order of Canada by the Governor-General. He'd been puffed up for days, preening himself for this imminent honour, and Max was glad not to have to listen to him, if only for a day.

The intercom rang. "Sorry, Max, but can you take a call on line four?" Dee asked.

"I'm on do-not-disturb."

"I know. I'm sorry. But this guy's been calling all week for Chaser. A writer from Montreal. Says it's really urgent."

"Why me?"

"Everyone else has gone to lunch."

"After this, I've done my bit, okay? I've left the country."

He punched line four. "Max Vellen."

"Hello, Mr. Vellen. Thank you for taking my call." The voice was gentle, educated, formal. "My name is Jonathan Pluman. I'm a writer in Montreal. Chaser Makepeace has probably mentioned me."

Max could not recall hearing about any Jonathan Pluman. "I don't recall offhand. Chaser's away for the day. What can I help you with?"

"Oh. I thought he might have mentioned my name. I'm doing a series of articles for you on communications. In three parts?"

A series? thought Max, alarmed. *On communications?* Who's going to end up editing this stinker? And why would Chaser have commissioned it? *Berger's* wasn't in the habit of running any kind of series. "Refresh my memory, if you wouldn't mind. There's been a lot happening here lately."

"Oh yes, I know. I follow the magazine closely. You may remember it was I who noticed the unfortunate similarity between the Sturgess essay and the Neil Postman passage in your April issue. Though I know none of us in what Mr. Makepeace calls 'the *Berger's* family' really wants to talk about that."

What was going on here? Max's whole body was alert now, and he had the receiver pressed tightly to his ear so he would not miss a beat. "Ah ha," he replied. "I didn't realize that was you. How long have you known Chaser?"

"Oh, not very long. Really just since he called me after I wrote that letter in the spring. We met when he was in Montreal about a month ago, and agreed on these assignments. Which is why I'm calling, actually. He's terribly hard to get hold of on the phone. I'm doing this writing instead of a summer job. And he had promised to give me an advance, which I need quite badly."

"There shouldn't be any problem with that," said Max, wondering how he could find out exactly what they were discussing. "How much did you settle on?"

"He said he would advance me five thousand dollars."

"What!!!?" Max mouthed to himself. The normal *Berger's* advance was five hundred or a thousand. "Tell you what," he said. "I can't okay a cheque that size by myself, but I'll speak to Chaser first thing Monday morning and sort it out. How does that sound?"

"I'd be very grateful," said Jonathan Pluman, and hung up.

Max looked at his watch. It was twelve forty-five. Everyone would still be out of the office on lunch. He walked once around the editorial section and saw no-one. Then he went into Chaser's office and sat at his big desk.

He checked the drawers — all open. Chaser had been in early that morning and must have rushed off to the airport without locking up. But apart from the bottom one on the left-hand side, which Max had already looked in, the drawers held nothing more interesting than chequebooks, bank books, and office supplies.

Max picked up one of several fat blue folders on top of the desk. It was labelled UNDECIDED. Inside were letters to the editor awaiting, Max assumed, Chaser's yes or no. Max riffled through the file, but he could see it was all recent mail received within the past ten days. The next file was labelled FOR PUB-LICATION. Max looked through it quickly. Another fatter folder was marked REJECTS, and contained nothing of interest.

A fourth folder was labelled COMMISSIONS. Inside were three sheets of paper covered with Chaser's ornate handwriting and flowery doodles. On the left-hand side of the pages he had written names. Beside them were brief descriptions of maga-zine assignments. In a column on the right he had noted dollar figures. Max was surprised to see that he had heard of none of the assignments, and not all of the writers either.

As Max read further, he realized that in this file Chaser appeared to be operating in a parallel universe, creating and assigning articles that had nothing to do with anything dis-cussed at editorial meetings. There were several names Max did recognize, including that of St. John Dunham, a down-at-the-heel freelancer who had emigrated from London as a young man. In the fifties, before the country had produced many writers of its own, St. John had been able to romp across the cultural landscape without much competition. He'd been lionized by *Berger's* and other publications. Twenty years later, with homegrown Canadian writers in ample supply, cultivated Brits had lost their natural advantage and the Dunham by-line had gone into eclipse. Chaser, Max speculated, was throwing St. John a lifeline with a few of Edward Clubb's dollars. But it seemed unlikely the article, described on the page as "Ex-beauty queen's dog cemetery outside Toronto," would ever make it into *Berger's*.

This file, Max guessed, housed Chaser's personal pork barrel, from which he repaid debts, rewarded longstanding support-ers, consoled unlucky old friends, and helped mysterious hang-ers-on like Jonathan Pluman — whose name was here too. All the note beside it said was, "Three articles on post-modern communications theory," and beside that Chaser had written "$12,000." Max was no wiser.

He placed all the folders back where he had found them, and looked at his watch. Ten after one. People would be drifting back in soon. As he rolled back Chaser's chair and stood up, he caught sight of a hair-thin fringe of blue alongside the editor's large leather writing pad. Max cocked his head over to the side to see what it was. Another blue file folder.

He pulled the folder out from under the leather pad and opened it up. Inside was a single letter dated March 30. It was signed by Jonathan Pluman.

CHAPTER 28

June 9

Chaser had visited Dot on Monday, saying she had called and asked to see him. "I'm just going out to take her pulse," he had told Max. "Back in an hour or two."

"Tell her I hope she's feeling a whole lot better," Max had said.

Later on, Chaser returned looking pale and anxious. "Dot seems to have made a miraculous recovery. She says she'll be back for the Wednesday editorial round-up."

And so she was. She swept into the office just as the meeting began and was as ornery as ever all through it, not giving an inch on Giorgio's deadlines or on story ideas she disliked. Max enjoyed the spectacle and was sorry when the meeting wound down.

"I guess that covers it," said Chaser finally. His eyes were darting anxiously around the table as if he badly wanted to flee the room. "Unless anyone has anything else."

"We haven't said a word about Maya McGarvie," growled Dot. Her chair was rolled back from the conference table and she was leaning her chin on a closed fist. Max could see that through her shades she was radiating contempt in Chaser's direction.

"Oh," said Chaser, "I didn't think that was still on."

"You bet it is," she snapped. "I've assigned a writer to

research it. He's done several interviews in Ottawa, including one with a prominent political wife who goes to Maya's ophthamologist."

Chaser fidgeted as he listened. "It's really not a *Berger's* story, though," he protested. "Unless you have someone who's seen him hit her, it's just gutter gossip. Fit maybe for *Poop*." He glared at her.

"We don't know what we have until we're at the other end of the interviews," she said in her deep, caustic voice. "If nothing else, we may have a juicy portrait of a marriage seen from the outside."

"I think we're buying ourselves a pack of trouble," he said, looking down at his pencil.

"You're saying the Prime Minister's wife isn't fair game? I think you're ducking a good story." She rolled her chair back to the table. "For your own reasons."

"Meaning what exactly?"

"Meaning I insist we go ahead with it."

"Then we'll go ahead with it," said Chaser in the hollowed-out voice of a man who has just been forced into bankruptcy.

A few moments later Chaser and Max were standing side by side in the men's room.

"Great meeting!" exclaimed Max. "Dot seems to have bounced right back from whatever she had."

"Uh huh," Chaser replied in a lifeless voice. "Amazing recuperative powers."

When Max returned to his desk, he found a note: "All I can say is thanks." There was a big heart drawn over Dot's initials.

As Max stared at the heart, he began to feel low. He thought of Betsy, then of Sarah. No true hearts for me, he thought. For solace he picked up the booklet he had been thumbing through over the last few days, a directory to rental cottages in the south of France, called *Vive la vie rurale*.

Vive la vie sans mal, thought Max. If you can find it.

CHAPTER 29

June 17

"Here's to three months of sweat, over and done," said Max, raising his tumbler of iced tea.

"I don't believe it's really done," said Leonard, lifting his mug of beer. "You'll be calling me tomorrow telling me I have to bag another interview." The weather was unseasonably warm. They were sitting on an outside terrace adjacent to a bar on Bloor Street.

Max shook his head. "Done. Fact-checked. Copy-edited. Not laid out on pages yet, it's true. We may have to cut a line or three. But basically it's history. You can lie back and relax until the mortar shells blow open your front door on publication day."

"I can't afford to lie back and relax. You didn't pay me enough."

"Tell me about it. I didn't pay me enough either. Which is one of about ten reasons why I'm thinking maybe this job isn't a great idea after all."

"Stop, Max! Don't do it. We don't need another hungry freelancer out here. Too many fingers in the pie already."

"Why not? I've been hungry before. I know how to wiggle my finger into the pie."

"You're nuts. You have a good job."

"I don't feel nuts. I feel remarkably rational. Especially clear-headed since I gave up drinking."

Leonard looked unconvinced. "That could be the problem. You're in some kind of toxic shock from withdrawal. What does the new girlfriend think?"

"I didn't tell you? I don't have a new girlfriend anymore. She gave me the heave-ho. That did send me into toxic shock. I fell for her in some kind of weird, mood-altering way that I couldn't easily shake off."

"Hormones," said Leonard. "The most powerful mood-altering substance known to man."

"It was a chastening experience. She seemed very interested in me. I thought we saw eye to eye on some of the contentious male-female stuff. It didn't last long. I was left feeling that I'd failed some kind of secret taste test."

"Maybe she just eats around."

"It got me thinking again about how I blew it with Sarah. You know I heard from her? After all these months."

"She sent you a letter bomb?"

"Close. She sent me a copy of a magazine article she's written about our relationship. No names, but everyone will know who it is. And she does quite a job on me. I was ready to strangle her when I first read it."

"I never really did hear her side of the story. I'll look forward to that," Leonard chuckled.

"You don't read *Canadian Woman*. I hope."

"And you've forgiven her?"

"Oh sure. She needed to vent it all. She wanted to embarrass me. So she did what she had to do. I can live with it. What interests me is that she hasn't wiped me out of her mind. So maybe there's still hope."

"Someone said 'Love is like a good cigar. You can relight it, but it never tastes the same.'"

Max shrugged. "You could also say charcoal burns better than wood. I'm going to call her one of these days. For one thing, I've never really made my peace with her."

"I wish you luck."

"How's your Ottawa love?"

"Still happening. In an infrequent, long-distance way."

"I've been avoiding this subject," said Max tentatively.

"Why's that?"

"I have something not so good to tell you. Do you remember introducing Danielle to Chaser Makepeace at the Red Cross Ball?"

"Uh huh."

"Somehow he's put it all together. He knows she's your source for the story."

Leonard's face turned ugly. "Where'd he get that?"

Max thought for a moment how best to massage the truth. "I didn't tell him. Chaser knows everybody. And he's a non-stop schmoozer. He must have mentioned her name to somebody in Ottawa who knew about her day job."

"Can we get him to shut up about it?"

"Ha!" Max scoffed. "Chaser is a motor-mouth. He won't shut up about anything, unless it's personally threatening."

"That's definitely another option."

"What you do have going for you is it's not in his interest to blab it around town right now. He's running your story in his magazine, and he'll look like a fool if he tries to discredit you."

"And after?"

"I'd say all bets are off."

"It was Danielle who wanted me to go." Leonard sounded uncharacteristically defensive. "She flew up as McGarvie's on-the-road press officer that weekend."

"Where's her animus towards the PM come from?"

The writer darted a wary glance at Max. "McGreedy treated her very badly at one point." Leonard looked across the terrace and grumbled, "She's not going to be happy with this news."

Max nodded silently, thinking, live by the sword. . . .

CHAPTER 30

June 28

"It's character assassination," snorted Clubb, waving the page proofs in the air. "It's . . . it's *smearing* our Prime Minister. Our *Prime Minister*! Doesn't anyone respect authority anymore?"

Chaser sat on the other side of Clubb's desk. He had his notepad on his knee. "I've written an editorial which I hope will provide some balance," he said meekly.

"An editorial? You're going to need a very long one to remedy the damage done by this article. In fact, you'd need a book. This is an outrage, Chaser. Do you think I purchased this publication to have my friends slandered in it? What does this man Leonard Freeman take me for? He must be laughing all the way to his bank."

"They don't get paid all that much, as I've mentioned before."

"Anything is too much for this . . . this . . ." Clubb waved the page proofs irritably again. "This crypto-Marxist, anti-elitist monkey shit." He brought his fist down hard on his desk, and the papers slapped the wood. "We're talking about public service. The good of the country. Tough decisions. McGarvie could be making four times as much if he'd remained in private life."

"But he didn't," said Chaser. On his notepad he wrote, "General Ripper, mad for revnge, finger on nuclr buttn."

"Eh?!?" Clubb crossed his arms angrily.

"What I mean is, he chose public service and willingly exposed himself to public scrutiny. He volunteered."

"Yes, and we should express our gratitude to him, not hurl mud in his face. If you publish this, *Berger's* will be behaving no better than a lewd street heckler who is arrested for public mischief. Which must be what Leonard Freeman does in his free time. His arrogance is stunning. I assume he believes he personifies *vox populi*."

Chaser wrote, "Blood thrsty Empror Tiberius. Lenrd Freeman to th lions." He said, "It's only one point of view, Edward. We'll publish other opinions over the course of McGarvie's mandate."

Clubb shook his head. "No. I forbid you to publish this. It's unworthy of our distinguished old publication. You know as well as I do it's a pack of lies."

Chaser was startled. "You forbid it? That would be a terrible mistake. It's already widely known the article is coming out."

"That makes no difference to me. What would I tell Bart McGarvie if this were published?"

"Tell him you've never met Leonard Freeman. Blame it on me. That's what I'm here for."

"McGarvie's going to take the heat when this comes out, Chaser. Not you."

"There is something else you could tell him. But I can't supply it just yet."

"What's that?"

"I could give you a name. Of someone who helped our writer. A source inside the PMO. It would be an appeasement."

"Give it to me, then."

Chaser's eyes widened. "I don't have it. But I will."

"When?"

"I'll work on it. I should probably have it by the time the article comes out."

"We're not publishing it. I just told you that."

Chaser wrote: "Godzilla." His eyes darted desperately around the room, then he said, "I have to tell you the facts. At this point we have no choice, God bless us. In a week the August issue goes to press. My hands are tied. It's physically impossible to do a switch now."

"For God's sake, Chaser, *Time* magazine publishes a fresh issue every week."

"*Time* magazine has an editorial staff of hundreds. We've got five."

"It's not even July yet. You have a month."

"You may remember that we're committed to have finished copies ready for distribution by about the middle of the month. Printing and stapling takes us a week at your plant. And we've already booked our printing time."

"Then cancel the issue."

Chaser wrote: "Goebbels reachs fr hs gun." He stared at his notepad for a moment, then said carefully, "Edward, we, *you*, would become a running joke in the advertising community. There is no possible explanation for cancelling an issue, other than gross ineptitude. We'd lose tens of thousands of dollars, maybe hundreds in the long run. Our relations with advertisers might never recover. From a purely commercial point of view, that would be very unwise."

"You're boxing me in, Chaser. That's not a place I like to be. I'm not happy in a box. Never have been." Clubb's anger had faded. He was now looking at Chaser as if he were a speck of dust on the carpet.

Chaser scribbled, "Bull in a box."

"Editors don't live forever, Chaser," the publisher added in an unemotional voice. "You should be more careful. You've been making some bad decisions."

CHAPTER 31

July 15

Max read from the *Tribune*:

Edward Clubb's Janus Corporation has purchased an interest in *Wellington* magazine.

In its August issue *Wellington* is publishing an apology to Mr. Clubb for statements made in an article published about him earlier this year. Mr. Clubb is dropping all legal action related to the case.

Until this week, *Wellington* was wholly owned by Emmanuel Rosenfeld, a Toronto real-estate developer and publisher.

Advance copies of the magazine's new issue were distributed yesterday. The apology occupies a half page and says in part that "the editors regret the excesses of the article and any offence caused to Edward Clubb and his family. The editors apologize for any inaccuracies in the portrayal of Mr. Clubb's business history, and regret any characterizations of Mr. Clubb that distorted the facts."

The editor of *Wellington*, Sharon Lutes, has resigned, effective August 1. Reached at her office, she said, "I wish the new management well. Manny Rosenfeld has been the best of owners and I'm grateful for all that he's done. I'd like to make it clear, however, that I played no part in drafting our apology to Edward Clubb."

The *Tribune* has also learned that *Wellington*, which has been without a publisher for two months, will soon have a new one. Chaser Makepeace, editor of the much larger national magazine *Berger's*, will soon step down to become *Wellington*'s publisher.

Reached at his office, Mr. Makepeace expressed surprise anyone was aware of his new appointment. "I can confirm it," he said. "There will be a press conference within the week." He refused to speculate on who might be the next editor of *Berger's*.

Asked if he considered his new job on the much smaller local magazine a demotion, Makepeace said it was his choice to leave *Berger's* and that he looked forward to the change. "I'll be running a smaller magazine, it's true, but one with large possibilities, a committed new ownership team, and a great staff."

The Clubb-Rosenfeld press release states that "this agreement brings to an amicable conclusion any and all outstanding legal matters relating to the article on Edward Clubb published by *Wellington* magazine in April."

Asked about Jeremy Glass, the writer whose piece triggered the libel suit, Mr. Clubb said, "As part of this settlement we will neither excuse Mr. Glass nor pursue him in the courts." Mr. Rosenfeld added, "The magazine's apology does not speak for Mr. Glass."

Reached at his home, Jeremy Glass said, "I withdraw nothing, I apologize for nothing, but I will also say nothing more about it. The capitalists have done their deal. I'll go on writing."

CHAPTER 32

July 22

One more week, thought Max.

Chaser had packed up and left the office. Dot, editor pro tem, was already interviewing for two junior editorial positions that Chaser's liberated salary had opened up.

"What would you like?" she had asked Max the day Chaser's departure had been announced.

"A part-time job," he said. "And all of August away from here." He laughed and added, "And hey, jobs for my cousins. And $50,000 in cash. Otherwise I sing to the cops."

Her pout expanded into a smile, and then the smile gave way to a grimace. "I don't really want a part-time editor. But I'll give it to you for a year. Just don't come back here in September and quit on me."

"What makes you think I would do that?"

"Because if you've thought of part-time," she said, "you've thought of quitting."

She'd released him until after Labour Day and he had immediately booked a flight to Europe.

He licked the brown envelope with two copies of the August issue in it and sealed the flap. "Leonard Freeman," he wrote on the envelope, and then wrote Leonard's address. The PMO had already acquired advance copies — Max could guess how. They had faxed a long letter of protest to Dot.

"Congratulations," she'd said in his doorway yesterday. "This" — she'd held up the fax — "shows we're doing our job the way we're meant to." She was a journalist of the old school: embarrass the powerful, and empower the voiceless. Whereas Chaser's motto would have been something like: massage the powerful, and never make a career-threatening move. "Arnold," Dot had added as she'd turned to go, "would have been proud of us."

Max took the brown envelope out to reception and asked Dee to express it to Leonard. The new issue was already spread around the visitors' waiting area. The cover line, "LET'S MAKE A DEAL," was splashed just above McGarvie's slicked-back hair. "Is Barton McGarvie Trading Away Canada's Future?" read the underline. McGarvie's face, a savage illustration, appeared with tiny, mean-looking eyes, and a venal, puckered mouth. Max thought Giorgio had commissioned brilliant artwork. Leonard would be pleased.

Max took the elevator down into the hot afternoon on Yonge Street. He had left half an hour early. He wanted to clear his mind of office clutter before he saw her. The meeting was not until quarter to six — there was time to browse in Lichtman's for a few minutes. He ducked into the bookstore and picked the fresh issue of *Poop* off the rack. He turned to "Mediocracy" first.

"Magazine hacks are all drooling hungrily at the sight of this week's two empty editorial chairs — at *Berger's* and at *Wellington*. You are all advised to suck in your tongues. As we go to press, both positions are about to be filled. The new head webspinner at *Berger's*, Dorothy Scrivener, is an ancient editorial arthropod with more kilometres on her spindles than a '48 Chrysler. She will now be laughing hard at bossman Eddie Clubb's jokes. And we have learned *Wellington* will soon announce that Liam 'Chubby' O'Chancre will be breaking chairs in that magazine's editor's office. O'Chancre, noted blowhard and social climber, is one of the few local journalists who has ever had a good word for Citizen Clubb, the megalomaniacal press monopolist who will soon be one of O'Chancre's employers. The other half of this new pair of *Wellington*ians, Manny 'Highrise' Rosenfeld, is said to find O'Chancre refreshingly upbeat on the subject of self-made millionaires.

"One small fly in O'Chancre's honey: our researchers tell us he has for the past several weeks known, in the Biblical sense, a female spellchecker on the *Wellington* payroll, Betsy Cerniak. Will the two continue to read the good book to each other after dark, or will conflict of interest cause Chubby O'Chancre to keep his travelling Bible zipped?"

Max felt his throat going dry. He had known he would eventually hear about Betsy's love life. But O'Chancre? *Poop* could be inaccurate about many things — possibly about most things. But they seldom mismatched bed mates. Irrationally, Max had the sickening sense he had been cuckolded.

He walked out of Lichtman's feeling betrayed and angry, then thought: Be grateful for small mercies. She'd been honest. What more could you expect of a ten-day affair? He had been hoping at least for a few delicious weeks of romance. But after Betsy's note, as he retraced his steps with her, he had begun wondering if her intentions hadn't been more business than pleasure.

Pictures of her making lusty love to Liam O'Chancre in a candlelit room flooded Max's mind. He could see them in bed, O'Chancre on his knees and palms, alternately grunting and congratulating himself on his sexual prowess, his big belly drooping over hers, his tonsured skull turned to see his shadow on the wall. Max could hear Betsy cooing, but her sounds grew ever more faint, and then he heard her lover loudly fart, after which the young sexual partners evoked no feeling in Max at all, other than detached amusement. He sauntered up Yonge Street looking forward to whatever might unfold in the next hour.

★ ★ ★

Sarah was waiting in Dooney's Cafe, feeling just a whisper of regret that she had agreed to meet here — of all places. This was where they had first had coffee. There were nostalgic associations that she could have done without. But when they had spoken on the phone this had somehow seemed the likeliest venue. And, tiny regrets notwithstanding, she had to admit she was also feeling a slight twitch of excitement.

She was sipping the spritzer she had ordered when she sighted him in the cafe's doorway — only five minutes late. He still looked shaggy and rumpled, like a tagless dog she had once taken home. His dark hair was still long and unkempt, his tie loosened (and, she thought, probably spotted), his face a day or two unshaven, his pants unpressed.

He saw her, waved, made his way to her table, and bent over to kiss her on the cheek.

"Sarah, you look great. Staying away from me must be a tonic." He slid into the chair opposite her and caught the waiter's eye.

"Hello, Max. I'm fine. And it's nothing to do with you."

"I'm sorry to hear that. I mean, sorry it's nothing to do with me. You know — my disturbed ego. I like to have an impact." He grinned stupidly, and asked the waiter for a lemonade.

"You did. I've done the necessary repairs, that's all. The damage is no longer visible."

Max's eyebrows shot up. "Damage? Is that all we were for you?"

Sarah smiled tolerantly. "Not entirely. But it wasn't all hearts and flowers either, was it?"

"I still think of you," he said, looking her in the eye. "Fondly."

"Don't get sentimental on me. It's good to see you again. But let's not stretch reality. Friendly, okay. Fondly, I'm not so sure."

"You don't have to feel the same way. I'm just speaking for myself. You were the one who was so angry, not me. I only got hot under the collar after you told me to walk. I thought I'd been done an injustice."

"Oh come on. You got off lightly."

"You didn't even reply to my letters."

"I couldn't. Letters were how we started. Letters meant hope and romance. I had no heart for letters after it had ended."

"Did you even read them?"

"To tell you the truth . . . no. I wanted to fumigate my life. Everything that had been Maxified around my place went into the trash. The letters too, when they arrived."

"For high crimes against love, the chopping block." He drew his index finger across his throat.

She nodded. "It made me feel better."

"You were wrong about me, though. I want you to know that. Difficult to pin down, yes, I admit it. Disloyal, no. That's a falsehood."

"You're not going to try and tell me now you were unfailingly faithful!"

"No. But I was arriving at that condition."

She shook her head and smiled sadly. "You were on a slow train, Max."

"Maybe. But I'd just about reached the destination."

"Let's not talk about this. There's no point to it now."

"I know I resisted settling in with you. I shouldn't have. In my own defence I can only say I've been a male wanderer for a very long time. Part of me is afraid to give that up."

"You don't have to give it up. Stay single."

"Yeah, right. I remember your cockroach joke. How did that one go? 'What does a woman do to get rid of the roaches in her apartment? She asks them for a commitment.' You apparently believe the single male is an extremely low life form."

"I think I was angry with you when I told you that one.

Anyway, what do you care what I think?"

"I still care."

"Are you seeing someone? How are you? Really."

"There's been nothing serious since we split up. As to how I am, I'm still subsisting in the dysfunctional world of writers and deadlines. I realized the other day that was part of the problem with us. I've worked in journalism so long I can hardly remember what normal, civilized behaviour is."

"You always exaggerate. There are viably married couples in your world. I've met some."

"Not so many. And even with the nominally viable ones, if you scratch the surface, you're likely to find one collosal ego being propped up and cared for by the other long-suffering partner."

"Jill thought you'd been seeing someone."

"She introduced me to a woman at the magazine awards and we went out for a couple of weeks." He tried to give her a wise look tinged with regret. "It was a mistake, but it's long gone. What about you? Are you in love?"

"That's an awfully personal question, Max."

"Okay, sorry." He looked away uneasily, then added, "I heard you were getting serious about some securities lawyer."

"No. He got serious about me."

Max held up his glass. "Stay for another drink?"

"I have to be somewhere for dinner."

"That's too bad."

"I have a life, Max."

"Ouch. Of course, you do. I was hoping we might eat together, that's all."

"I agreed to have a drink with you. I'm still not entirely sure what you had in mind."

"Oh. Okay. I think partly I want to make my peace with you. I've had a crazy year. Not just with you, but with everything. I want it to be different. I'd like you to give me another chance."

He grinned like a child.

Sarah thought his expression looked so open she could blow through it. "You're nuts, Max. We ran each other through a wringer. There's no juice left."

"So, maybe a wringer is good. We've been drying in the wind for six months and now we're ready to put each other on again," he said brightly.

"After it ended, I told myself you were someone who hadn't grown up, at least not entirely. A manchild. I'm not trying to insult you. It's just an observation."

"You shouldn't kill off the child in yourself," he said defensively. "You lose that, you lose your essence."

"That's one point of view," she said.

"I'm going to Europe for a month. Wanna come?"

"Aren't you still at *Berger's*?" she asked, surprised.

"Sure. I've got a month off. The new editor likes me."

"I'm glad. You weren't exactly in a state of harmony with Chaser."

"She's letting me have part-time in the fall."

"Good for you." She looked at her watch. "I'll have to go soon."

"Yeah. I've rented a *gîte* south of Bordeaux. Second two weeks of August."

"You what!?!?"

"I thought you might be interested in coming for a visit."

"I couldn't possibly do that."

"Why?"

"Because we aren't seeing each other anymore."

"No. But we could start again. Right away. Before I leave."

"Max, if we ever did begin again, that's not the way it would happen."

"So we'll make it happen your way."

"I didn't say that."

"But you do think there's some little quark of a chance, some micromillimetre of light trying to squeeze through?"

"Probably it's just a rogue particle on the loose today," she said as she stood up. "I should get going."

"We'll see each other again?" He stood up and faced her.

"This is a bit rushed. Sure, if you think so."

"I hated your article."

"I know. You said. I've had lots of calls, though. People seemed to relate to it."

"Yeah. Me too. That was the problem."

"Enjoy your month off."

"If I write you from France, will you write me?"

"I suppose I might, if I can stifle my envy."

"If I write you from France, will you *read* my letter?"

"Yes, Max."

As he leaned forward and brushed her cheek, he felt her lips give him a light, friendly peck.

He watched her walk to the door, the planes and angles of her familiar body visible to him beneath her loose green-and-blue sun dress as it swished back and forth.

He thought: first thing tomorrow, cancel the expensive *gîte* south of Bordeaux — forfeit the deposit. It was worth a try. Maybe, it's a long shot, but maybe. A whole life could be built on slim possibilities.

As she stepped out onto the sidewalk, Sarah saw a blimp in the sky advertising fruit juice. She pictured herself in it, high in the summer light, looking down at Max. He was running along Bloor Street, dodging pedestrians, his head tilted up, his right hand raised and waving a small white speck — a letter.

THE END

ACKNOWLEDGEMENTS

For their generously given time and helpful advice I am very grateful to Mark Abley, Carole Corbeil, Ernest Hillen, Anne Michaels, Gary Ross, Eric Wright, and Ronald Wright. I am especially grateful to my partner Alyse Frampton for her patience and wise counsel as I wrote and rewrote this book. Thanks too to my publisher Jack David and my editor Kevin Connolly, both a pleasure to work with.

I am grateful to the Ontario Arts Council for its support.